# Katrina Class

## The Chronicle
## of Unwelcomed Sinners

by
Roy LeBlanc

ISBN:   978-1-7349226-3-9

This book is printed on acid-free paper.

Printed in the United States of America

This book is a work of fiction. Names, characters, places, and incidents either are the products of the author's imagination or are used fictitiously. Any resemblance to actual events or locales or persons, living or dead, is entirely coincidental.

"In three words I can sum up everything I've learned about life: it goes on."

Robert Frost

"This is not a 9th Ward nightmare. Nightmare implies that people have the capacity to dream. In the 9th Ward nobody dreams."

Unknown

Acknowledgments


Kenny - The real Katrina hero.


Isabella - A remarkable young writer with wisdom and insight beyond her years.

# 1

FALL ORIENTATION IS ALWAYS AN exciting time for incoming college freshmen everywhere, especially so at Tulane University. New Orleans is a great place for personal discovery. It is an ancient city that embraces change, but clings to the history of traditional ways as Spanish moss hangs eternally from the branches of Audubon Park oaks. Moss absorbs nutrients from the steamy dampness of summer heat. Living in New Orleans challenges your soul in a similar way. Breathe deep; it's in the air.

Three hundred years ago, Bienville founded New Orleans on a small plot of high ground surrounded by swamps and marsh lands claiming it for the King of France. Since then, a determined Mother Nature has contentiously fought epic battles to reclaim it. She slings hurricanes at New Orleans like a heavyweight champion throwing knockout punches. In recent history, the worst storms have been made more destructive because of the environmental devastation encouraged by the petrochemical and shipping industries. People living in low-lying areas of the southern parishes used to gravitate to the relative safety of New Orleans and her strong levees. This was before the oil and gas industry dug thousands of miles of canals crisscrossing the marshes and swamps.

The linear canals encouraged salt water intrusion, killing the wetlands, marsh grasses and bald cypress trees that held the deltaic land together and helped protect the city from hurricane floods. In testimony before the Natural Resources and Environment Committee of the Louisiana legislature, an oil company CEO said, "We did it because it was not illegal at the time."

Then the back swamps to the north of the city were drained to create the neighborhoods of Lakeview, Gentilly and New Orleans East, encouraging growth and development in below sea-level areas close to the lake. Adding insult to injury, global shipping interests and the Army Corps of Engineers dug the Intercostal Canal and the Mississippi River Gulf Outlet, bringing seawater to the doorsteps of New Orleans.

Hurricanes have a way of entering the history of New Orleans and becoming a part of the fabric of our culture. We remember Audrey, Betsy, Camille and Katrina the way other cities memorialize hometown athletes. Here, hurricanes mark the time. History rolls along and the storms, they keep coming. They considered the hurricane of 1915 to be a hundred-year storm. They were almost right. Katrina slammed into New Orleans 90 years later.

Many hurricanes start off as low pressure systems moving westward across the African continent, enter the Atlantic, and under the right conditions become tropical disturbances. The warm waters of the Caribbean and Gulf of Mexico are perfect for nurturing killer hurricanes headed for Louisiana. Until the 1950s, they were named for the year in which they struck land.

During the Hurricane of 1915, a steam locomotive and seven passenger cars were caught unprepared on a stretch of track near Rabbit Island in the Lake Catherine area. The engineer tried to make a run for New Orleans, but the 130 mph hurricane force winds blew the speeding train off the tracks into the swampy marsh. Some passengers survived the flood waters by climbing Bald Cypress trees plentiful in the swampy land. Twenty-two people were never found. Eight of the lost were children. They were included in the 275 killed in South Louisiana that night.

The heavy engine and passenger cars sunk deep into the soft muck and disappeared. Recovery was impossible. The train was forgotten and considered an urban legend until the 1990s when a work crew laying fiber optic cables along the track right-of-way discovered the lost engine.

Hurricane surges enter Lake Ponchatrain from the Gulf through Lake Borgne and Lake Catherine. The lakes are connected to the Gulf by a short, eight-mile-long, deep water tidal pass called the Rigolets. It is a French word for trench pronounced in New Orleans as the 'Rig-uh-leez.' During the 1915 storm, a small, wooden-hulled cargo ship with twelve crewmen searched for the channel leading to safety from the rampaging open gulf waters. The captain manned a searchlight looking in vain for channel markers that were already washed away; visibility was zero. Water began to flood the engine room. Radio distress calls went unanswered.

"Full revolutions! I need full revolutions. Hard rudder!" the captain barked desperately to the helmsmen.

The watch officer reported the flooded engine room and the wheelhouse was taking on water from broken windows. The ship was never seen again. Over the years, local fishermen have reported hearing a ship's bell and emergency horn. Some have claimed to have heard a captain shouting orders. The ghostly sounds always stop at 11:46 p.m. The eye of the 1915 Hurricane passed directly over the Rigolets and into the city of New Orleans at that exact time.

In 1969, the first year of the Jazz Fest, the Ole Miss Rebels led by quarterback Archie Manning defeated the Arkansas Razorbacks 27-22 in the Sugar Bowl at Tulane's Willow Street Stadium, Neil Armstrong walked on the moon and Hurricane Camille slammed into the Gulf Coast.

Camille formed in the usual way, but became a powerful Category 5 with winds over 190 mph, and carried swarms of tornados as it approached New Orleans. It was on a deadly track heading for Lake Borgne in a westerly direction, straight up the Rigolets. The highest wind speed was reported by a Transworld Drilling Company platform about twenty miles east of the storm's path at 197 mph. It was a worst-case scenario for New Orleans with a twenty-foot-high wall of rising water potentially forced into Lake Ponchatrain. The protective levees and pumping stations surrounding the city would surely fail.

New Orleans was spared at the last minute as Camille turned east, placing the city on the weak side of the storm's eye. It clipped the boot of Louisiana and slammed into the Mississippi Gulf Coast. Bay Saint Louis, Pass Christian and Long Beach were destroyed by the wind, tornadoes and surge. Wind drove pine needles into the walls of homes as if they were ice picks. The mayor of Pass Christian said he was mayor of a city in 'name only,' as everything was destroyed. Camille came ashore on the night of August 17, 1969, remembered as Woodstock weekend everywhere else. We all assumed no storm could ever top Camille, until 2005 when Katrina took an almost identical path.

# 2

**NEW ORLEANS WAS THE WEALTHIEST** city in America before the Civil War. Even into the 1930s she stood proud as 'queen of the south.' Her economy was bigger than Dallas, Houston, Atlanta, Memphis or Birmingham. The port of New Orleans was third behind New York and Amsterdam. New Orleans' banks, like The Canal Bank, Whitney and Hibernia, were some of the largest financial institutions in the country.

The French Creole LeMoyne family first settled here in the 1750s after the French and Indian War, but never figured out how to make any money. Some of the mansions on Saint Charles Avenue have been in the same families for generations. On the other hand, Louis LeMoyne inherited a rundown shotgun camelback on Montegut Street in the upper Ninth Ward. It was sparsely but tastefully furnished with mostly second-hand items purchased from a consignment shop on Canal Street.

Louis was taught to believe in the American dream, and he was determined to achieve his version of happiness. Some people work their entire lives and accomplish nothing, earning only failure, disappointment and more work. Farmers used to affix a carrot to a stick and attach it to the bridle extending beyond the mule's head, but just out of his reach. The ass faithfully plowed fields all day long believing he was getting closer and closer to the dangling carrot in front of him. Louis chased his dream with similar optimism.

After years of struggle, the LeMoyne family felt almost middle class. Louis did okay for himself and his family, especially so when you consider that they started out penniless living in a 400-square foot apartment on Louisa Street. As a kid in the rundown, shabby, rented apartment, Louis used to corner rats in the kitchen. Like some unfortunate family from a John Steinbeck novel, they didn't have much of anything. Still, Louis was raised with middle-class Catholic values. Five years as an altar boy reinforced his strong Catholic upbringing.

The parish church paid each altar boy two dollars for the wedding or funeral they served. The altar boys were divided into two crews: A and B. "Crew B report to the church," Sister Mary, the school principal, would make announcements as necessary. Individual teachers had no idea which boys served in each specific crew, so when an announcement was made all the boys left their classrooms, and those not needed at the church hid behind the 'old' school gym smoking cigarettes and playing paper football.

Each Friday the altar boys pooled half of all their weekly earnings together and bought a carton of smokes for the next week. The cigarettes were wrapped in a black trash bag and hidden under the back-church steps. Once this caper was discovered, the school principal, Sister Mary, dragged Louis to the church and forced him into the confessional. She said he was, "willful and naughty." Louis had to say the Rosary five times and three Hail Mary's. He recited the Act of Contrition ten times and received a month of afterschool detentions.

Usually afterschool detentions involved cleaning the lunchroom floor or picking up trash around school property. The lunchroom floor was a mess after three hundred kids ate lunch. Sweeping and mopping took hours, but collecting trash on the playground was even worse. The parish priest stood on a bench and pointed out each individual piece of litter he wanted picked up. "I want that one. There's another." The priest pointed here and there as Louis ran back and forth for hours until the school's playground was completely clean. Louis could pick up only one piece of trash at a time, and run back and place it in the trashcan near the priest. Then the priest pointed out another on the other side of the playground. If Louis walked the priest emptied the trash can. "Clean that up, too," he said.

On certain holy days, the crucifix was placed at the altar and parishioners came up one by one to kiss its feet. Altar boys stood on each side and wiped it clean for the next in line. An old lady was next. She wore caked-on makeup and heavily applied red lipstick. Kissing the statue passionately, she left lipstick everywhere that was impossible to wipe away. Louis and the other altar boy began laughing as they unsuccessfully tried to remove the red marks. "We need bleach!" Louis said quietly.

"Report to the principal's office immediately," Sister Mary barked over the school intercom system early the next morning. Louis had no idea who the people were waiting for him along with Sister Mary. She was furious.

The people in Sister Mary's office were members of the parish with a special needs daughter. They accused Louis of laughing at her during the service. The family was next in line behind the old makeup lady. Louis had not even noticed the family. "I was laughing at that old lady, not your daughter!" No one believed him.

Louis was forced to apologize and go back to confession. "Forgive me, Father, for I have sinned. Again!" Louis said as he entered the confessional. He spent another two months in afterschool detention after saying the Apostle's Creed fifty more times.

The parish priest said the Devil was gaining control of Louis's soul. "You are in danger of becoming lost in Purgatory. A soul roaming the earth trapped forever between heaven and hell." The priest said everything Louis did wrong was another sin moving him along the road to Purgatory. That scared Louis to death.

Louis and Jan met at Resurrection Catholic Elementary School. They both attended Catholic high school and were married after graduation. It was common practice for Catholics to marry young, especially if they were enjoying premarital sex. Marriage was the only way to atone for sins of the flesh and avoid Purgatory.

On Mardi Gras day, 1982, Jan dressed as a tasteful but sexy, catholic school nun. It was a homemade costume she designed and sewed herself. She caught the eye of a freelance photographer, who happened to be on the parade route. He snapped a few photos and said she was a natural beauty. "One of God's grand slam homeruns," he said. Jan's photo turned up on the cover of *Gambit* magazine. She received offers from talent agencies around the country, but turned them down. She preferred to marry Louis and start a family.

On schedule, Louis and Jan started a family and soon had the added responsibility of raising a child. Birth control was also prohibited by the church and sinful. Their daughter, Willow, was born a year later. As obedient Catholics, Louis and Jan were taught to stay married regardless. Divorce was never considered seriously, even as the stress of life's struggles robbed them of the few dreams they managed to remember. They always loved each other, but were unprepared for the tempest of regret that consumed the romance they once shared. Marriages end when bitterness turns to contempt, even Catholic ones.

Still fearful of Purgatory and lost souls, Louis believed that sex outside the marriage was sinful, so he was oblivious to the advances of other women. He wasn't sure if the years had changed Jan's views about marriage. At first everything was wonderful. Jan prepared home-cooked lunches, including soups and salads, hamburgers or grilled sandwiches, and she had everything ready when Louis arrived home. Sometimes they skipped lunch all together and spent the time in the bedroom enjoying each other's attention like newlyweds. Once Jan surprised him by greeting him at the front door in an open bathrobe and nothing else, and they spent an hour on the living room floor.

Things changed. Jan stopped cooking and seldom bothered to get off the sofa when Louis arrived home. "There is leftover fried spam in the fridge. Make yourself a sandwich or something."

Jan purchased stylish new clothes, joined a gym and made appointments at trendy uptown salons. It was all very expensive and much more than Louis could afford. Although Jan reassured him, Louis had his doubts. He knew she had male acquaintances. "They are all just friends," she told him. "Stop being childish."

Jan invited a new 'gym friend' to visit her at home. He was nervous about Louis. "If my husband shows up, admit nothing, deny everything and make counter accusations. Works every time," she joked.

That afternoon Louis left work a few hours early. He did not recognize the gray Pontiac parked in the driveway. Jan was sitting on the couch with a man Louis did not know. "This is Dave. He is my new friend. We met at the gym. He just happened to stop by."

Louis noticed the open bottle of wine and two glasses on the coffee table, but said nothing about it. "Nice to meet you." Louis held out his hand in a friendly manner. The idea that Jan had become restless never occurred to Louis before this. He was not stupid; only too trusting and too Catholic. "She is my wife for better or worse, simple as that," he told a prying coworker.

# 3

LOUIS WANTED TO SAVE HIS marriage and give Jan more of the material things she wanted; he worked hard, saved some money and started a small business. He made some investment decisions, but his timing always seemed off. Louis watched cable financial news shows on a regular basis, and felt he understood macroeconomics and investment banking. Jeff Krueger was the Jerry Springer of financial news. His daily investment show focused on easy money, and was not considered serious investment advice by most financial professionals. Nevertheless, it was popular with wide audiences. Investment experts paid a fee to appear on the show. Krueger never disclosed this fact. His shirtsleeves were always rolled up; he was sweaty and he yelled a lot. Most considered the show to be silly financial porn. Still, Louis believed that Jeff Krueger and his experts were brilliant, and he sought to profit from their advice.

Louis started buying gold bullion and numismatics in the 1990s, and had a few gold Krugerrands, silver Morgan dollars and some other US gold coins. Most of the coins were purchased when gold was two-hundred and fifty dollars an ounce. Louis had to sell them at an inopportune time to cover unexpected monthly bills. He discovered that some of his coins were placed in fake plastic squares so they would appear to be uncirculated. Some of his silver coins were artificially aged with shoe polish and cigar smoke, and some were filed down and stamped with bogus rare dates. Louis eventually made a few thousand dollars on the authentic coins he had left.

The LeMoyne family always dreamed of owning Gulf-front property. Planning to roll his coin proceeds into a new investment, Louis began searching for the most inexpensive beach property available. It took decades for the Mississippi Gulf Coast to recover after Hurricane Camille. Vacant beachfront lots, barren cement slabs and condemned buildings remained untouched for decades. During that time property prices were significantly undervalued.

Louis and Jan managed to purchase a small, commercial, beachfront lot for about $21,000. The property was owner financed with a two-thousand-dollars down payment. It had been owned by the same family for generations, so they also owned the valuable beach rights across the highway. The rights were included with the purchase. Property values shot up once the Mississippi casinos appeared. Louis listed the property and soon had an offer for $150,000. Afraid the buyers would back out, Louis sweetened the pot and threw in the beach rights for free. "Let them have them," he told his listing agent. Today those beach rights would make Louis a rich man if he had not given them away. Nevertheless, he did have the $150,000 to invest. That was more money than Louis had ever dreamed he would have.

Louis invested $50,000 of his real-estate profits in a "sure thing" investment program that was guaranteed to triple his original investment. His total income could have been $300,000 once his name reached the top position on the list. "Dare to dream big. A money-making phenomenon!" the salesman guaranteed in unrealistic returns. The program turned out to be a worthless get-rich-quick scheme. Louis sent $10,000 each to the top five names on a long list and mailed thirty solicitations to new participants. His name was added to the bottom of the list. If everything went well, he expected to receive thirty $10,000 checks. It was a classic scam. Louis received nothing.

Louis was introduced to a well-known New Orleans wealth manager called 'The Iron Lung Broker.' He contracted polio in the 1950s, and for the next forty years he spent every day in an iron lung breathing machine. The broker learned about business while a patient at the famous Georgia Hall Polio Treatment Facility in Warm Springs,

Georgia. He chose to study markets and finance as part of a rehabilitation program offered at the facility designed to teach personal independence to polio survivors. The broker called clients and prospects nine hours a day while enclosed in the breathing machine. He convinced Louis to invest $30,000 in a Master Limited Partnership (MLP) involving offshore crew boats and supply vessels. Louis invested in an ownership percentage of three boats. The broker called them the 'Tiger Fleet,' and had the boats painted LSU colors. "You can't lose with LSU!" he said.

Eventually, falling oil prices caused day rates charged by the boats to drop by 50%. Operating expenses exceeded revenue and the boats were mothballed. "You should have read the offering documents and prospectus. Didn't I tell you that?" The broker said Louis learned a valuable lesson about investing. "It's not about making money; it is about managing risk. Did Jeff Krueger forget to mention that?"

The iron lung broker did not worry about laws, regulations or compliance. He thought no penitentiary in the country could accommodate his seven-foot-long, eight-hundred-pound yellow breathing machine. He was mistaken.

The Securities and Exchange Commission investigated the broker for securities fraud, revoked his license and gave him a four-year prison sentence. The broker insisted it was all a small misunderstanding. Eventually, Louis recovered ten cents on the dollar.

Willow was raised in the inherited camelback double on Montegut Street near Saint Claude Avenue. Bob Dylan made the street famous when he mentioned it in his song, "Tangled up in Blue." It was an area of natural high ground, unusual in New Orleans. It was less expensive to live in this area because flood insurance was not required, saving hundreds of dollars each year.

Trying to provide a comfortable home for Jan and Willow, Louis converted the inherited double into a single home with about 2,000 square feet: three bedrooms and two baths. He did almost everything himself, working on weekends and late evenings. Louis knocked out a wall that separated two upstairs bedrooms and made one large room for Willow. He modernized the upstairs bath with two vanities and a modern shower, and learned to do tile work, but he did not do sheetrock. It was hard and difficult. Louis always preferred to hire professionals for that. He used marble tiles on the kitchen countertops and bought stainless appliances with a Home Depot credit card. The floors were done with artificial wood laminate that snapped into place. It all came out quite nice. Louis considered it a great accomplishment to own a remolded home free and clear.

The neighborhood was mixed zoning of residential and light industrial. The L&N railyard was across the street and the old Zetzman 7-Up bottling plant was at the end of the block. Freight trains began rolling at 4:30 a.m. every morning and a fleet of soft drink delivery trucks left an hour later. They all rumbled past Louis's house, so alarm clocks were not necessary.

Once Louis finished the home renovations, the city reappraised the property for tax assessments. Since it was now valued at more than the allowable homestead exemption, Louis faced an unexpected property tax bill. It took him three weeks to get an appointment with the elected tax assessor.

"What can be done about this? I can't afford a big bill like this every year. I would never have renovated the house if I had known this."

The tax assessor listened politely, showing little interest. He checked his watch twice.

"I get ten to twenty people in here every day asking for the same thing. Nobody likes to pay taxes," he said, and then changed the topic to fishing. The assessor had a passion for fishing and he loved his 16-foot aluminum flat boat. "The boat itself is great, but the motor is worn out. I sure could use a new twenty-five horsepower outboard. Yes sir, a new motor would be just the thing."

Louis understood this was a shakedown, but a new motor was expensive. He didn't have the money. "Thanks for your time." Louis shook the assessor's hand and left the office.

"Sorry we couldn't reach an agreement; perhaps next time. Don't forget to vote." The assessor closed his door.

Jan did not work, but she maxed out credit cards at the Biloxi casinos. She also spent any extra money the family had playing the dollar slot machines at the Rivage, where she claimed to have a foolproof system for winning. "They make me feel special, like a movie star! I get free meals and free drinks. The employees know my name. I feel important when I am there. It is glamorous and I love the elegance of it." Occasionally Jan showed Louis a publicity photo of her with a giant check, usually for five-hundred dollars or less. She never talked about the money she lost.

"Everyone eventually loses at those places. The odds are never in your favor," Louis said, hoping to curtail Jan's expensive Biloxi habit.

"Loses!? You mean like your fake silver coins, iron lung broker or stupid chain letter foolishness? You got no room to talk. At least I get dinner and drinks when I get screwed."

Melba's Ice Cream was located near Montegut Street on Franklin Avenue. Louis and Willow walked across the L&N tracks to Franklin Avenue and Melba's. They always invited Jan, but she declined because she was watching her weight. Louis seldom went out to eat or spent money unnecessarily, but he looked forward all week to ice cream on Saturday afternoons with Willow. It was the highlight of his week.

They especially enjoyed Melba's, not only because the ice cream was wonderful, but also because the shop attracted so many interesting characters. Louis and Willow enjoyed people watching. One man sat at the same table always eating a large bowl of vanilla ice cream. He drove an expensive car, wore nice clothes, and liked to show off his gold bracelet and diamond Rolex. He concentrated on enjoying his ice cream and never spoke or even said hello. "Do you think he is a bank president or something?" They were only guessing.

"I want chocolate or maybe strawberry with sprinkles and whipped cream," Willow reasoned after considering her options.

"I'm going to try a nutty-buddy this time!" Louis and Willow playfully argued all week about the best flavors, never reaching a consensus. "I guess we just need to try them all," she said.

# 4

THE MONTEGUT STREET LOCATION AND zoning worked well since Louis could rent an old warehouse nearby. It suited his small startup home maintenance and river sand business perfectly. Parking for employees and his old dump truck was adequate; walking home for lunch was an added benefit.

Using his remaining money from the Mississippi property invest-ment, Louis purchased a secondhand dump truck and used it to haul river sand from the spillway to residential lots around the city. The Bonnet Carre Spillway diverts flood water from the Mississippi River into Lake Pontchartrain. River sand sediments deposited after the spillway opened are available to anyone willing and able to haul it away. This keeps flood waters flowing freely to the lake the next time the spillway is needed. It also created a great business opportunity for anyone in New Orleans with access to a dump truck. Each delivered load of sand sold for $185. Louis averaged two or three deliveries each day, and almost all the revenue was pure profit.

The sand was used to fill low areas in yards caused by the subsiding soil. They call it sand, but it is a chocolate-colored mud that carries rich nutrients washed down from the center of the continent. Sci-entist called it alluvial deposits; locals called it river sand. City flood officials ran the pumping stations around the clock. They lowered the water table so much that some neighborhoods sank six inches each year as soil dried out. Flood protection in exchange for broken foundations and cracked driveways were the trade-offs New Orleans homeowners faced.

Spreading river sand was a New Orleans summer community tradition. Kids played in the giant sand piles until neighbors pitched in with wheelbarrows. They spread it around sinking yards the way Pennsylvania Amish communities joined together to raise barns. The major difference between New Orleans and the Amish in Pennsylvania was beer and boiled crawfish. New Orleans sand parties involved alcohol, Cajun music and dancing. The celebrations eventually moved inside, because the mosquitoes got bad at night.

"Hey mister! Where you bringing that sand?" Five young boys on bicycles followed behind Louis's truck as he turned onto Jewel Street in Lake Vista. The address was an upper middle-class, brick, single-family home on a double lot near the lakefront.

"Stand back, boys." Within a few minutes, Louis placed six square yards of beautiful river sand exactly where instructed.

The boys were trying to ride their bikes over the sand hill like motorcycle stuntmen. It was impossible since the sand was so soft. When their front wheels got stuck they fell over face first, laughing all the while. Four neighbors were already pushing wheelbarrows down the street ready to help; two were wearing Saints jerseys. One wheelbarrow was full of ice and beer. It was heavy and hard to maneuver, especially with only one hand. The other hand held an open Dixie longneck. Fifty pounds of crawfish were boiling on the back patio.

The lady of the house paid Louis's invoice and invited him to stay awhile. She asked many questions about his business. "William-Mark, my husband, is lazy. I wish he owned a business. All he does is sit around all day and drink beer while I work! I manage a law firm. He does nothing! But he did show initiative once. He read that tilapia was becoming a popular and profitable fish, so William-Mark converted our swimming pool into a tilapia breeding colony and backyard fish farm! He said they grow fast and called them aquatic chickens. He said it was easy money, but when early fall temperatures fell below 65 degrees all his tilapia died. He did not realize that the temperature information he studied applied to in-ground pools. William-Mark was using our above-ground pool, which cooled down much quicker in colder weather. The entire economic misadventure became an enormous mess!" she said.

"Where you get dem crawfish?" William-Mark called out to his wife. He was already on his fifth beer.

"I got um from Seafood City on the corner of Paris and Saint Bernard Avenue. The same place I always get um. Best prices in town," she said.

"Dat place is king of da straight tails! That's why da prices are so cheap!" another drunken neighbor said.

When crawfish are boiled, their tails wrap down and under their bodies. If a boiled crawfish has a straight tail it was already dead. No one eats the straight tails except tourists.

"Da last time I went to Seafood City I tru half of dem away!" William-Mark was complaining, but still eating.

French Cajuns are descendants from original settlers after the French and Indian War. They left Quebec and settled in Louisiana. Creoles are French and Spanish from the colonial days, but also have mixed blood from the East Indies and Haiti. Cajuns are found mostly in the Acadian Parishes to the West of New Orleans. Creoles are common in New Orleans, especially the 7th Ward. Cajuns and Creoles are very different from a New Orleans 'Yat'. William-Mark would be affectionately called a Yat. His descendants were from Germany and they settled in parts of Midcity, Gentilly, and most recently in Chalmette. They say 'dis' instead of this, 'dat' instead of that, 'da' rather than the, and 'dem' for them.

Louis left about forty-five minutes later. The men were still eating and drinking, the boys were still trying to jump the sand hill and the party was moving indoors because, as expected, the mosquitoes were bad! Not a single wheelbarrow of sand was spread.

Louis's sand deliveries generated enough cash to build and grow the business. Bayou Contracting Shoppe still hauled sand, but they also repaired foundations, replaced roofs, remodeled and fixed plumbing problems. Jan suggested the extra 'pe' in the name because she said it made the business classy. Over the years Louis expanded the business, eventually owning three dump trucks, a bulldozer and various other pieces of heavy equipment.

He also owned the New Orleans franchise for Level Lock Foundation Repair, a company that specialized in cracked foundation repair and home elevation enhancement addressing flood insurance problems for houses built in the lowest lying areas. Many older homes were built with crawl spaces underneath; they could be lifted with huge jacks, and then back filled with river sand or placed on taller footings. Louis raised the base elevation of only two or three houses a year, but it was a profitable part of his business. Bayou Contracting employed one person to answer phones and run the office (his sister-in-law did that) and five full-time workers. New Orleans is full of historic homes. Louis considered it a privilege to work in such an interesting city.

He also traded services from time to time. He replaced a roof in exchange for a truck engine rebuild and he leveled a foundation for a surgeon's office on Napoleon Avenue near Baptist Hospital in exchange for medical services.

"That covered the cost on my appendectomy," Louis said.

As you may have guessed, Louis did not have much formal education, although he was runner-up in a citywide high school essay contest. The winner won a scholarship to Brother Martin High School, the runner-up received a year's subscription to the *Times Picayune* newspaper. So, Louis attended Francis T. Nicholls Public High School on Saint Claude Avenue. It was built in 1940 at the old MaCarty Square location that was once a monument to WWI veterans from the area. Louis ate his school lunch every day under a large, marble arch memorial inscribed with the names of 1,231 WWI heroes.

Louis worked hard and read a lot, especially books about the Crescent

City, and he enjoyed onion rings, but that is another story for another day. Louis loved reading Southern fiction as well, and had many favorite authors, especially Walker Percy. He also loved New Orleans and Tulane University, but the closest Louis had ever been to the university was watching Green Wave football at the old Willow Street stadium, affectionately called 'The Sugar Bowl'.

He was there in 1973 with his father when Tulane beat LSU 14-0. At the time, 85,000 fans were at the 'Sugar Bowl'. Louis remembered watching all the Tulane players leaving the bench and pilling on each other every time the Green Wave scored. Louis still had the faded green and white Tulane pennant from that game.

His dad always tried to avoid game-day traffic. They drove down Canal Street to City Park Avenue, took a left at the cemeteries and turned onto Bamboo Road. They turned onto Earhart, and then to Carrolton and finally Claiborne Avenue. It would have been faster to take a direct route to the stadium straight down Claiborne Avenue like everyone else, but Louis's dad had to avoid congestion because slow-moving traffic caused his old Chevy to overheat. The worn-out car smoked more than Humphrey Bogart and was nearly in a comatose condition. They were lucky to get that far.

After the games, they spent a few hours walking the campus, waiting for the traffic to clear. Louis's dad knew the names of all the Tulane buildings and their purpose. The oaks with Spanish moss and historic buildings were greeted like old friends. "This is where Tulane holds graduation ceremonies." He always reminded Louis of that each time they walked past McAlister Auditorium.

Louis learned to love Tulane. He visited the campus often with his father for many years. It was there, after a winter walk, that Louis met Kathy. She was beautiful in a demure sort of way, wearing a snug-fitting black dress over a very attractive petite figure. She looked beautiful and posh like Audrey Hepburn in the opening scene of "Breakfast at Tiffany's." Kathy walked over to his table, pulled up a chair and confidently introduced herself. She was quick-witted with natural charisma and irresistible magnetism. When she spoke, her eyebrows were animated, crunching together when she was puzzled or asked a question. They arched up, expressing surprise. She must have been terrible at poker.

"You look like a real Tulane fan!" She joked about his matching Green Wave jacket and shirt. Kathy finished a BS in Engineering Physics at Newcomb College, Tulane's college for women, and then earned a Masters in Computational Science from Tulane's School of Science and Engineering. She enrolled in Newcomb as an undergrad student to get the unique acorn graduation ring, an old family tradition. Wearing the oak leaf ring proudly, she said her mother and grandmother both finished at Newcomb College.

Kathy was the most beautiful uptown girl Louis had ever met, and she seemed interested in what he had to say! Conversation flowed effortlessly for hours. She eventually talked about her husband. The marriage was failing and they were profoundly unhappy. A counselor said Kathy and her husband were two of the most incompatible individuals she had ever met. "I still don't understand how love can die so quickly and so completely. It is doubtful we will stay friends, because we do not even like each other. It is all very sad," she said. "People change, but I don't even know him now. All he does is eat ice cream and smoke cigarettes." Kathy said that he recently took a short trip to Atlanta.

"The hotel refrigerator was stocked with many pint-size ice cream containers. When he checked out, the desk clerk said there must be some mistake, because he was charged for a total of two gallons of vanilla ice cream. He agreed and said that was incorrect. It was actually three gallons." Kathy laughed as she finished telling the story.

"Still, he was surprised when I moved out. He was in the bathroom when I said I was leaving. He asked me to bring back more ice cream!" Kathy said he did not take her seriously at first and thought she would never leave. She was most upset about not being able to remarry in the Catholic Church. "I will be forced to pay for this youthful misjudgment for the rest of my life. I know leaving an unhappy marriage should be easy, but as in engineering the simple is always the most difficult to accomplish," she said.

As a trained engineer, Kathy had expected the pieces of her life to fit perfectly in place, like Lego blocks snapping together. Human nature is not science, she discovered. "There are no engineering formulas for predicting the rhythm of love, hate, jealousy, companionship, friendship, broken hearts, disappointments and restlessness. Life has a clever habit of shuffling unanticipated events in confounding ways. Like a Nancy Drew 'whodunit' mystery, there is always an answer, but correctly reading the essence of clues and motives along the way is difficult. Still, life's random surprises can bring welcoming change leading in unforeseen but wonderful directions. It is this hopeful unpredictability that makes being alive worthwhile," she reasoned.

Louis had to save his money all week to take his family to see a movie at the Lakeview Theater. Kathy's grandmother owned the theater. Louis's unfortunate economic circumstances did not seem to bother Kathy. It was the start of a cherished friendship between them. She wondered why Louis loved Tulane so much.

"Imagine being a student here. I can't think of anything I ever wanted more. Just wasn't in the cards for me. Things could have been different. I came real close," Louis confessed in response to Kathy's curiosity. He explained how close he came to winning the Brother Martin High School scholarship essay contest. "Then I would have been qualified for Tulane admissions. I was real close," he said.

Louis said his dad had a similar story. "He dropped out of school after only the eighth grade to find work. Then he spent the next forty years operating a dry-cleaning machine in a laundromat on North Miro Street. On weekends, he used a small aluminum flat boat with an old Johnson Sea Horse motor to fish in the marshlands around the Rigolets and Lake Borgne. Dad was never proud of being a dry cleaner, but life has a way of kicking you down and keeping you that way. We always had food on the table, but usually it was something cooked in pots, like red beans, butter beans or cabbage. Dad was very proud. He never allowed me to eat dinner or supper with friends because he did not want neighbors to think he could not provide. He never had a childhood. His only pleasure in life was watching Green Wave football in the Willow Street stadium and that old boat," Louis said.

Tulane supported the construction of the Louisiana Superdome on Poydras Street, however the university planned to keep The Sugar Bowl for college games, high school football games and other sporting events. But Louisiana politicians with their skullduggery antics screwed the university. They did not want Tulane's stadium competing with their expensive new dome stadium. Two months after the Superdome opened, state inspectors condemned the Sugar Bowl as unsafe and ordered its demolishment. The President of Tulane announced the sad news. Louis's father stood on the Claiborne Avenue neutral ground and watched wrecking crews go about their work. It was the only time Louis saw his father cry.

Louis's daughter, Willow, was very smart. He thought she could be the first in his family to attend college, maybe even Tulane. There is a joke in New Orleans. "What is the difference between the University of New Orleans and Tulane?" The punch line is, "The annual tuition charged by UNO is equal to the weekly spending money given to most Tulane students." It is not funny, but does make a good point. Tulane is expensive, but it is money well spent. Nevertheless, the university had a program that allowed children of all employees to attend Tulane free of charge. A doctor from Thailand moved his family to New Orleans and worked as a campus landscaper to receive the tuition waiver for his three college-age children. Many others did the same. The university never had problems filling job openings.

The university gave each Louisiana state senator and representative one tuition waiver each year. The scholarships were intended to go to deserving students unable to afford the expense. It is a deal that goes back to the 1880s involving Tulane property tax exemptions. These scholarships all went to powerful friends and wealthy political families. Also, every member of the Louisiana Board of Elementary and Secondary Education awarded Robert C. Byrd scholarships annually. These awards are supposed to go to needy students as well, but per newspapers this board is another Louisiana den of political snakes. Louis didn't know any politicians or influential people, so he did not expect any help from elected officials. He wrote a letter to the editor expressing his disappointment with this situation. Disappointment is a powerful word; it can't be rebutted. In the end, it made no difference, because no one cared enough to bother.

One Sunday afternoon Louis spent thirty dollars and took Willow on a guided walking tour of the French Quarter. The tour guide pointed out an old building and said it was built for Napoleon if he escaped captivity on Saint Helena Island as planned by conspirators in New Orleans.

"That's wrong. This building was built twenty years after Napoleon already died. Everybody knows that," Louis said.

The guide suggested he become certified, and then he could lead his own tours. He called Louis a "smart ass."

That would-be Louis's dream job, a professional tour guide in historic New Orleans. But Willow needed to go to college, and Louis needed to make enough money to pay for it somehow.

# 5

A FEW YEARS AGO, A well-known Louisiana 'oil man' died unexpectedly of heart failure. His Subchapter "S" oil and gas exploration company was large and successful. The 'oil man' claimed to be the wealthiest man in Louisiana with a total net worth of more than $200million dollars. Having no children, he left nearly his entire estate to the benefit of public school children in New Orleans. Having grown up poor to a single mom in Houston, he learned the value of education as a student on scholarship at LSU. He also realized the importance of moving Louisiana's economy away from its dependence on the oil and gas industry, and believed that oil patch jobs were not a solid enough foundation to build a modern Louisiana economy on.

"Education is a generational thing. Often the expectation for college success is determined by the education achievement level of the parents. Without family support, academic success is unlikely," he said at every occasion. The oil man believed education was an important tool used to escape poverty. His scholarship program evolved into a statewide reform movement.

Before desegregation, many Louisiana school districts did not build high schools for creole students. Most local school boards offered agriculture training or nothing at all. Academic study beyond the eighth grade was not available to most creole kids. Those few that did make it to the eighth grade used out-of-date hand-me-down textbooks salvaged from white schools. Since it was impossible for creoles to attend secondary school, college was completely out of the question.

Because they lacked educational opportunity, creoles also suffered economically. The entire situation was a devastating "Catch 22." The innovative scholarship program funded by the oil man's wealthy estate intended to help level the playing field and improve the neglected New Orleans public schools in the process.

The program was different than all others because it provided enrichment and academic support throughout the high school years. Students enrolled in the program met each week with advisors and counselors specifically assigned to them. They reviewed and tracked student progress. The full-time counselors also provided advice on goal setting, effective communications, life skills and study habits, and ACT practice tests were offered every six months.

As part of the program, students spent two weeks every summer living in real college dorm rooms and taking special classes on college campuses. Even the US military offered summer living space at the Belle Chase Naval Air Station and the Algiers Navy Yard. The goal was to keep kids off the streets and out of trouble during the long, hot, New Orleans summers. With the successful completion of each high school year, more and more college expenses not covered by financial aid were waived. Eventually, hardworking students could cover the entire cost of a four-year university education.

Lesley was the Executive Director of the scholarship program from its inception, and did a remarkable job designing and implementing all aspects of it. Her successful efforts were recognized by Tulane with an Honorary Doctor of Humanities Degree awarded by the College of Liberal Arts. She was asked to deliver the commencement address the following year. Tulane commencements are known around the world for being unique celebrations, recognizing scholarly achievement with jazz music, Mardi Gras beads and thousands of people celebrating and doing the 'second line' in the Superdome.

She was introduced by Tulane's president, took a deep breath and stepped to the podium.

"I want to take a moment to thank my husband, Clarence. He has always loved and supported me," she continued after a short pause. "No child should be condemned to a lifetime of failure and disappointments simply because they were born in the wrong school district in the wrong city in the wrong state." Lesley's voice was a little shaky, but her nerves were settling down.

She looked up from her notes and became more confident. "During the last fifty years Louisiana high school drop-outs could easily find well-paid work on rigs, production platforms or crew boats. High school was an unnecessary inconvenience and college was a worthless expense, since oil patch jobs were available, secure and lucrative. These jobs are disappearing and Louisiana has found itself at the bottom of all fifty states in the measurements of academic achievement. Economic concentration and specialization is harmful, making a state's economy vulnerable in the face of random economic or natural events. When the oil price drops one dollar per barrel, Louisiana's education budgets lose twelve million dollars." Lesley went on discussing other similar examples like Japan's dependence on the automobile sector, Botswana's reliance on diamonds and Egypt's tourism industry.

"Quality public education was unnecessary when a booming oil industry was offering on-the-job-training and secure careers, even for drop-outs. Nevertheless, in today's globally competitive world a high school diploma is just not enough. If Louisiana's economy is to be modern, competitive and diverse, we must address the crisis in high school dropout rates, college costs, economic diversity and sustainability."

Lesley stepped away from the rostrum and walked across the stage as she made more important points. She discussed Junior Colleges and Quick-Start job training programs. Lesley said Louisiana's lack of a competitive community college system and articulation agreements with four-year public universities created academic dead ends. "Charter schools could break the hold corrupt school officials have over the entire system, but current funding formulas won't allow it," she explained. All Minimum Foundation Funding (MFP) dollars for public schools were allocated based on enrollment figures in early October.

"I believe every smart child in New Orleans should have the opportunity to attend college regardless of the financial wherewithal of their family or color of their skin. Too often college opportunity has been stolen by mediocre inner-city schools, corrupt officials and outrageous costs. Why would any student study hard if high school was unnecessary or if college was financially out of reach?

"Once Louisiana's economy modernizes away from oil and gas dependence, then inner-city schools will work harder to meet university admission requirements, and New Orleans families will support academic reforms with renewed enthusiasm. Success should not be limited by poor quality underperforming schools, or how much a family earns or the price of oil. It does no good to be disillusioned with the corrupt, unscrupulous and inert nature of government functionaries if we are unwilling to resist them and work for real education reforms. We need an academic rebirth in this city and this state!" The standing ovation lasted a long time. Tulane faculty members were the first to stand and the last to sit. Tulane's president rose to shake Lesley's hand.

"Well said. I could not agree more. We need to work together reforming this system. Education reform should be this state's most important and urgent endeavor," he whispered in her ear.

New Orleans has many reasonably priced Catholic girls' high schools like Cabrini and Saint Mary's, but even these schools were financially out of reach for Creole families of modest means. Willow attended Warren Eastern Public High School. The LeMoyne family had no choice in the matter. since this was the public school designated for their neighborhood. It was a typical urban school with discipline problems, tired teachers and politically connected administrators. Ninety-five percent of all students qualified for the free lunch programs. No one was held accountable for the school's

45% dropout rate or high number of social promotions.

An idealistic new math teacher was eager to start his first day as a certified Warren Eastern teacher. He went into the boys' bathroom to break up a commotion. Two boys defecated in their hands and threw it at him. "I quit!" he announced to the principal, never to return. He went to California seeking a new career working in Silicon Valley. The only thing Warren Eastern High School was ever known for is the fact that Lee Harvey Oswald attended there before going to Dallas.

Under the circumstances, Willow did the best she could. She was on the yearbook committee, the National Honor Organization and the Library Club. Her GPA was a 3.8, placing her near the top of her class. All her classes were designated as 'Gifted and Talented,' and were supposed to be college prep. She took the ACT college entrance exam as a high school freshman. Willow scored a 12, low for college early admissions standards, but outstanding for a New Orleans public high school freshman.

"I'll never get to a good university. I won't even get into a backwater community college at this rate." She felt defeated and asked if she could get a job in her dad's business and forget about college. "It's totally hopeless." She was discouraged.

Lesley met Willow at Warren Eastern. She was there interviewing the brightest students. "If you fulfill the program requirements, then we will see to it that you will go to college." She explained everything in detail. Willow was thrilled and looked at high school with a renewed enthusiasm.

For the next three years, Willow did everything expected. Her ACT scores climbed steadily from a 12 to a 30. She also took the SAT and scored a 1295, well above the national average. Willow took the hardest classes and met with counselors and tutors three times each week. She sat-in on evening writing classes at Delgado Community College. Willow also signed up to help immigrant students learn English. On Tuesday and Thursday mornings she tutored six students at the English as a Second Language lab in the Warren Eastern library. She graduated at the top of her high school class. "I can't wait to follow your college success. You are going to do great," Lesley told her.

Willow learned to stay safe by avoiding particularly dangerous high school bathrooms as much as possible. That is where rapes happened. A recent assault at the school was classified as aggravated trespassing when a neighborhood vagrant hid in a bathroom stall. School administrators and police called the attack 'trespassing' to avoid negative publicity. When walking the halls between classes, Willow tried hard to look purposeful and confident, even though she was constantly scared to death.

She rode the public service bus every day. Willow never stood at a bus stop alone, never flashed money and carried only a few one-dollar bills at a time. She sat near the driver and did not sleep on the bus, even when exhausted. Always aware of her surroundings, she was never able to be caught off guard. When possible, Willow used the hidden batture trails to avoid the delinquents and hoodlums stalking public transportation. The little-known land between the levee and the river was wooded with dense undergrowth, but the footpaths were peaceful and isolated, especially during the summer low water stages of the river. It was perfect for avoiding the violent drug gangs roaming the city. Willow was street smart.

Holding down weekend and evening jobs on those days she was not working on her scholarships, Willow insisted on contributing financially to the family. She worked as a bank teller for two years for a small bank with five local branches. "They say tellers are the bank's window to the community; it's most important employees. I handle thousands of dollars each day, but my pay is minimum wage. How is that possible?" Willow turned down an opportunity to enter the branch manager training program because it required a full-time commitment for two years and she planned to go to college.

Willow worked in the bank's main office on Canal Street. She was the only creole employee. The president's office was directly behind the teller line. He thought it would be a good idea to have live birds in the lobby. "No other bank does anything like that. Our customers will love it," he insisted.

The massive brass cage was large enough to hold fifteen white doves. It was situated directly in the center of the lobby. "They look like pigeons!" Willow did not see how this would attract customers. It took Willow about thirty minutes to balance her teller drawer, if everything went well. Then she had to clean the bird cage and change the paper at the bottom of it. This was a filthy job that took another twenty-five minutes. Willow would go home, eat dinner, and then study until she fell asleep. She quit the bank to take another job that did not involve birds.

Willow enjoyed her new job working at the Hilton Riverview Hotel. Starting as a pool person, handing out clean towels to hotel guests, she moved up quickly. "Creole girls are the world's most beautiful. Successful men fly across the country to be near them. It's just human nature." The hotel manager said Willow was smart and beautiful. "You should never clean bird cages again," he said.

Willow soon became the hotel's concierge, assisting guests with restaurant reservations, booking transportation and managing a team of bellhops and doormen. Willow also coordinated special events with the convention center. She earned a decent wage and tips nearly doubled her overall income above that. The hotel was directly connected to the New Orleans Convention Center, the River Walk shopping center and food court. Hotel kitchens catered events at the convention center and supplied many of the food court vendors.

Hidden passages linked everything together. "I love moving around unseen. These secret tunnels and passageways are really cool." Willow said they reminded her of Disney World, as she'd read that all operational support was hidden from guest view. She had keys to the many non-descript doors in the Convention Center that allowed servers and workers to magically appear wherever necessary. "Someone could hide here for months in these catacombs and no one would ever know," she said.

Tulane receives about 30,000 to 40,000 undergraduate admission applications each year. At times, that is more than any other private university in the country. Of that number, they accept about 1,200. For her admissions essay, Willow wrote about her family.

"New Orleans Creole families never had much good luck. My grandfather spent his life operating a dry-cleaning machine, but he loved Green Wave football. He never missed a home game at the Willow Street Stadium. My dad inherited his love of Tulane from his father. No one in my family has ever been able to afford college." She discussed her struggles in public high school and her family's financial situation. "I want to attend Tulane, not only for myself, but for the generations of my family deprived of great dreams." Finally, she explained how proud her grandfather was the day he was told his granddaughter would be named 'Willow.'

Willow received her acceptance letter on a Saturday morning. Her heart pounded as she pried her fingers into the envelope, tearing it open from the top. She ignored her discouraging mother, who said she didn't understand all the fuss and didn't see any difference between a good community college and Tulane. "Dreams are like demons, trust me. I know from experience. First they overwhelm you, and then they consume you. You are better off without them."

Willow unfolded the letter, but kept her eyes closed for a long time. Her mother showed little interest.

"I'm in! I'm going to Tulane!" Willow ran back and forth around the house.

She ran down Montegut Street to her dad's shop. He could hear her excitement from a block away. Neighbors came out on their porches as Willow ran by.

"I'm going to Tulane!"

# 6

THE YEAR 2004 WAS THE worst hurricane season in memory, and things seemed to be getting worst. Florida was hit by four or five major category 4 storms. Hurricane Charley was a category 4 that made landfall near Fort Myers with 145 mph winds. Frances and Karl were also category 4 storms. Powerful Hurricane Ivan slammed into the Alabama Gulf Coast. New Orleans was targeted in Ivan's warning area, but the storm turned north sooner than expected, sparing the city. Louisiana's good luck became Alabama's misfortune. The beach towns of Gulf Shores and Orange Beach received a devastating direct hit. Parts of the Fort Morgan Peninsula were nearly sliced in half by Ivan's powerful surge, which reached north past the intercostal waterway in some places.

Everything that was stored under the raised homes on West Beach was washed out past Little Lagoon and deposited on Fort Morgan Road. The road was blocked with jet skis, furniture, boats, construction debris and the wreckage from destroyed beachfront homes. The National Guard used heavy equipment to clear a path. The narrow single-lane passage was like a canyon with fifteen-foot-high walls of rubble lining each side. Entire families combed the mountains of debris hopefully searching for lost personal items. Desperate men started fistfights over the limited water and MREs provided by the guardsmen. The ready-to-eat meals were Army surplus from the first Persian Gulf War. They provided the only nutrition most storm survivors would have for weeks.

That weekend was also the LSU/ Auburn football game in Auburn, Alabama. It was one of the biggest SEC games of the year. Evacuees from the beaches were sent away, making room for the football fans. "Sorry, the LSU fans made reservations last year. There is nothing we can do." Hotel managers showed no sympathy, and the Louisiana fans were short-tempered because some of their rooms were not ready on time. "The storm is not our problem. Geaux Tigers!" Their cavalier attitudes were fostered by the sense of security provided by the massive fail-proof wall of levees surrounding New Orleans. Tulane played in the Sunbelt League, and their smaller games were not an inconvenience for anyone.

Meanwhile, Louis decided to sell Bayou Contracting Shoppe and apply for employment at Tulane. This was the only way to cover the tuition difference for Willow's scholarship. The scholarship paid 100% of the cost of a public university. Families choosing a private university had to make up the cost difference. Louis was happy about selling the stressful business, and looked forward to spending days at such a beautiful place as the Tulane campus. It was certainly better than his musty, poorly ventilated and hot old warehouse.

Louis had grown tired of the obstacles and hardships faced by all small business owners. He would not miss meeting payroll every week. There had been many Thursday nights when he woke at 2:00 a.m. throwing-up because he had no idea how he would make payroll the next morning. Louis did try to keep his sense of humor. "I sleep like a baby—I wake up every two hours and cry," he said. Many times, Louis covered business expenses with personal credit cards. Often the paychecks he wrote to himself were placed in a bottom draw and never cashed. He shredded them at year's end.

The Willow Street Stadium was long gone, but memories of the times he spent there with his father could never fade. He would always love Tulane, and was incredibly proud of Willow. Louis scheduled a meeting with the senior associate vice president for facilities services. He planned to verify the job's tuition benefits first, and then if all went well with the interview he would see a business broker about listing his company for sale.

Tulane campus maintenance supervisors earned an annual salary of about sixty thousand dollars and generous benefits, including health insurance and a 401k retirement plan as well. The tuition benefits made the opportunity even more attractive for Louis. He accepted the position without delay.

"See you in two weeks. You will love it here." The facilities vice president was happy to hire a worker as skilled and dependable as Louis.

Louis calculated the value of his business to be about three-hundred thousand dollars, but he would be willing to sell for two-hundred and fifty thousand if the sale closed quickly. At this price, he could pay-off debt and have a cash cushion available as he started his new career at Tulane as a groundskeeper. Louis's hard work was finally paying off and he looked forward to having financial security. Louis even hoped to buy a new Chevy, his first new car ever. He expected Bayou Contracting to sell fast, but was willing to offer owner financing on a small portion of the purchase price if necessary. Louis understood that most business brokers charged an 8% commission on the purchase price.

Jan was happy Louis would finally make some real money for a change. "It's about time. Finally, I can live the decent life style I've earned. I'm tired of living like a dog on the street. I want to spend money. Everybody gets to chase dreams except me. That needs to change," she said in a smart-alecky tone while mentioning her desire to spend a summer in Paris. She warned Louis about screwing things up. He looked at Jan the way an enlisted Army recruit looks at an overbearing superior officer. He wanted to say exactly what was on his mind, but decided it was in his best interest to keep quiet. Financially, Louis believed things were finally going well.

MBI Brokers had been selling small businesses in New Orleans for decades. They asked Louis to bring all the necessary paperwork, including income statements and tax returns. "So, the warehouse lease is short term and the owner has a first refusal right on subleasing or lease transfers? The trucks are leased as well, and you claim that revenue is greater than presented because you under-reported cash and bartered on some large jobs. Correct? Does this business actually own anything?" The broker also reviewed the lease documents. "It seems you signed all the lease paperwork as Louis LeMoyne." Louis was puzzled and wondered how else he was supposed to sign his name.

"These documents should have all been signed 'Louis LeMoyne, President Bayou Contracting Shoppe.' You are personally on the hook with the banks. They are not likely to give up that guarantee, regardless of who wants to buy the business. However, they may release you from the obligations if you pledge collateral, like the deed to your house." Louis learned that underreporting income and revenue was a bad idea. A new buyer was not likely to accept his word that revenue was more substantial. "In a business deal everything has to be verified. If it can't be proven, it doesn't exist."

The broker explained 'goodwill' and the intangible value of some businesses. "McDonalds, Ford, Bank America, Pizza Hut, all these companies have tremendous intangible value built up over decades of marketing. It is basically the consumer's positive familiarity and name recognition. You haul sand and fix cracked driveways. Your sand is no different than any other. Most likely, the business has no goodwill value."

The broker pounded numbers into his calculator for a long time, and then looked up over the top of his reading glasses. He furrowed his eyebrows and typed something on his laptop. "There is nothing here to sell. No tangible value at all. All you can do is try to owner-finance a deal with a significant down payment, but you will still have to make all the monthly lease payments yourself. The new owners will basically be buying nothing except a customer list, and if the buyers fail to make payments, then the banks will still force you to pay or they will compel you to file bankruptcy and most likely take your house as well. The franchise agreement with Level Lock Foundation Repair is strong and worthwhile, but this is only a very small part of the business. You do maybe two foundation repairs a year. Perhaps your best option is to forget about Tulane and keep running Bayou Contracting until all the lease terms are satisfied. If you are lucky, maybe you will break even. Sorry we don't have better news, but this is business. I'm not here to tickle your belly." The broker handed

Louis an unexpected bill for three hundred and forty-two dollars; 'balance due for business valuation assessment services,' it read.

If he did not sell the business, then he could not take the Tulane job offer. Without the Tulane job, Louis could not afford Willow's tuition. Kathy reminded Louis that he could take Tulane classes through the School of Continuing Studies as well. "You know, the tuition waver applies to you and Willow." It had not occurred to him that he could be a Tulane student. Louis had to find a way to sell Bayou Contracting. Owner financing seemed to be the only real option at this point. One potential buyer came to mind. Louis called William-Mark. Louis had only met him that once when he delivered river sand to his front yard and stayed for a crawfish party.

"Your timing is perfect. I just got laid-off from da dish industry job, but it was not my fault. Business got slow. But my wife is nagging me to death. She says dat I should be a go-getter and she says dat I drink too much beer, so now I drink more gin. I keep it in a bottle marked HOLY WATER. She will never figure dat out." William-Mark had been washing dishes at a local seafood restaurant. He liked to say he was employed in the 'dish industry.' That sounded much better than saying 'dishwasher.' Louis explained what he had in mind and discussed his owner-financing ideas.

"My wife will sure be happy about dis. Do you think my DUIs will be a factor? It was only a few beers," William-Mark asked.

# 7

THE NEW ORLEANS FLOOD CONTROL systems were constructed well over a century ago. The original levee to the north of the city also served as an elevated railroad track still in use today. Pumping stations moved flood water through the 17th Street Canal, Orleans Canal, New Basin and Lower Line canal out to Lake Pontchartrain. Over the years, additional land was reclaimed and filled between the pumping stations and the lake, creating entirely new neighborhoods of Lakeshore, Lake Vista, Lake Terrace, Lake Oaks and Lake View. The levee system was simply extended further out as the city expanded, but the pumping stations were not moved north. After a century of continuous city development and growth, the stations were located miles from Lake Pontchartrain with massive levees lining the canals and protecting the new neighborhoods. The extended canals also created a flood path deep into the heart of New Orleans.

The Orleans Levee Board was responsible for the upkeep and ongoing maintenance of the drainage canals, levees and pumping stations surrounding New Orleans. Levee Board appointments were a favorite way of paying off or settling political debts. Most appointed members knew nothing about levee construction or flood protection. Instead, the politicians built a casino, two marinas, operated an airport, built a multimillion dollar overpass on Hayne Boulevard and restored an expensive 1930s WPA fountain at the airport. The Levee Board also had its own police department and developed a research park on its property. Bally's Casino generated profits of about $4.6 million dollars and boat slips at the marinas brought in another $1 million. Some of this revenue was used to purchase a jet for board member travel.

"Official business," of course.

The board also leased prime commercial property on West End Boulevard to a politically connected businessman for the bargain price of one dollar a year. The location was used as a popular lakefront grill and breakfast restaurant. The Marina Grill became famous for its deep-fried Onion Mum. Packing twenty-five hundred calories, it was extremely fattening but sinfully wonderful to eat. One Onion Mum was enough for four to share. The politically astute restaurant owner gave each levee board member a gold Rolex. The watches were valued at twenty-thousand dollars each. "Please accept this gift as a token of my appreciation indicating how much I value our friendship." The restaurant owner claimed his sweetheart lease arrangement had nothing to do with the expensive gifts.

Three board members became regular visitors to Amsterdam, claiming they were studying Holland's flood control systems. They were arrested for using levee board credit cards to pay prostitutes. One card was used twenty-three times in one weekend. Like New Orleans, Amsterdam is a port city with a long tradition of prostitution. In Holland, prostitution is legal and regulated, but not in Louisiana, and the taxpayers certainly did not like paying the bill.

The Levee Board also raised funds by leasing canal bottoms to a fiber optics company running communication lines around the city. The contract was poorly written by Levee Board lawyers; thus, the clever company could charge fees for overpasses and power lines crossing their canal bottom right-of-ways. The resulting legal entanglements lasted for years and cost taxpayers millions of dollars to finally settle.

Distracted from the mundane task of levee upkeep, the board members cared more about land development, revenue and travel junkets than flood protection. Patricia LeBlanc lived a few blocks from Lake Pontchartrain on Fleur de leis Boulevard and the Seventeenth Street Canal. She believed water was seeping under the levee onto her property. Her lawn was always soft and wet. Even in the summer nothing would grow and a large Magnolia tree died. The heavy equipment needed to remove the dead tree sunk deep into the saturated yard. "Small sand boils develop in the levee when the pumping station is running. They shoot water a few feet!" Patricia explained all this to the Levee Board, but it took them three months to send an inspector out. He arrived with a caviler attitude.

"No problem with the levee; it's strong and safe. Perhaps you have a leaking water pipe." The inspector suggested Patricia call a plumber.

Incompetent inspectors did not notice Nutria eating away at the levees. They are swamp rats that can grow to twenty pounds and live six years. They eat large amounts of vegetation and they burrow into shorelines, riverbanks and levees. The swamps, marshes and drainage canals around New Orleans created the perfect breeding ground for these multiplying pests. Concern about the nutria's effect on levee strength, the Jefferson Parish Sheriff ordered his deputies to shoot nutria on sight. Jefferson Parish is directly to the west of Orleans Parish, but its levees were maintained by a different and separate political entity.

"Shoot em! Shoot em!" the sheriff said.

It was not unusual to see the Jefferson Parish sheriff deputies parked along canals shooting five or six nutria at a time. The Orleans Levee Board refused to kill the giant rodents, deciding instead to study the issue. They considered the feasibility of trapping and relocating the nutria to the Lake Borgne area. "We don't have any right to just kill them," the board president suggested. A relocation program proved to be too expensive, so nothing was done. Uninhibited, nutria continued to eat away at the Orleans Parish levees.

The Mississippi River Gulf Outlet 'Mr. Go,' as it was affectionately called, was dug by the Corps of Engineers as a shortcut for oceangoing ships using the Port of New Orleans. It saved significant time and money, since the freighters did not need to take the long journey up the Mississippi River. Instead, they entered New Orleans from the East. Mr. Go linked Lake Borgne, Bayou Bienvenue near the Rigolets and the Industrial Canal to the open Gulf, passing through the heart of the New Orleans 9th Ward. A lock at the Mississippi River connected the entire system to the river. The north mouth of the Industrial Canal flowed freely into Lake Pontchartrain underneath the Seabrook Bridge. The bridge was operated by the Orleans Levee Board. Local news media carried a few stories here and there about the weak and poorly managed levee systems, but no one put down their beignets long enough to pay attention. When it came to flood control, the official attention span was shorter than a fruit fly's.

Louis loved to fish near the Industrial Canal River locks and the Claiborne Avenue Bridge. "Best catfish fishing in town," he believed. On long summer evenings, he often walked the short distance down Saint Claude Avenue with his cane pole and orange, five-gallon bucket from Home Depot. The bucket served a dual purpose as a comfortable portable fishing seat and it held his catch on the walk back home. The fishing was great because the canal connected directly to the lake and gulf. Sometimes he preferred to just sit and daydream. On these days Louis still held his cane pole so police would not chase him away, but on the end of the line he tied only a plastic float and sinker, no hook. Louis enjoyed watching large ships pass nearby, dreaming of visiting the many faraway places they have been.

# 8

EACH YEAR THE TULANE FREEMAN School of Business organized a conference that attracted business leaders from around the country. The Freeman students analyzed the performance of Gulf Coast businesses, and then presented their findings during the conference. Discussion also focused on corporate and social responsibility. Business leaders, students, Tulane faculty and community leaders participated in organized discussions about difficult issues of the day. For the first few years the event was a local effort drawing little attention beyond New Orleans. However, the accuracy of the reports and importance of the discussions began to attract wide international attention. Now it is one of the largest business gatherings in the nation. Hedge funds, mutual fund companies and investment banks all seek spots on the policy making conference agenda.

Ironically, the conference also attracted charlatans promoting investment plans suitable for the end of the world or collapse of the nation or World War III. They recommended gold and silver, or Armageddon food supplies and bomb-proof safes. These con artists and frauds held their events at local hotels, trying to ride the coattails of Tulane.

Being in New Orleans at the same time as the Tulane/Freeman Conference created an air of credibility. Many people tried to make a name for themselves in the competitive world of economics, finance and investment banking also showed up. Seen and be seen. Included in this group were broadcast personalities.

Jeff Krueger set up at a local television studio and broadcast his finance show live from New Orleans for three days. He arranged interviews with business leaders and attempted to capitalize on Tulane's success just like everyone else. His daughter, Sloan, was Willow's age. It would be a great career move for him if she attended Tulane's business school. Sloan would rather enroll at a northeast university like Yale or Princeton, but she was willing to consider New Orleans. "Can I have a new Mercedes convertible? Will you ship it to Tulane?" Jeff agreed to Sloan's terms and they picked out her new car. "Daddy, I want a blue one with black interior and black convertible top."

Lesley thought it would be helpful for Willow to tour Tulane's freshman student housing. She especially wanted her to see Butler House, the honors dorm. "Kathy would be the perfect tour guide since she is a Newcomb girl and loves Tulane's campus. She was also an undergrad honor student. When Kathy studied engineering, it was still considered a man's profession. There were only two females in her graduating class. She is a remarkable woman." Lesley said Kathy was caring, intelligent and resolute, a perfect role model for Willow.

Kathy and Willow rode the Saint Charles Avenue streetcar to Tulane. "Each Tulane building is filled with its own set of unique memories. It may be the distinct smells of plaster walls and wooden floors or the ambiance of an out-of-the-way quiet study spot. Maybe a certain classroom awakens memories of a favorite professor or college friend. In these cherished old buildings, we are ever mindful that every generation will eventually yield to the next. I love these buildings like family." Kathy smiled at Willow, took her hand, and showed Willow where lovers had long ago carved their initials on a banister in Gibson Hall. Kathy rubbed her fingers over the letters: RM&KS 1948. "Do you think they are still in love? Do they even remember each other? I like to think they grew old together with lots of grandchildren around when they celebrated their 60th wedding anniversary." Kathy enjoyed showing Willow around the beautiful campus while explaining her appreciation for its remarkable history.

"Monroe Hall and Butler House are the best freshman dorms. They are both nice, but Butler is the honors dorm. It is also where they assign the children of politicians, oil sheiks, business leaders and celebrities. Amy Carter, Jimmy Carter's daughter, lived in Butler! It is quieter, but you will still get the freshman experience. Each floor tends to have its own personality. One floor may have a fantasy football competition going and on another floor students may be wandering back from too much beer. Butler still has the quiet kids, nerds, party kids and sorority girls; it's just that they are all honors students, like you." Kathy and Willow visited the bookstore. Willow bought a Tulane shirt for herself and a green wave coffee cup for her dad. They relaxed at PJ's coffee shop near the student center.

"I like Butler. It's perfect." Willow decided to apply for housing at Butler House. Kathy knew she would have a most wonderful freshman year. "Remember, regardless of your chosen field of study, you will qualify for Newcomb's acorn ring at graduation. It is very special. Newcomb grads are always proud of that ring." Kathy showed Willow her ring. "My mother and grandmother had one just like it," she said.

Like most colleges, Tulane uses dorm room assignments to bring students from different cultures and socioeconomic backgrounds together. Learning to get along and respect differences is an important part of the university process. Willow received her letter assigning her dorm room and introducing her freshman roommate, Sloan Krueger.

# 9

**WILLIAM-MARK VISITED THE WAREHOUSE ON** Wednesday morning and inspected the equipment belonging to Bayou Contracting Shoppe. He started up one of the dump trucks and seemed surprised that the transmission was not automatic. Louis explained how simple driving a standard is. "It just takes time to get the hang of it."

William-Mark was also concerned that the engine sounded funny. "Anything wrong with it or no?"

"It's a diesel!" Louis said. "That is exactly how it is supposed to sound."

William-Mark looked at him suspiciously. "Really?"

"What about dat nice little aluminum flatboat back dere in da corner? I love dat old school Johnson Sea Horse motor. You don't see those much anymore."

Louis explained that the boat was not for sale. "I will never sell it for any price. The boat belonged to my father. It is not a part of this business. I plan to move it to my house and store it under the carport."

He inspected the warehouse structure by walking around the exterior and climbing onto the roof. William-Mark questioned the lack of air conditioning in the office area. "The fans work fine." Louis was getting annoyed.

William-Mark also noticed indications that the roof leaked in a few spots. "Will these multiple leaks damage da equipment?"

Louis said no and did not bother to explain that bulldozers and dump trucks are not affected by water dripping from a roof. "If it worries you, just cover everything with plastic when it rains."

William-Mark reviewed the paperwork and customer list. He examined the lease documents, profit and loss statements and balance sheets with little interest, and casually flipped through the QuickBooks spreadsheets. It was the same packet Louis had prepared for the MBI business brokers. "Dis all looks to be in order. I like da strong PBT." William-Mark was trying his best to sound knowledgeable about bookkeeping. Of course, he had no idea what 'Profit Before Tax' was. But most of his questions concerned the cash income generated by the business each month.

"Does dis business really generate dat much cash? Holy smokes, dat's a lot of tax free money!" He explained that waiters at the restaurant were required to share ten percent of their tips with the dishwashers. William-Mark appreciated the fifteen bucks a night extra income. "I kept dat little secret from da IRS and my wife. It's my beer money!" He was proud of his cleverness and winked at Louis as if he was now in on some important top-secret intrigue.

"Da IRS will not worry about you and me. They have bigger fish to fry." Louis was guilty of playing some games with the IRS, but he learned to respect them. On the other hand, William-Mark was a little too cavalier.

The owners of the laundromat where Louis's dad operated the dry-cleaning equipment had the same reckless attitude. They did not report the revenue from quarters collected in the self-service washing machines and dryers. IRS agents checked the model numbers on the machines and verified the amount of water each wash cycle used. They compared that to the monthly water bills. The owners faced thousands of dollars in fines, penalties and taxes, and nearly went bankrupt. "I can't believe the IRS spent so much effort auditing this tiny business! Don't they have bigger fish to fry?" The surprised owners reported everything after that unpleasant experience.

Louis knew William-Mark was a fool, but he had no alternatives at this point. He explained how the owner financing would work and the amount of cash he expected as a down payment. "My god! Forty thousand dollars is a lot of coin!" William-Mark held his chest with his right hand as if he was having a heart attack. He fanned his face with his left hand and motioned for Louis to bring him a chair. "I was expecting something in da neighborhood of about twenty-five hundred dollars down. My God! You're giving me a coronary!"

Selling a business is a complicated endeavor, and Louis did not understand price negotiations or tactics. He caved on his down payment price immediately. "We can talk about it. The forty-thousand dollars is not carved in stone," Louis said, desperate not to lose his only prospect.

Suddenly feeling better, William-Mark smiled and held out his hand to shake. "Now were talking. Got any beer around here?"

Louis agreed to accept a few thousand dollars upfront cash offered by William-Mark's wife. She planned to borrow most of the funds on a home equity line of credit. "That way the payment is a tax deduction for us." She seemed to know what she was talking about. Louis would receive another ten thousand dollars after one year if everything went according to plan. Moreover, Louis negotiated a monthly payment of three-thousand dollars for five years based on profitability. All the equipment leases conveyed to William-Mark and he was responsible for everything else, including maintenance and insurance as well.

The banks rejected William-Mark's credit. "We wouldn't even qualify him for a used car loan," one exasperated loan officer told Louis. "It's not that his credit is bad, it is the fact that he has none; that's the issue! He has never even had a credit card in his name!" William-Mark said that he could make all the payments each month from the company's revenue.

"Who needs credit? I will make da monthly payments directly to da lenders. The fact dat da leases will remain in your name makes no difference. I promise!" Despite William-Mark's assurances, Louis still felt unsure. But he reluctantly agreed, having no other options available.

The warehouse lease was another issue. Hidden in the middle of page three was a sentence that gave the building owner, Leon, the right to reject any sublease or lease transfer. Although Louis read the agreement carefully, he did not think anything about this when he signed the long-term documents a few years ago. It seemed of little consequence at the time.

"I will approve the sublease agreement only if you personally guarantee my payments. If William-Mark does not pay on time, then you will. That needs to be a rock solid contractual obligation!" The warehouse owner, Leon, also asked about guarantees. "If he doesn't pay, how do I know you can? I only deal in certitude not happy talk." He asked many questions about Louis's financial situation. "Don't you own your house free and clear?" Leon asked.

"I'm not interested in stealing anyone's house, but I would feel much better about all this if my name was temporarily added to your deed anyhow. Once the lease is up in five years we will remove it. Think of this as my insurance policy. It is like a car airbag. Most likely you will never need it, but when you do you sure are glad to have it. Oh, one more thing. For all my trouble, stress and risk, I want a one-time cash payment of ten thousand dollars, also refundable after the five-year lease is up. Be aware that if William-Mark is even one day late on a payment, then I keep the ten thousand dollars for my trouble. A contract represents gain and detriment for both parties. My gain is your detriment. That's how this all works," Leon said.

Louis could not believe that one short sentence on page three of a fifteen-page lease agreement could cost him his home and ten thousand dollars.

"What are you upset about? I have a five-year lease you signed. Twenty-one hundred dollars per month over five years is one hundred and twenty-six thousand dollars. I think a ten-thousand-dollar good faith payment is more than reasonable. I'm being generous!"

Louis knew he was getting screwed by everyone, but felt powerless to stop it. It also did not occur to him that if his name remained on all the leases, then he would be on the hook for most state and federal tax obligations. Louis had strong natural intelligence with considerable capacity for logic and problem solving. Without formal education, he lacked business reasoning skills and the ability to think critically, making him an easy mark.

The Orleans Parish Office of Conveyance is in the basement of the Civil District Court building on Loyola Avenue next to city hall. It is dimly lit with yellowed florescent lights. The countertops are covered with a green Formica surface, and the terrazzo floors look like they have not seen a mop since the Nixon administration. City real estate deeds and transactions back to 1857 are stored here. Across the hall is the office of the Orleans Parish Civil Sheriff. Process servers sit on wooden benches, waiting for their turn to serve subpoenas. They all carry pistols and look tough like they enjoy bar fights.

Political groups and parties fight hard to control the Conveyance Office because the twenty employees are non-civil service. It was one of the last sources of classical political patronage remaining in New Orleans. The office notarizes documents and records mortgages, leans, encumbrances and changes to existing deeds, but is run by political hacks and corrupt political bosses. It seems reasonable to expect that public officials working in important offices should be hired based on education, experience and merit rather than political cronyism. In New Orleans, there was no distinction between corrupt politics and inefficient administration of public offices.

The clerk assigned to the intake desk had been a 'wheelman' for SOUL, a large, 9th ward political organization. During legislative sessions, he drove political leaders back and forth between New Orleans and Baton Rouge. He was reliable and loyal, never repeating anything he saw or heard in the Cadillac limousine, and was rewarded with a lucrative job at the Conveyance Office. The clerk finished a GED from an adult education program and attended the Orleans Regional Vocational Technical Institute for one year. He had no formal legal training, but he loved spicy Popeye's fried chicken and always kept a ten-piece box on his desk. Greasy fingerprints were left on every document he touched.

Louis brought his driver's license and amended deed; the documents were reviewed, date stamped and filed away. His title abstract for the Montegut Street property went back to its origin in 1803 as part of a land grant. Louisiana was purchased for France in that year. It is considered the year of origin of New Orleans' property abstracts proving satisfactory for title deeds. "Everything seems to be in order. You are adding one additional name as an equal equity owner for this property on Montegut Street. Correct?" Louis paid a fifty-dollar recording fee and received a greasy receipt. He asked the clerk if he could remove the new name at any time. "Sure, whatever you want. Lawyers are in and out all day long doing that. All you will need to do is pay a new recording fee and some court costs," the clerk said without looking up. "Now move along. Next?"

Louis gathered his documents, including the ten-thousand-dollar certified check, and met Leon at a local coffee shop. He was already sitting at a table near a window when Leon walked in. "A round of drinks and fresh horses for my men!" Leon thought he was funny, but Louis did not laugh.

"I have everything you asked for," Louis said, ignoring Leon's stupid horse joke.

"I'll have a large coffee with one sweetener and cream, two jelly doughnuts and a shot of expresso on the side. Now we can get down to business." Leon looked over everything. He held the certified check up to the light, verifying the authentic watermark stamps.

"How do I know I will get this money back and your name removed from my deed when everything is said and done?" Louis felt that he should have some type of written agreement.

"Not to worry! Louisiana uses the Napoleonic Code. With our laws, you don't need to write contracts down. If we agree and shake hands on a deal that is sufficient. The fact that we act to carry out the agreement confirms the existence of the deal in a legal sense. It's how important things get done here!" Leon asked Louis to repeat after him, "Napoleonic Code. Napoleonic Code."

Leon finished his coffee and doughnuts, stood up and shook Louis's hand. Then he wiped his mouth with a napkin and tossed it on the table. "Wish I had more time, but got to run. It's a pleasure doing business with you." He got in his Corvette and drove away leaving Louis with the unpaid check. Louis felt like the tiny sandpiper birds that rummage around open jaws of giant crocodiles. The powerful jaws could slam shut at any time without warning. He hoped to get out before that. Louis called Tulane to confirm his start date. He would sleep well tonight with the knowledge that Willow would be a student at Tulane soon. Louis only wished his father had lived to see this day.

# 10

"ARE YOU DOING ANYTHING EARLY tomorrow morning? Can we meet at Holy Name of Jesus church at 5:45? Please don't be late." Aware of the overwhelming stress Louis faced, Kathy wanted to share something restorative with him. Holy Name of Jesus is a Catholic gothic cathedral on the campus of Loyola University directly adjacent to Tulane overlooking Audubon Park Lagoons. It is more like a church found in Renaissance Europe or Notre Dame Cathedral in Paris.

Louis arrived early and parked in a spot reserved for Loyola faculty. He was wearing work clothes with his name stenciled over his left pocket and an American flag on his right sleeve. The first faint traces of light appeared on the horizon, but it was still a dim and grayish early morning. Birds were beginning to sing as they always did right at sunrise. Kathy was waiting near the old Burk Observatory building. She ran towards Louis with her hand outstretched. She pulled him in her direction.

"I am so glad you are here. Hurry! Hurry! We don't have much time." They entered the church laughing and out of breath. It was dark, empty and damp, filled completely by the sun's absence. They sat close together near the back, holding hands. "Thank you for coming," Kathy whispered. She nestled her head against Louis's shoulder. The massive stained and leaded glass windows were remarkable, still their brilliant detail was not apparent in the darkened sanctuary.

Louis sat quietly, happy to be with Kathy. She smiled and held his hand tighter. "Just a few more minutes." She playfully poked him in the side.

Morning's first rays of sunlight began pouring in through the windows with hopeful radiance, chasing away Louis's blues. Kaleidoscopes of gold reflected from the altar's Tabernacle among a sunrise colored by mosaics of stained glass. Individual beams of sunshine advanced from pew to pew to pew, blanketing the sanctuary in warmth. They watched the cathedral awaken from a lonesome night. Louis had never experienced a more beautiful dawn. He was not embarrassed or ashamed by the overwhelming emotion he felt. Somehow his worries seemed less hopeless. For the first time in his adult life, Louis wept.

"When life's troubles became overwhelming, my grandmother found strength here. She believed this was God's way of holding her hand. It was a gift of another day with the confidence that God still had faith in her." Kathy said she loved her grandmother dearly and thought of her often, especially here at Holy Name. "I actually thought life would be easy for me. I thought misfortune was something that only happened to other people. I never dreamed things could become so difficult. It helps to know someone cares." Wiping away his tears with her right index finger, Kathy hugged Louis. "I'm so glad you are here with me."

Louis and Kathy began meeting for coffee every Tuesday morning. Larry's Marina Grill was a few blocks from her house. They always sat in the same corner booth near the back. Kathy lived nearby at 623 Robert E. Lee Boulevard in an area of expensive homes near the lakefront across from Mount Carmel Academy and close to the Levee Board's marina. The home belonged to her grandmother, and Kathy was living there until difficult issues with her marriage were resolved. It was also a perfect location since Kathy loved to jog. She ran ten miles a week along the Lake Pontchartrain levees. "623 Robert E. Lee. I just love saying that!" She said the address sounded like part of a song.

Most of the other diners at the Marina Grill were professionals in sharp-looking tailored suits and driving expensive BMWs and Mercedes sedans. The parking lot looked like a German car dealership. The mayor, city councilmen, levee board members, school board members and other local politicians were usually present as well. These officials did not act like servants of the city's voters, but had a habitual sense of ruling entitlement, a divine right. They leaned in close and spoke in whispered tones, discussing dark secrets of corrupt political deals. They slapped each other's backs and walked around like they owned the place. The bastards probably did own it. Louis never saw any waiter ever leave an elected official a bill. It was restaurant policy. "Good thing they hang around here every morning cutting silly deals. We would be in trouble if these dimwits had to make life and death decisions." Kathy agreed. "That would be truly terrifying!"

On most Tuesday mornings, Louis was the only person at Larry's dressed in work clothes and driving a truck. Once he was mistaken for a delivery person and told to go around to the back entrance. "Hey buddy. Deliveries go round back!" Kathy was offended about that, but Louis just laughed. "Nothing to get upset about. It happens," he said. Living nearby, Kathy usually arrived first and had coffee already ordered. Sometimes they ate pancakes.

Louis liked pancakes, but he craved the famous fried onion mum. It was not available until dinner. "I sure would love to try that. I bet it is like a giant delicious onion ring!" Louis pointed to the photo on the cover of the menu.

Kathy explained how unhealthy it is to consume twenty-five hundred calories for breakfast. Her eyebrows were pointing up. "Think of your cholesterol levels!" Louis said he would be willing to take that risk. They laughed.

The next week Kathy was waiting in the corner booth as usual. She had coffee ordered and was looking over the morning newspaper. She greeted Louis with an enthusiastic embrace. "Sit down. Sit down. I have something special for you." She assured Louis he would love it.

The head cook came out of the kitchen and looked in Kathy's direction. She gave him a nod. A moment later he reemerged from the kitchen with a perfectly fried magnificent mum.

"I could get fired for this, but your friend is very persuasive. She said you have been craving the onion mum. Enjoy."

Although the marriage was essentially over, Kathy's husband was still controlling, jealous and threatening. He liked to be called Stewart. He had a problem controlling his temper, especially when angry, which was most of the time. On more than one occasion Kathy considered a restraining order. Stewart paid a private detective to follow her every move, disclosing her friendship with Louis and their Tuesday morning get-togethers. Still Kathy did not expect her husband to show up at the grill.

He stood over the table near her, pounding his fists. A gold bracelet rattled against his diamond Rolex sounding like coins jingling in a pocket. Louis recognized him as the unfriendly man from Melba's that was always eating a large bowl of vanilla ice cream. Stewart never worked a day in his life, but inherited millions from his father's oilfield service company. Originally the family's wealth came from less than honorable circumstances. Afraid of being drafted to fight in the trenches of World War I, his grandfather became a dentist. He read an article about the Army's dental training program, and after a few short courses he began pulling a lot of teeth, whether necessary or not. After the war, he returned home with buckets of gold fillings.

A real 'man of leisure,' Kathy's husband lived off proceeds generated from a family trust. It was invested exclusively by Lehman Brothers. He did manage to finish a BA degree in General Business. It took him nine years. Even then, Stewart was awarded the degree only after his grandfather funded the college's stadium renovation.

"So, is this the Creole guy you meet every Tuesday morning? Tell me? Is he your boyfriend, lover or your lawn guy?" He pointed his finger near Louis's face. "This is between me and my wife. Stay out of it or I'll drop you like an easy putt!" He advised Louis to stay seated. Louis did not play golf, so was unmoved by the threatening metaphor.

Kathy was upset and embarrassed. Louis placed his hand on Kathy's shoulder, giving her a reassuring smile.

"Please leave," She asked her husband over and over, burying her face in her hands.

Louis was not aggressive. However, it would be a terrible mistake for anyone to push him too far. Trying hard to control the anger building inside him, Louis calmly set his coffee cup down on the table and stood up. Standing next to Kathy, he spoke softly, "No one is going to hurt you."

Louis made his living with his hands. He hauled building materials and sand; he repaired heavy equipment daily. Louis never had a gym membership, nevertheless he was built like a linebacker. Not easily intimidated, Louis's forearms were bigger than this out-of-shape knucklehead's legs. "Kathy asked you to leave! I suggest you listen." Louis said he did not want to hurt anyone. "Just leave."

Surprised by Louis's overwhelming physique, Stewart stumbled a few steps backward and wisely backed away. He turned and stormed out the door.

"Kathy, it's not your fault. Everything will be okay." Louis was reassuring and calm. "It's not your fault."

Kathy felt safe with Louis. He gently tucked an arm around her and held her tight. His powerful embrace wrapped Kathy in a protective blanket keeping her from harm. "Thank you," she whispered in his ear while running her fingers through his hair. She rested her head against his chest. "Your heart is racing." It was not because of the scuffle; it was pounding like a steam locomotive because Louis was falling in love. He thought his opportunity to feel this kind of intense passion had long since passed. Louis was struggling to find reasons to resist. They held each other very tight, hand-in-hand. "Please take a chance," Kathy said softly.

Like a hamster scampering round and round in a run-about ball, Louis was a prisoner torn in two between his traditional Catholic views on marriage and his longing to love Kathy. Louis valued their friendship above all else, but tried hard to remain devoted to his unsatisfying marriage to Jan. Most importantly, Louis did not want to risk losing Kathy. He was amazed that a beautiful uptown girl like Kathy could love a working-class Creole man from the 9th Ward. It seemed impossible to him. Lacking confidence, Louis was afraid to cross the line between friendship and love, risking the companionship he cherished. "Please take a chance with me," Kathy said again.

After a nervous pause, Louis responded with a question, foolishly concealing his true emotions. "What happens when I start the Tulane job?" Louis's new schedule would make their Tuesday morning coffees at the Marina Grill impossible.

"Don't you worry about anything." Kathy reminded him how often she was on Tulane's campus. "There is a delightful coffee shop on Carrolton Avenue near Saint Charles. Dante's opens early and serves great coffee. It is quiet and romantic." She said it was a favorite spot among Tulane students and locals. "They have sidewalk tables on the avenue. The area is like Paris, but with more passion and much more soul." Kathy loved watching bygone streetcars rumble along the tracks. "It is enchanting and charming, just like you." Louis preferred spending his time in the historic areas of New Orleans as well. The Lakefront was very nice, but everything there was new, well-kept and too perfect. Kathy reached across the table and placed her hands over Louis's. Like vines their fingers intertwined together, hands linked. As a Catholic, Kathy understood, not wanting to be responsible for the pain and heartache caused by another failed marriage and broken family. She suddenly became serious and seemed sad. Kathy's smile disappeared, eyebrows crunched.

Concerned, Louis asked what was wrong. "Is it something I said?"

"Dante's has fresh pastries, croissants and wonderful chocolate donuts, but they don't serve onion mums!" Kathy's bottom lip extended out in a contrived pout. Louis loved her spontaneous humor. He leaned in across the table; the kiss was warm and gentle.

# 11

ONE HUNDRED YEARS AGO, THE industrial revolution dramatically impacted the lives of common people, like Louis. Today's technological advancements are affecting lives as profoundly and completely as heavy industry changed those in the last century. Lifelong employment in Louisiana's oil industry is no longer guaranteed as old industrial skills become obsolete.

Unprofitable and environmentally harmful jobs have been shut down or relocated to developing countries, creating unemployment, bankruptcies and profound uncertainty for those individuals left behind. The Industrial Revolution used motors, machines and assembly lines to amplify the strength of human muscle. The new economic revolution multiplies the power of education and knowledge. Somehow, Louisiana's economy is still based on obsolete fossil fuels with an outmoded public educational system stuck deep in the industrial revolution.

Over 20% of Louisiana's population live below poverty rates, and in New Orleans the statistics are much worse. The city's public schools continued to sink deeper and deeper into a quagmire of failure. The odd thing was that Louisiana ranked high in educational standards and administration oversight, but extremely low in student performance and graduation rates. The politicians all gave each other high fives, but only 25% of fourth graders could read. The only light of hope to be found anywhere on the New Orleans educational horizon was Lesley's scholarship plan.

At the root of these economic and social problems was a spectacularly failed New Orleans public school system. The entire organization was maintained for the benefit and protection of officials, careers and jobs. School children in New Orleans have paid a high price for this failure of leadership while the politicians exploited them for their own selfish objectives.

Everything in the school system was structured from the top down to protect elected officials from accountability for the failures they created. The convoluted organizational chart deliberately made sure blame could not be assigned to anyone important. Each elected Orleans Parish school board member gave out jobs and contracts to political cronies like holiday presents. Every individual school needed substitute teachers, bus drivers, cafeteria workers and custodians. Board members had total say regarding employment decisions in their districts. The legal requirement for full board approval was only a formality, since elected members never challenged what others did in their own districts. It was considered professional courtesy. Local school board members became powerful lords of their political realms.

The board also appointed the superintendent, who was responsible for running the schools on a day-to-day basis, but his hands were tied because he answered to elected board members. They evaluated performance every six months, and a simple board majority could cancel the superintendent's contract essentially at will. The saying goes that a majority vote of tenacious board members could make water flow uphill, placing the enfeebled superintendent up the proverbial 'creek without a paddle.' The *Times-Picayune* said, "It is a good thing the Parish superintendent is not female. He has to say yes to everyone!"

Running a school system is big business. Insurance, construction, supplies, transportation and land purchases all created tempting opportunity for political graft. The Orleans Parish School System auctioned thirty-five surplus school busses to the highest bidder. The estimated value of each bus was twelve thousand dollars. Three certified bidders entered offers. The first bidder needed only two busses and the other bidder wanted six. The final bidder was a front man for a school board member who owned a transportation company. The school board member called the others, "Drop your bid and I will give you the busses you want for free." The front man then offered $3,500 total for all the busses. When the other bidders dropped out he won the auction by default. Eight busses were given free to the other two bidders as promised. The school board member purchased twenty-seven busses for $3,500 total price. The investigation turned up nothing improper.

"The auction was properly advertised. We can't help it if no one shows up to bid." The superintendent defended the board. Soon thereafter, his wife started a political consulting and PR firm. She landed lucrative contracts with many school board members. Corrupt politicians only trust other politicians when they have something on them. The board members knew they could trust the superintendent once they began funneling money to his wife. He would not rock the boat, because he grew accustomed to the money and he could not rat anyone out without implicating himself. The more dishonest the superintendent became, the more he was trusted by the other scoundrels. Twenty percent of the school bus scam profits were paid back to the superintendent's wife in the form of 'Election Day' consultant contracts.

Since most bids were rigged, repairs and maintenance on schools and facilities were always second rate, shoddy and overpriced. The deferred maintenance and inadequate funding took a heavy toll on all New Orleans public school buildings, but the system was most corrupt in the poorest areas of town. Thus, children most at risk had the most neglected facilities. Many studies have linked the physical condition of New Orleans school buildings with poor academic performance. It was a vicious cycle.

Lesley spent a lot of time in these schools. "I saw a school principal brush a dead rat under her desk with her foot. She was hoping I did not notice." Lesley said schools in New Orleans East had the worst rodent infestations because of the low land and nearby marsh areas. "Rats and mice are part of the problem. However, the real issue is the snakes rodents attract." Lesley said she was afraid to visit some of these schools.

Nearly all schools had leaky roofs, causing black mold to grow undetected in attic crawl spaces and some older buildings had no insulation in walls or attics at all. The windows were old and drafty single-pane type, the putty long since worn away. "Winter winds are strong enough to blow papers off desks, even with the windows closed! Children wear coats all day long if they are fortunate enough to own one. Their breath is visible in the frigid air. A small space heater in the front of each classroom is simply inadequate," Lesley said.

Leaky bathrooms were another issue. The foul smells frequently caused illness. "I wanted to throw-up myself," Lesley said after visiting a high school. The school board says they try to maintain the newest structures as their priority. The budget leaves nothing for the older buildings. Some of the schools in New Orleans are over one hundred years old. They should have been condemned long ago.

The Louisiana State Board of Elementary and Secondary Education had the authority to declare the Orleans Parish school system 'educationally bankrupt.' This would allow the state to take over all operations and fire the Orleans Parish superintendent.

This state education board is the same den of political snakes that awarded scholarships to wealthy politically connected families. The president of the state board was from New Orleans. He dropped out of the Orleans Parish schools in the tenth grade and began working for inner-city political organizations. His seat on the State Education Board was a political gift rewarding his loyalty. The GED certificate he received was presented by the State Department of Adult Education to avoid embarrassment should the media discover the President of Louisiana's highest education board was a high school dropout. His main objective was protecting the power of political groups and the corrupt political patronage in the Orleans Parish schools.

The board president personally handled the educational bankruptcy issue when it was placed on the state's monthly agenda.

"I move that this item be referred back to committee for further study and review. Do I have a second? All in favor? Any opposed? Motion carries. Next item." The issue was dead before other members realized what happened. The president then moved that the remaining agenda items be considered in 'global,' approving everything with one single vote. "All in favor? Any opposed? Motion carries." He hammered his gavel, ending the meeting.

"This system will never change. It needs to be completely rebuilt from the bottom up. A renaissance is possible only if the current New Orleans system is gone completely!" Lesley was fed up with political corruption and disappointed with the state's inability to change.

# 12

**TULANE OFFERED ORIENTATION SESSIONS FOR** out-of-town incoming freshmen called the Fall Welcome. The overnight two-day programs were held from May to June as a kick-off to the new academic year. Orientation offered incoming students the opportunity to explore campus life, make friends, eat on campus, meet their new roommates and sleep in college dorm rooms for the first time. New Orleans culture was introduced with Creole cooking in the Common's cafeteria, and Cajun bands were playing Zydeco music at the university center. Upperclassmen were available to answer questions and show the new freshman around campus and the residence halls. Fall Welcome follows with Move-In day just before the semester starts.

As promised, Jeff Krueger decided to transport Sloan's new Mercedes convertible down to New Orleans. He contracted with National Transport, a company specializing in moving classic cars. Usually they shipped only Packard, Rolls Royce and other expensive classics, so Sloan insisted on using them. "Daddy, my car can't arrive at Tulane on a beat-up trailer full of old Fords and Chevys! I would be so humiliated!" She warned her daddy that they had better not scratch it. "Make sure sweaty workers don't drive my car around." The company promised that one Bentley, a Lotus Europa, a Maserati and two Jaguar XKEs would be on the transport, nothing else. Jeff paid over four thousand dollars for the special arrangements and a guarantee that

Sloan's Mercedes would arrive safely at Tulane the morning of Move-In day.

Jeff was worried about Sloan being so far from home for the first time. He also did not want her subjected to the inconvenience and danger of using commercial air travel each time she wanted to come home to New York for a weekend. Especially, Jeff did not want some over-weight, balding, middle-aged TSA agent putting his hands on his daughter as if she was a wanna-be terrorist.

He contracted with VistaFlight, a private business aviation company providing worldwide point-to-point travel arrangements with guaranteed jet availability and no positioning costs. They had experience flying into and out of dangerous and hard-to-reach destinations, including during and after natural and manmade disasters. VistaFlight was the only aviation company able to reach their stranded clients after Hurricane Andrew destroyed much of South Florida. They had similar success rescuing clients after the Indian Ocean tsunami reached the Maldives and after Iraq's surprise invasion of Kuwait. Sloan was given a stainless-steel card, similar in size and appearance to a credit card. A coded number on the card guaranteed that a jet would be waiting at the New Orleans Lakefront Airport within two hours of her call, guaranteed! "The peace of mind is worth the expense," Jeff said. "Even under the most difficult circumstances, I know my daughter can get home safely." Sloan looked at the card and asked if she could fly her friends to Cozumel. "Please Daddy! Please!"

Sloan spent the day with a private personal shopping guide. They went to all the most expensive Manhattan shops, traveling from store to store in a black limo. She spent thirty-five hundred dollars at Chloe, their first stop. Next on the list were Prada, then Lanvin, Tom Ford and finally Brunello Cucinelli. Sloan spent the day trying things on and meeting designers. She liked Tori Burch most. Sloan's other dorm room items came from expensive stores as well. Her sheets and pillowcases were one-thousand thread count Egyptian cotton.

Valuable art was selected for her dorm walls. Picasso created the 'White Clown' as part of a 1930s-gallery showing in New York. The lithographs were used to promote the exhibit. Picasso created two hundred copies. They come up for sale very seldom. The Picasso was purchased at a gallery located between 10th and 11th Avenues. There are more art galleries located here in these few blocks of New York than in any other city. "Only the best for my little girl." Jeff was unmoved by the twenty-five thousand dollars Sloan spent.

Louis and Willow were discussing the essential items on Tulane's dorm room supply list. Jan said she was tired of hearing about Tulane and left for the evening. "Tulane, Tulane, Tulane. I need a break! I'm going to Biloxi!" Louis told Willow that her mom was going through difficult times. "But I know she loves you very much," he explained.

Willow said she already had many of the required items on the list. "Sheets and pillows; I think I have this covered. College students wear jeans and t-shirts most of the time. I have two pair. We're good!" Willow had saved a few dollars from her part-time jobs and knew her family was experiencing difficult financial circumstances. She did not want to ask for anything more. "I'm just happy to be going to a great college. None of this other stuff is all that important."

Pushing himself away from the dining table, Louis picked up a chair and carried it into his bedroom. He found the exact right spot directly in front of his closet and set the chair down on the carpet. He pushed down on it, making sure the chair would support his full weight. The ceiling was made of insulated square tiles supported by a sturdy metal frame. Louis installed the tiles himself to help insulate the rooms and to give the house a modern look. He carefully stood on the chair and reached for the ceiling. Willow watched. "My goodness! What are you doing?"

When Louis pushed on the corner of a certain tile it popped up. He reached his hand inside the opening and fished around for a few moments. From time to time he had a few extra dollars. Sometimes he got tips from the sand deliveries. Occasionally, jobs paid in cash. Usually Louis could set aside ten or twenty extra dollars a week. He had been secretly saving for Willow's college since the day she was born. The four thick rolls of small bills were held together with rubber bands. He handed them to Willow. "This is for you!"

With this money available, Willow would be able to concentrate on her Tulane studies without working a part-time job at nights and weekends. Management at the Hilton Riverview refused to accept her resignation as permanent. "You are the best employee we ever had. We don't want to lose you." Her manager suggested she take a few weeks and get settled in at Tulane. The manager would not accept her keys. "Then perhaps we can work something out convenient around your schedule; maybe just a few hours a week at first." Willow enjoyed her job and did not want to burn bridges. She agreed to give it some thought.

Willow could not wait to meet her new roommate; she was so excited. The Tulane t-shirt with Mardi-Gras colors looked great with her new jeans. She believed Walmart clothes were the same as those sold at expensive mall stores like Penney's and Dillard's. "No one can possibly tell the difference." She removed the Walmart tags just to make sure. "Sloan and I will be great friends. I just know it!" Willow encouraged her dad to walk faster. Arriving at the dorm room first, she wondered which one of the dozens of girls wandering around the building was her roommate. Willow watched families come and go. She did not pick a dorm bed because she thought that should be something they would decide together as friends. A girl and her dad exited the elevator and walked in Willow's direction. She was dressed like a movie star on the red carpet. "That's her! I know it!" Willow ran back in the room. "They're here! They're here!" Sloan's dad knocked on the door. "May we come in?"

Louis was thrilled to meet Jeff Krueger and explained how much he enjoyed the investment show. Louis said he had learned so much from watching it. "I tell you what, buddy. Give me your address and I will have my people send you a framed and signed photo of me standing inside the New York Stock Exchange. How does that sound?" Jeff patted Louis on the back in a condescending way.

"I'm Willow. I'm your new roommate! It's wonderful to meet you! We are going to have a great year together!" Finding it difficult to temper her excitement, Willow wore a huge smile and offered a friendly hug. Sloan looked at her father. "Daddy, is she black?"

# 13

LOUIS HAD A BUSY WEEK ahead. He planned to spend a few days with William-Mark making sure he was ready to hit the ground running. They had a lot to get done and William-Mark still needed to learn how to drive dump trucks! First Louis planned to move his father's old flat boat out of the warehouse and store it under his carport. He took down the 1973 Tulane-LSU pennant from the office wall and carefully packed it away. Louis told William-Mark to meet at the shop for 6:30 in the morning. "Dat seems really early!" he complained.

Louis expected to spend the next few days at the shop teaching William-Mark how to run a business, but Tulane called and asked him to start sooner than originally planned. This storm season had seen an unusually high number of powerful hurricanes that wreaked havoc across the Gulf Coast. The university was taking no chances. "When a storm enters the Gulf, it's all hands on deck. Most likely we won't see any impact from Katrina, but you never know with these things. Hurricanes have a mind of their own." Tulane's grounds supervisor seemed to be on edge. "We need you here as soon as possible."

Tulane was concerned more so this time around because the previous summer was the worst hurricane season in memory. Hurricane Charlie was a category 4 that made landfall near Fort Myers with 145mph winds. Frances and Karl were also category 4 storms. Powerful Hurricane Ivan slammed into the Alabama Gulf

Coast. New Orleans was targeted in Ivan's warning area, but it turned north sooner than expected, sparing New Orleans.

Louis had been so busy that he neglected to pay attention to the daily news. He did not know that a storm had formed in the Atlantic and was expected to cross into the Gulf of Mexico as a Category 3, then head up the west coast of Florida striking Tampa and Apalachicola before crossing the panhandle and heading into Georgia. The warm waters of the Gulf of Mexico created favorable conditions for further strengthening. "This could become the most destructive storm ever recorded, a strong Category 5. Everyone living on the Gulf Coast should pay attention to this one." The Weather Channel did not want to encourage panic, but said this could be a life or death situation. Early reports predicted Katrina's worst effects would reach only as far west as Mobile, Alabama. New Orleans was well outside the expected impact zones for now, but the city's residents were advised to stay alert.

William-Mark was already thirty minutes late. "Where have you been? You're late!" Louis said.

"Yea, I know. Ain't dat something?"

William-Mark sat in a chair across from Louis's desk and placed his feet up. "So boss, what's on da agenda?"

It was unusual for Jan to wake up early. She displayed very little interest in selling the business and did not care to know any details until now. Louis was surprised when she showed up at the Bayou Contractor's warehouse. "How about coffee and donuts?" Jan bought fresh coffee and a dozen donuts, six glazed and six jellies. She handed William-Mark a jelly donut and placed the box on Louis's desk. William-Mark thanked her for bringing his favorite.

Louis poured his own coffee. He liked it black with one pack of sugar, but turned down the donuts. "Thanks, but no thanks." For a moment, he wondered how Jan knew what William-Mark's favorite donut was. He chalked it up to coincidence.

She was dressed in tight jeans and a low-cut shirt exposing attractive cleavage. It was obvious she was braless. "I have to look after my interest for a change! If I had done that from the beginning I would be living in Hollywood now having dinner with directors and producers." Jan sat in a chair next to William-Mark and playfully placed her hand on his knee while looking directly in Louis's direction.

Jan acted as if she was the one to whom some injustice had been done. "I have created a lovely home. I have been a good wife. I have never neglected Louis. I have never failed to have a hot meal waiting for him at the end of the day. Louis keeps secrets and hides things from me. I can't trust him anymore. Everything in this marriage is 50/50, including this business. It's the Napoleonic Code! I gave up Hollywood for this!" Jan said to William-Mark. She was furious to learn Louis had been secretly saving money for Willow's college. "All these years I sacrificed, did without and let my dreams die while he had fat rolls of cash stashed away in our bedroom ceiling! What else is he keeping from me?" She gave Louis a cold stare. He was not sure how things with Jan got so far off track.

"I should have told you about the money. You're right." Trying to avoid a confrontation, Louis apologized to Jan and did not say what he thought. He felt better just thinking this way.

'You're upset? Everyone has something to be upset about. Indians are upset about Americans taking their land. Tulane is upset about the hurricane. The Russians are upset about the French and German invasions. The Palestinians are upset because the Jews returned to the Middle East, and the Jews are upset because Europe supports the Palestinians. PETA is upset because you had fried SPAM for breakfast. I'm mad because an Iron Lung broker stole my money. Everyone is mad about something. Get over it!'

Louis was not guilty of having an affair with Kathy in any physical sense yet, but she consumed all his daily thoughts. Although they saw each other only on Tuesday mornings, he missed her dearly whenever they were apart. Louis fell asleep with thoughts of Kathy and wished she were next to him. On the rare occasions when he made love with

Jan, he got through it by thinking of Kathy. Loving Jan felt like a conjugal prison visit. This difficult situation reminded Louis of an old joke. A man says he has been with the same woman for years. The punch-line is: 'Don't tell my wife. She will kill me!' It didn't seem all that funny anymore. Could all this trouble with Jan be his fault? Louis wondered why he felt so guilty.

"Don't worry about anything, Louis. I will be here in the morning to open the warehouse. You go to Tulane, they need you. I will spend the day showing William-Mark the ropes around here." Jan smiled at William-Mark. "Right?"

William-Mark replied enthusiastically and said he would love to come in early. "At da crack of dawn!" he added.

Under normal circumstances Louis would be assigned to a team of Tulane tradespeople that maintained, repaired and operated campus and building systems. He would also handle equipment changes and environmental controls. Louis would help oversee regulatory compliance with applicable environmental regulations and safety codes as well. His experience owning Bayou Contracting was helpful in this new role.

"The only time Tulane shut its doors was during the Civil War. Hurricane Katrina won't change that. That's why we prepare." Wilson, the campus grounds supervisor was happy to see Louis, and walked with him over to a small dump truck painted Tulane colors and owned by the university. "First, I need you to move all this river sand to points around campus. Crews are waiting to fill sandbags." He told Louis to start near the Claiborne Avenue side of the campus first. "That is the area most likely to flood."

"Do you think the levees will fail?" Louis asked in a concerned tone.

"Certainty not. These levees are stronger than Hoover Dam, unless someone puts a voodoo curse on them!" Wilson was only half joking. "The real problem will be rain." He said the city's pumping stations could handle one inch of rainfall per hour. "Anything over that amount and the streets start flooding."

Louis was an expert behind the wheel of a dump truck and had the job done quickly. He expected to spend the afternoon moving equipment and computers to higher floors and helping with sandbags. "All of that computer stuff is insured and backed up. Nevertheless, most of it will be moved later as events dictate; we have teams of tech people for that. But that is not our top priority right now." The supervisor hired Louis partly because of his love for New Orleans' history and culture. "Our task is much more important. We have to protect the history of Tulane."

"First, we need to go to Tilton Memorial Hall." Two priceless, Tiffany stained-glass windows overlook the foyer. "We have metal panels designed to protect the windows. They need to be installed." Tilton Hall also houses the Amistad Research Center. "This is the nation's oldest and most important independent archive focused on the history of African Americans and other ethnic minorities. For the past twelve hours, faculty and staff have been boxing and categorizing everything. We need to get it all moved safely to the second floor. This is an important undertaking. I need you to oversee this." Louis was honored to be around so many important books, and he was impressed with the professionalism of the Tulane workers. They wore white cotton gloves and treated the historic documents with the respect and reverence they deserved.

"Once the Amistad Center is secure we will head over to the Woldenberg Art Center building and repeat this same process at the Newcomb Art Gallery." The Newcomb pottery program was designed to teach self-reliance and financial independence. It became one of the most significant American art potteries of the twentieth century. Each unique piece was inspired by the flora and fauna of the Gulf South, and collectively created a distinctive southern art form. Today Newcomb pottery is critically acclaimed, highly sought after and extremely valuable. "The world's largest collection of Newcomb Pottery is right here on campus in the Newcomb Art Gallery's permanent collection. We have a plan to safeguard it as well," Wilson said.

"Then we need to check in on Tulane's mummies." Louis had no idea Tulane owned mummies.

"Two, 3,000-year-old Egyptian mummies were discovered in a forgotten storage room under the stands of the Sugar Bowl stadium during the demolition. No one had any idea how they ended up at the university or how they were completely forgotten for so long. You never know what you are going to find when you clean up. Today our mummies are in Dinwiddie Hall's first floor under the care of the Anthropology Department." Louis was looking forward to seeing authentic Egyptian artifacts. "We should also look after Tulane's extinct tree species." The Meta Sequoias were found in a remote area of China during World War II. "Tulane was one of several schools to receive seeds for a propagation program." Louis understood the importance of these trees. "They are a Tulane treasure," Wilson said.

"Finally, we will stop at the library and check on the Latin American collection. They say this is Tulane's crown jewel. It is a collection of records and manuscripts from the Spanish colonial era. The collection even has letters from the Spanish explorer Hernan Cortes!" Wilson said that all of this was most likely just a precaution. "Better safe than sorry."

Katrina did not take the expected turn to the north and drifted slightly further westward as it approached the warm open waters of the Gulf of Mexico, having moved across South Florida. Hurricane watches and warnings were moved west to Mississippi, Alabama and parts of Louisiana. "The city of New Orleans is not in danger from this storm, now." Mayor Ray Glapion did not want to issue an evacuation notice because of the possible potential legal liability on the part of the city for closing hotels, schools and other businesses unnecessarily. "I am not evacuating the city, but citizens are free to leave if they decide to do so." Mayor Glapion refused the advice of the Director of the National Hurricane Center, who pleaded with him to issue the mandatory evacuation order for New Orleans. "I will take it under consideration," Glapion said.

This was nothing unusual. New Orleans mayors have a long history of lying about such things. "Rumors! There is no reason for alarm in New Orleans," Mayor Arthur O'Keefe said during the great Mississippi River floods of 1927. In truth, the river was "angry, wide, high and fast, swirling in whirlpools, the current sweeping logs, lumber, the bodies of mules and horses past the city. In some stretches it had risen higher than the levee and was contained by planks backed by thick walls of sandbags," according to the newspapers. Mayor O'Keefe insisted anyway, "New Orleans is absolutely safe from any threat of flood from the river."

In 1965, Hurricane Betsy flooded much of New Orleans. Victor Schiro was mayor. "Don't believe any false rumors unless you hear them from me first," he said after the storm hit.

Mayor Ray Glapion continued this tradition and insisted Tulane maintain the scheduled 'Move-In' day, as any delay could cause an unnecessary panic. "Besides, we have hundreds of school busses available to move people to the Convention Center and Dome if the city loses power for an extended period."

A National Oceanic and Atmospheric Administration (NOAA) buoy in the southern Gulf of Mexico recorded 68-foot-high waves before it was destroyed by Katrina's strengthening punch.

# 14

**THE QUEEN MARY OCEAN LINER** is now docked in Long Beach, California. The famous London Bridge is in Arizona, and the Eiffel Tower Restaurant sits on Saint Charles Avenue in New Orleans. Who knew? The Cubans love cigars, the Swiss love watches, the English love fine suits, and in New Orleans they love food. In 1981, French engineers inspecting the Eiffel Tower discovered that it was leaning towards one side. The hundred-year-old structure was sagging from its own weight. They determined that the famous restaurant at the top was too heavy and responsible for the tower's structural problems.

The restaurant was removed and the pieces stored until a new location was found, but French culture officials decided that the restaurant could not be reopened anywhere in Paris using the name "Eiffel Tower." The owner had the eleven thousand pieces packed in crates and stored away. "Without the Eiffel name it is just like any other French restaurant," the owner said after listing the crates for sale. The French officials agreed, and did nothing to block or stop the sale. Even France's National Institute for Preventive Archaeological Research failed to recognize the historic and cultural significance of the restaurant.

American investors spent millions of dollars to have the restaurant moved to New Orleans and reassembled. The Restaurant de la Tour

Eiffel was built at the edge of the Garden District on top of a sixteen-foot-high metal frame structure like the top of the original tower in Paris. "It looks like a giant bird cage," some people said. Others appreciated the romance of having a true Parisian Café in the city, especially one that had counted Picasso, Brigitte Bardot, Charlie Chaplin and Charles de Gaulle as regular patrons.

Picasso had lunch alone once in the Eiffel restaurant when he realized he had forgotten his wallet. The quick-thinking waiter told him not to worry. He returned to the table with a napkin and pin. "Sketch something and we will call it even." The young waiter explained how much he loved Picasso's work. The simple female figure drawn on an Eiffel restaurant napkin and signed by Picasso recently sold at auction for nearly three-hundred thousand dollars.

De la tour Eiffel was open late every night and served hot soufflés, iced champagne and café au lait into the wee hours of the morning. The elaborate desserts became famous with the New Orleans late night crowd. After a long day working at Tulane, Louis thought it would be nice to see Kathy for a late-night coffee. "Do you have any plans for later?" Kathy was wearing a red dress with a zipper in the back and a string of pearls around her neck. She was waiting under the Eiffel sign, checking her watch. Her blond hair and fair complexion complemented the dress perfectly. Louis stepped off the streetcar. She was so happy to see him.

"It has been such a long time. I missed you!" Kathy stood on her toes and hugged Louis around his neck. He reminded her that they had coffee at Dante's just last Tuesday. "I know, I know, but it seems like eternity whenever we are apart." A long ramp led from the street up to the restaurant's main entrance. "This is quite a climb. If the city floods this is where I want to be," Kathy joked.

Louis and Kathy held hands across the table and talked like lifelong friends. She suggested a bottle of champagne. "Let's do something different. We have coffee all the time!" Conversation came easily. "Do you realize Picasso may have sat in this very booth?"

Louis rubbed his hand across the top of the table. "Fascinating."

Youthful college-age lovers sat side by side in an adjacent booth caressing each other's hands, unaware of anyone else. "I like the way they love each other. They have that lover's look," Kathy whispered quietly. "Do you think passion and love is only for the young?" Answering her own question, Kathy said youthfulness was not defined by birthdays. "Life can be wondrous like that at any age if you are in love!" Kathy was sounding like a whimsical author writing a romance novel about yearning. It was not something anyone would expect from an engineer. "Do I sound like a mushy romantic fool?"

"People do fall in love," Louis said, "and there is nothing foolish about that."

"You think it is difficult to control for every variable in an engineering problem? Understanding human nature is even harder. Love is more challenging to grasp than the tiniest fleeting particle in physics ever was," Kathy admitted.

The pianist started to play a Louis Armstrong song about kissing and dreaming. Kathy mentioned that with the hurricane approaching she would take the opportunity to get away and planned to spend a few days in her hometown of Greenville, Mississippi until Katrina passed. "I'm looking forward to visiting with family for a few days, but I will miss you." Louis did not know Kathy had family in Greenville. "It's just for a few days."

Greenville has produced many great southern writers. "Shelby Foote and David Cohn are from Greenville! My favorite writer, Walker Percy, is also from Greenville. I can't believe you have family there! 'The Moviegoer' and 'Love in the Ruins' are my favorite books!" Louis was elated and asked Kathy if she had ever met any famous Greenville writers.

"Yes, Walker Percy is my uncle!" Kathy said his writing had a magical way of questioning the ability of science to explain basic mysteries of human nature. "My family was surprised by my decision to study engineering instead of creative writing, journalism or literature. I was somewhat of a rebellious black sheep, but I wanted to do something different. They thought I was switched at birth with someone else's baby. In fact, I'm a quixotic romantic hiding behind a thin engineering school veneer. That is one reason I think I'm falling so hard for you. I'm a covert romantic at heart." The first champagne bottle was finished. They ordered another.

Louis knew that the Mississippi Delta area was a relative oasis of calm for blacks during the early twentieth century. He did not know that the tranquility was largely due to the efforts of Kathy's family. The Percy family owned banks and made it possible for blacks to finance farms and businesses, and mortgage property. Kathy's great uncle, LeRoy Percy, believed 'noblesse oblige' benevolence was the responsibility of the elite. Showing great courage, he also took on the Klan. "Let this Klan go somewhere else where it will not do the harm that it will in this community. Let them sow dissension in some community less united than Greenville." Kathy said she was proud of her family's remarkable heritage and remembered hearing about her uncle's speech when she was a young child.

Eventually the waiter brought the check. "Can I get anything else for you two lovebirds?"

"We must have that lovers' look, too!" Kathy said after the waiter left.

Before Louis could open his wallet, Kathy pulled out a card from her purse and slid it with her index finger across the table. She maintained eye contact and had a mischievous grin. Her eyebrows were raised. Louis was old-fashioned and insisted on paying. "Put that away," he said.

"This is not a credit card. It's a hotel room key!"

As the moth is lured to the candle's flickering flame, Louis stared at the key card, powerless to resist. "Cur non," he said, Creole for 'Why not?"

The night had turned cool and breezy. An unexpected strong gust blew away apprehension as oak branches offered little resistance and willingly moved in rhythm with the wind. Kathy held her hands outstretched and spun around in circles, enjoying the pleasant evening.

They had to wait on the Saint Charles Avenue neutral ground as a streetcar passed. An elderly lady sitting alone smiled and waved from an open window as the streetcar made its way to its next stop. Trumpet music from a nearby all-night jazz club filled the air. "Hurry," Kathy ran ahead across the avenue encouraging Louis to catch-up. She turned around and ran backwards for a few steps. She motioned with her hand, "Come on."

The Pontchartrain Hotel was directly across the avenue from the de la Tour Eiffel. It was an elegant old hotel that somehow managed to maintain class and grace even through all the economic ups and downs New Orleans faced over the years. Confederate Jasmine covered the columns supporting the portico where parking attendants greeted arriving guests. The lobby's registration desk appeared to be made of colorful marble. Closer examination showed that the counter was made of thousands of tiny pieces of hand carved oak, cedar and cypress all inlaid on a heart pine base. It was beautiful and stunning.

Hotel management decided to rearrange the lobby. To protect tradition, the old grand piano was moved only one inch a day so that the regular guests would not notice anything different. Louis and Kathy's room was on an upper floor providing views of the nighttime New Orleans skyline and Saint Charles Avenue. Kathy opened the window. They admired the city lights and watched streetcars make their way along the tracks. Jazz music carried by the cool night breezes filled the room. "It is hard not to fall in love in this romantic city." Kathy turned towards Louis and made the first move, admitting that she had been lonely for a long time.

Louis was having trouble with her zipper. "Here, let me help you." The dress fell to the floor in waves around her feet. She was even more beautiful than Louis imagined. Kathy's body was firm and tight, toned by years of long runs on the levees. Her buns fit perfectly in Louis's large hands. He picked her up and carried her over to the bed. Sitting Kathy on the bed's edge, he placed his hands on her knees and spread them apart. Kathy leaned back and reached out to Louis, pulling him down towards her. She pushed the pillows to the floor. Louis wanted her so badly, but he knew he could not last. He kissed her neck first and worked his way down. Kathy's breasts were firm. She held her left breast while Louis sucked her erect nipple. His right hand was between her legs. Unselfishly delaying his own pleasure, Louis was patient and used his tongue for a long time; he was skilled and gentle. Louis loved the taste of her. At one point Kathy seemed to lose complete control and had a long spasm, punctuated with soft sounds of pleasure.

After her third orgasm, Kathy reached for Louis and pulled his face up to hers. She was out of breath and breathing heavy; her heart raced. "That was remarkable! Now it's your turn." She held him with both hands and guided him in. Kathy thought her husband was large, but Louis was twice that size. Stewart was like a roll of dimes by comparison. She was warm, moist and inviting. "I want all of you. Don't be shy." Kathy loved the feel of his deep thrusts and encouraged him to keep going. "Enjoy it!" she said repeatedly. Kathy had another climax and was completely exhausted. Never had she felt so satisfied.

After the loving, they both had that mildly awkward feeling all new lovers experience, but they stayed locked in a tight embrace. "I have never experienced anything like that before. Nobody has ever made me feel this way." Kathy said she was in love. This was the most passion Louis had felt in decades. It was the first time he had been unfaithful to his marriage and he was surprised by the massive Catholic guilt he felt building inside. His stomach was in knots. Louis decided he should head home before Jan grew suspicious or worried. He slipped out of bed and began dressing, making up an excuse about work. "I was hoping we could stay together longer, but I understand. You should go. It is very late." Kathy kissed his forehead and asked him to stay just a few more minutes.

"I'm sorry," Louis apologized while heading out the door. She wondered if she would ever see him again. Kathy had a terrible feeling that he was leaving forever.

When Louis arrived home the house was quiet, dark and lonely. Jan was not walking the floors. She was not worried about his whereabouts. She was not in any type of a jealous rage. She was, however, sleeping quietly. Louis would prefer anger to indifference any day. He took a quick shower and quietly slipped into bed, careful not to wake her.

Louis looked over at Jan. The streetlights shone through the thin, half-open bedroom curtains, providing just enough light to see that she was sleeping peacefully. Louis did not need light to see the obvious. A few years ago, Louis's friend, John, had a major heart attack. It was unexpected because he was in good health. Happily married for over twenty years, John had two children, a nice home and a Dodge minivan. His wife was called from the hospital emergency room. She told the nursing staff that she was busy with work, but would get there soon. She showed up two days later. "I could have died and you were too busy?" John asked his disinterested wife. It was an epiphany moment indicating another happy life masquerade was suddenly over.

In New Orleans, Formosan termites swarm at night around the streetlights. Unable to sleep, Louis lay awake in bed watching the flying insects circle around and round. He did not know how much timed had passed. Louis felt like a misbehaving child that decided to run away from home but could not get past the front yard because he was too afraid to cross the street.

# 15

IT WAS LATE SUMMER, EARLY fall, usually a wonderful time of year in New Orleans. Mums, Sage, Black-Eyed Susans and other flowers were in bloom. The light breeze was sweet with fragrant scents. Bees moved about from flower to flower. Wildflowers grew along the streetcar tracks and sidewalks. The air was less humid than normal for this time of year. It was a beautiful day, cool and fresh with an intense, cloudless blue sky. Hurricanes need energy and they absorb it from the atmosphere like French bread soaking up a bowl of gumbo. Thus, the days immediately before and after big storms are usually the best weather of the year, beautiful like this day was. It was a nasty and tricky deception played by Mother Nature luring the inexperienced into a false sense of calm before delivering the knock-out hurricane punch.

The highlight of Tulane's Move-In day is always the speech given by the university's president to welcome the incoming freshman class. This year he talked about the time between hello and goodbye. "Your time here is very short, only four quick years. The experience will shape your life forever." He advised the new students to make the most of everything the university and city had to offer. New Orleans is a great place for personal discovery he explained. "It is an old city that embraces change, but clings to history as Spanish moss hangs from the branches of Audubon Park oaks." The freshman class spent the next few hours getting to know everyone. "I'm David from New York. I'm Susan from California. I'm Isabella from Spain." They all had a turn to introduce themselves. Willow was thrilled to make friends from around the world. Sloan stood up and talked about her daddy. "He is very rich and very famous! He calls the president of the New York Stock Exchange by his first name. Does anybody want to go to the Caribbean? I have a jet available anytime!" She passed around the jet card for everyone to see.

The logistics of Move-In day are complicated and challenging. "It's like organizing the D-Day invasion year after year." Tulane administrators were the best around, but still felt challenged by the massive task at hand. They made many helpful suggestions. "Don't bring anything of value that needs to be insured. Don't bring large items, and remember that everything you bring to Tulane will eventually need to be moved back home. Streetcars run directly in front of the campus. There is no need for anyone, especially freshman, to have a car." Sloan ignored all the advice and did everything she was advised not to do. She shipped the Picasso, expensive clothes, jewelry and of course her new Mercedes.

Federal Express had the moving contract each year. They accumulated everything the students shipped at one central location in the Midwest, then moved it all to Tulane at one time. It took a fleet of tractor trailer trucks to get everything to New Orleans for Move-In day.

The FedEx convoy lined up on campus along Drill Road adjacent to the student union, with the Quad on one side and Warren House to the right. The spectacle of so many trucks reminded Louis of the Mardi Gras day truck parades. The Krewe of Elks has over one hundred trucks and follows directly behind the Rex parade. The Krewe of Crescent City follows behind the Elks. The FedEx trucks were not decorated in purple, green and gold, or full of costumed riders throwing beads and doubloons, but every New Orleanian loves a truck parade nonetheless.

Willow could move everything she needed in the trunk of Louis's car. Her side of the dorm room was neat and organized. Louis moved her bed to another wall and set up Willow's computer desk. "We should wait for Sloan since we don't know how much space she will need."

Willow was looking forward to getting off to a good start with her new friend. Six large unpacked FedEx boxes addressed to Sloan were neatly stacked in a corner. Willow made her bed with the new Walmart sheets. "I hope these colors match with Sloan's."

Sloan arrived three hours late. Willow offered to help her get settled in so they could get finished quickly and then go to dinner together. "Oh, don't worry about my stuff. I'm going to be moving to another dorm room in two days anyway." She said that her father's friend from Goldman Sachs had a daughter at Tulane. "Daddy thinks my college experience will be more rewarding if I room with her. He already called the dean and arranged everything. It's nothing personal." Sloan was chewing gum and wearing sunglasses inside. She thanked Willow for the dinner idea, but said she already had other plans. "I met a really cute boy. I might even sleep with him," she said.

"What about your reputation?" Surprised, Willow said it was only the first day of the first semester.

"OMG! That *is* my reputation!" Sloan offered a mock frown.

Hurricane Katrina did not take the earlier turn north as expected. A strong category 5, the storm was now heading directly for the mouth of the Mississippi River and Grand Isle, a worst-case situation for New Orleans, just like 1915. Mayor Ray Glapion called an emergency press conference. "We advise everyone who is able to leave the city to get out now. However, as shelters of last resort, the Superdome and Convention Center will be open for those choosing to stay." The mayor also activated the traffic Contraflow plan converting all highway lanes to flow in one direction allowing more people to get out faster.

Other New Orleans mayors had the sense to protect city assets by moving firetrucks, police cars and school busses to bridges and overpasses as hurricanes approached. Mayor Glapion did not see the need for such precautions. After the press conference, he left on a helicopter with his family for the safety of Houston, Texas. "I wish I had better news," he said while boarding the Louisiana National Guard Huey.

Willow advised Sloan to return from her date early. "The weather is going to get really bad, really fast!"

"How can that be possible? The weather is beautiful." She said Willow was acting like a mother hen. "You are worse than my daddy," Sloan whined.

Over one-hundred thousand New Orleanians did not own cars and could not leave the city or get to the shelters. Following the city's Emergency Management Plan, efforts were activated to pick up these people from twelve different locations around the city and transport them to the Superdome. It's ironic that Tulane's football team had practiced in the Superdome just the day before. New Orleans Regional Transit Authority buses ran for hours. Police and fire crews drove through low-lying neighborhoods with bullhorns directing everyone to get out. Eventually over twenty-six thousand desperate people were packed into the Superdome, and many more were sent to the Convention Center. The plan seemed like that employed by the Americans to evacuate Saigon during the fall of South Vietnam with similar tragic results.

The shelters were expected to be used for only a few hours, and then everyone would make their way home after the danger passed. Consequently, no previsions were made for long-term emergency power, water or food. Many people were sick, some were gang members, and many were armed, but most just stood around outside waiting for directions that never came. They were all hungry, thirsty and scared. Everyone was expected to fend for themselves. "At least they are alive," Mayor Glapion said in a caviler tone before leaving town.

The New Orleans lakefront airport was built early in the twentieth century on a manmade peninsula extending far out into Lake Pontchartrain. It was the city's only airport until Armstrong International was opened in the 1950s. The lakefront airport was now used primarily by small commuter and private airplanes. With runways extending out into the lake, the airport was on the wrong side of the flood levees. The entire facility was already under three feet of water and Katrina was still off in the Gulf of Mexico with the first storm outer bands just beginning to cross over the southern tip of Plaque-mines Parish. Authorities also closed Armstrong International to com-mercial flights, making the airport available only to emergency and military aircraft. New Orleans was effectively cut off.

The Contraflow plan called for implementation fifty hours before the storm hit. Since Mayor Glapion had waited too long to issue the evac-uation orders, everyone with a car was trying to leave New Orleans at the same time. Even with the Contraflow plan in force, all roads head-ing out were bumper to bumper for many miles. Interstate 10 head-ing east to Slidell and north to Baton Rouge was gridlocked, as were US 90 and US 61. It became clear that with the storm approaching fast, many people would be forced to ride it out on the highways.

The Marines stationed at the Marine Reserve Headquarters near the lakefront were ordered to evacuate. They left in gray navy transport helicopters. Amtrak sent a special passenger train to the Union Pas-senger Terminal (UPT) to move its employees and their families north to safety. The train had three hundred empty seats available and was only a short walk from the Superdome. The multiple urgent calls about filling the empty seats Amtrak officials placed to the mayor's office went unanswered. With time quickly running down, the half-empty train pulled out of the UPT and headed for Saint Louis. Thou-sands of evacuees standing around the Superdome watched it speed out of town with whistles blowing and bells ringing. Normally, Amtrak rules allowed a top speed of 40mph within city limits. This train reached 80mph.

When people from New Orleans ask 'where you from' they are usu-ally talking about what high school you attended. Brother Martin, Jesuit, Holy Cross and Saint Augustine are the largest boys' Catholic schools with the greatest football rivalries. The season was just getting started. Message boards were confident that the season's opening games would be postponed for only a week or so. "This gives Jesuit an advantage since they need another week of practice before Brother Martin kicks their ass." Everyone was hopeful that Katrina would be just a minor inconvenience like all the other hurricanes over the last twenty years had been.

With Katrina now targeting New Orleans, and following the mayor's advice, Tulane encouraged students to evacuate. Many followed the school's suggestions and left with their parents. In a short time, students went from setting up dorm rooms to evacuating the city. The four-hundred students that remained were transported on buses to Jackson State University in Mississippi where they were housed in the school's athletic center. "University operations are to resume Wednesday," message was posted to Tulane's website. Willow missed the last bus because she was worried about Sloan. "At this point it may be best to stay on campus. I will be there first thing in the morning." Louis believed Tulane's stone and brick buildings were the safest place in New Orleans for Willow to be. "Tulane's buildings are safer than Montegut Street. That's for sure!" he said. "If it does flood, go down the street to the Eiffel Restaurant. That place is more than twenty feet high."

Sloan's new boyfriend picked up a small stone and tossed it at the streetlight adjacent to the secluded bench, enveloping the hidden area in darkness. They were behind Louise Hall near the old power plant. Tulane students have been making out there for generations. Sloan lay back on the bench and raised her skirt up above her hips. She pulled her pink panties to the side and arched her back. Her friend fumbled around awkwardly; his hands were shaking. "Is this your first time?" Sloan asked in an impatient tone.

He continued to wrestle with his own belt buckle. "Oh god! Oh god!" Suddenly, his body tensed. He stood ridged for a moment.

"OMG! Are you kidding? I haven't even touched you!" Frustrated, Sloan lay back on the bench and looked at the night sky. Her friend apologized and explained how embarrassed he felt. He asked if they could try again later. "Where have all the stars gone?" She ignored his question about another date, but was suddenly worried about the rapidly changing weather.

"I don't have time for little boys. Besides, it is hard to fake enthusiasm a second time." Sloan told him to leave. "Get lost!" She stared at the suddenly scary night sky. The stars were all gone, hidden by thick clouds moving fast across the sky. The wind was picking up. Tree branches swayed violently, and campus lights began to flicker on and off. It was a very bad idea to miss the Jackson State busses.

She fumbled around in her purse and found the VistaFlight card. "Due to the hurricane... your call cannot be completed..." Sloan ran across the dark and deserted campus. Lightning flashes provided the only light. She stopped repeatedly and tried to redial VistaFlight with the same result. "Due to the hurricane... your call cannot be completed..."

"Get your jet in the air and pick up my daughter!" Jeff Krueger was calling VistaFlight every ten minutes demanding that they get a flight to New Orleans. He called other private jet companies as well. He also called a helicopter service and the US Coast Guard. The answer was always the same: "Travel to New Orleans now is impossible."

The VistaFlight CEO explained that the New Orleans lakefront airport was submerged under six feet of water and the international airport had been closed by the government. Winds were gusting at 130mph. The city was completely shut down. "We don't even know where Sloan is because all phone networks are down as well. Most likely she is with the Tulane group at Jackson State." Krueger was assured that Sloan would be picked up first thing in the morning when things cleared up. "Everything is on standby and ready to move. We will find her ASAP."

Willow was standing in front of Butler House worried about Sloan. "Hurry. Come on!" She motioned for Sloan to run faster, but Sloan had on dress shoes and her hands were covering her ears. "Run Sloan!" She pumped her arms hard and kicked off the Prada shoes. Menacing thunder sounded like bowling balls rolling down a lane. Driven hard by the wind, raindrops stung like hornets. The snapping tree branches popped louder than rifle shots. "It's ok! These are the first outer bands. They are like outstretched fingers bringing energy to the storm's eye. Things will die down in just a few minutes. The actual hurricane is still hours away." Willow tried to calm Sloan down, although she had never seen storm feeder bands this powerful. "It is going to get very windy, noisy and scary. I have seen twelve of these storms since 1988. We will be fine. I promise!" She held Sloan tight.

"Tulane did not say anything about this in the brochures," Sloan cried. After a few minutes she began to regain her composure.

"What about my Mercedes?"

# 16

GREENVILLE, MISSISSIPPI IS THREE HUN-
DRED miles north of New Orleans. The night sky was still clear
and star filled. Kathy and her cousin sat in antique wicker rockers on
the back veranda of the Percy family home, enjoying the pleasant
evening. They had been close since childhood and could talk about
everything. The rockers were salvaged from the nearby Whitney Plantation after it was condemned from too many years of neglect and dis-
interest. The Percy home was on a ridge overlooking acres of
manicured land with mature hardwoods, wisteria and azaleas surrounding a white trellis. An old, unused pole barn stored a rusty tractor. It hadn't run since the Carter administration. Off in the distance
the peaceful Mississippi River reflected starlight as a single tug pushed
three barges south towards Natchez. Nephews and nieces enjoyed
sweet tea and chased lightning bugs with butterfly nets and mason
jars. "I have five!" They excitedly yelled a new total each time they
caught another. "I have eight!" The pitter-patter of their running feet
carried across the otherwise quiet evening. Kathy sipped a mint julip.
Unharmed, the insects were always set free later.

Kathy's cousin could not wait to hear about her new romantic interests. She was happy Kathy had finally left her loser husband. "We
have so much to get caught up on." After learning everything about
Louis, even about his Creole heritage, the cousin looked around and
then leaned forward on her rocking chair. She lowered her voice to a
soft whisper. "So? Did you two lovebirds do it yet?"

Surprised by the unexpected question, Kathy's eyebrows went up. Bright red splotches appeared on her neck. She blushed. "Oh my! You bad girl!"

The answer was clear without words. The cousin fanned herself with her left hand and padded her forehead with a damp napkin borrowed from her cold drink glass. She advised Kathy to never play poker. "You would most certainly lose every hand." They both laughed.

Then Kathy confessed to harboring a broken heart because Louis was too loyal and too Catholic to end his profoundly unhappy marriage. Kathy thought perhaps Louis felt their lovemaking had been a mistake. "Don't worry, my dear. These things have a way of working out. Don't ever lose hope!" The cousin tried to cheer things up.

"I have a confession to make." The cousin admitted to an addiction for reading explicit romance novels. "But I only read them when Stewart is out of town. He doesn't approve! Luckily, his new job demands a lot of travel." They both laughed some more. "My favorite book has a plot set in the antebellum period. A beautiful southern belle, 'Caroline,' is kept locked safe in a large sugarcane plantation on Bayou Lafourche near Thibodeux. Her father expects her to marry the son of a business partner, a man she does not love. Caroline goes along with the arranged marriage because she does not wish to disappoint her father. But every night she quietly slips out her bedroom window and runs into the arms of her Creole lover waiting under the live oaks. There must be something about these Creole men!" Kathy smiled and agreed enthusiastically.

"You have no idea!" she said.

"Don't you remember Grandmother and Grandfather always talking about that famous speech Franklin Roosevelt gave from his train, the Ferdinand Magellan? It was the one about race relations and the diversity of America's armies."

Kathy said she did remember. "How could I forget? They loved FDR. The president said everyone banded together to battle Japan and Germany. Irish, Polish, Italian, French, Scandinavian immigrants and Blacks all did their part."

"Yes, but do you remember that Thanksgiving Day when Grandfather stood on a chair and did his best FDR impersonation?" Kathy remembered and said that was one of her most cherished childhood memories. I was six, but still remember the words Grandfather spoke while he looked across the dining room directly at me. "Do you think it was too much brandy talking or too much of that sweet muscadine wine he liked?" Kathy said it was Grandfather's passion for FDR, not the alcohol.

Grandfather stood on a chair and delivered lines from the famous speech: "The Murphys and the Kellys, the Smiths and the Joneses, the Cohens and the Carusos, the Kowalskis, the Schultzes, the Olsens, the Swobodas, and right in with all the rest of them, the Cabots and the Lowells. Among American citizens, there should be no forgotten men and no forgotten races." Kathy said Grandfather knew the president's speech by heart.

"Perhaps that is why we don't discriminate in our selection of lovers. Creoles have a little of everything in their blood. They are as diverse as Roosevelt's armies!" They both agreed and said Grandmother and Grandfather would approve. "They would love Louis!"

Kathy looked in the direction of the television playing in the living room. She enjoyed visiting with family, but was keeping one eye on the Weather Channel as well. Through the windows she could see dramatic graphics with projected computer paths all dead center directly over New Orleans with one word, 'WINDY,' highlighted over the city. "I hate the Weather Channel. The 'cone of impact' always includes a major media market. They seem to enjoy all this a little too much!" Kathy suggested they go check her laptop.

"I don't think those people on TV should be allowed to capitalize on a tragedy like this. Let's go inside." Kathy's cousin could see her concern. "Everything is going to be just fine!" She reached out for Kathy's hand.

The National Weather Service indicated that Katrina was weakening somewhat as it began to approach land. More importantly, it seemed to be taking a very slight, last-minute eastwardly jilt towards the Mississippi coast, which was encouraging news for New Orleans, but terrible for Biloxi. Nevertheless, as Katrina's eye approached the southern tip of Plaquemines Parish, a massive wall of water was already being pushed into Lakes Pontchartrain, Borgne and Maurepas. Mississippi would get wind and temporary surge; New Orleans would get persistent flood water.

Louis and his father used to fish in the Lake Borgne area. The area was dotted with old forts built by the French and Spanish during colonial times. Some were tiny with space for only two or three cannons protecting small inlets; others were massive. A few were well preserved, and some were ruins or just piles of old bricks. These were the first New Orleans area structures to face Katrina head on. They had survived centuries of storms, tides, floods and war. Katrina claimed them all in a matter of minutes.

Water was rising fast in the Mississippi River Gulf Outlet 'Mr. Go' and the Rigolets, backing up into the industrial canal where Louis used to sit and watch ships come and go. Flood water was surging into Lake Pontchartrain and reaching dangerously high levels in the canals. The Orleans Levee Board said the levees were "strong and safe," but those protecting the Lakeview area along the 17th Street canal were growing weaker under the pressure and bulging like over-inflated balloons. This was the exact area were Levee Board inspectors found no problems and blamed wet backyards on leaky pipes.

The communities of Shell Beach, Delacroix, Yscloskey and Chalmette in the eastern-most part of Saint Bernard Parish were already inundated. Saint Bernard was on the wrong side of the major flood protection levees and the wrong side of the industrial canal. Average elevation across the parish is three feet. Katrina's serge was over 30 feet. Nearly all structures were heavily damaged or destroyed completely.

Just a day before, people sat on benches, watched pelicans and enjoyed a pleasant sunset on the Mississippi coast. They spent money in the casinos and ate dinner at popular Gulf-front restaurants. Expensive and historic waterfront homes were built on gently rising land directly across from the beach. Unlike south Louisiana, most everything in Mississippi is above sea level, so levees and pumping stations were not necessary. But nothing protects the Mississippi coast from storms except a thin line of offshore barrier islands.

Thirteen casinos were confidently built on floating barges to comply with Mississippi gambling laws. Voters wanted the revenue gambling generated for schools, but did not want the sinful businesses on Mississippi soil. The tax money was all dedicated to education, thus securing voter support. Mississippi politicians reduced existing education budgets by the amount of new gambling revenue. Gambling money did go to schools as promised, but elementary and secondary budgets remained the same. Floating casinos became a metaphor for political horse trading. It was too difficult, expensive and probably impossible to move the giant barges inland. Katrina's powerful, right front quadrant was heading directly for Gulf Port and Biloxi.

Most of the Mississippi casinos were washed hundreds of yards inland and were destroyed. The Hard Rock Hotel and Casino opened the day before Katrina struck. It was also a total and complete loss. The President Casino was moored at the Broadwater Beach Resort and Marina. It contained thirty-eight thousand square feet of gambling space and over nine hundred slot machines and was one of Jan's favorites. It broke free and was found one-half mile away after the surge washed back into the Gulf. It would be a very long time before Jan could play the Biloxi slot machines again.

Hancock, Harrison and Jackson Counties were devastated. Two hundred and thirty-six people died in Mississippi, and sixty-seven were lost and never found. Total damages along the Mississippi coast amounted to over one hundred and twenty-five billion dollars. "We will not simply rebuild, but we will build back bigger and better than ever," per the Mississippi governor's promise.

Willow and Sloan hunkered down in a third-floor Butler House bathroom. It was centrally located with no exterior walls or windows. They padded the floor and sides of a shower stall with blankets, pillows and chair cushions. Although they were protected by multiple cinderblock and brick walls, the entire building still swayed back and forth each time it was hit by powerful wind gusts. "The water is sloshing around in the toilets! I hear it!" Sloan was scared. Some of the old wood-frame windows on the north side of the dorm building were blown out. Willow ran up and down the hall, closed the doors and returned with more pillows. Sloan sat in a corner of the shower in the fetal position with her hands covering her ears. Willow held her as a mother would comfort a frightened child. "It's all going to be okay," Willow promised.

All Willow could offer was reassurance. As a child, she always felt safest in the arms of her father. He used to sing a song on stormy nights. Willow remembered the words. She sang the same song tonight in a soft comforting tone.

There's a big old storm a coming,

Big old storm tonight.

There's a big old storm a coming,

Better shut your windows tight.

There's a cold, cold wind a blowing,

Cold, cold wind tonight.

There's a cold, cold wind a blowing,

Better shut your windows tight.

There's rain, rain, raindrops falling,

Rain, rain, rain tonight.

There's rain, rain, raindrops falling,

Better shut your windows tight.

Katrina's last-minute move towards Mississippi spared New Orleans a direct hit from the storm's most powerful quadrant. Hurricanes rotate in a counter-clockwise direction. With the eye moving east, New Orleans was hit by dryer and weaker winds circulating back from the north. Unfortunately for Mississippi, they were hit by south gales coming directly off the gulf. The wind weakened dramatically over land before crossing across Louisiana and rotating back over open water.

New Orleans did not experience the wind calamity predicted from such a powerful hurricane. The city's wind damage was inconsequential compared to the devastation and ruin in Mississippi. Under normal circumstances this would have been very good news for the city. By now most people in New Orleans were feeling somewhat lucky compared to the Mississippi coast. But Katrina was not an ordinary storm; its massive surge already pushed a wall of water into Lake Pontchartrain before the shift east. Now all that additional water was being pushed south across the lake back towards New Orleans, piling up against the already weakened levees.

# 17

**LOUIS HAD FINALLY FALLEN ASLEEP,** but woke just an hour or so later. It was late morning; the winds had died down and the sun was beginning to shine through. The cloud cover was breaking apart, indicating that the worst was over. He made a pot of coffee using an old-fashion percolator on a gas stove. Electric coffee makers are fine, but Louis kept his father's old 'stove coffee pot,' especially for situations like this. The sound and aroma of hot coffee bubbling into the clear glass lid reminded him of his childhood. His father always called the morning's first cup 'caoua,' a French word pronounced like kah-wah. Louis could get by without electricity, but not without coffee.

The coffee was ready just as the morning sky began to clear. No one knew how long the electricity would be out. Louis wanted to pick up the downed tree limbs and other debris littering his front yard. The house lost a few roof tiles, but otherwise seemed to be in good shape. He checked email while his laptop battery was still fully charged. "University operations are to resume on Wednesday, August 31st. Classes will resume on Thursday September 1st, but not later than September 7th. We must assess the campus condition and commence repairs and cleanup. Contact your supervisors for essential work schedules." Louis was asked to return to Tulane that afternoon. That worked out fine, because it still gave him time to take Willow to lunch. Louis expected everything to be back to normal real soon.

Restaurants would reopen once electricity was restored, most likely in a few hours.

Pine tree branches are easy to break apart and clean up. Louis filled two trash cans with front-yard debris and wheeled them to the curb. He returned from the garage with a rake. Water, about an inch-deep, covered Montegut Street. Louis thought that was very strange, but assumed the city pumps would clear it up soon; perhaps the generators were out at the pumping stations. Within a few minutes, water was rising over the curb. He dropped the rake and watched the water for a moment. It was now over the grass and lapping at his shoes. Louis bent down low on one knee. He made a cup with his hand and tasted the water. It was salty. "Jan! Jan! Get up! The levees have failed. We've got to move now!"

When Louis got out to the shed, water was already reaching his waist and rising fast. He climbed into his father's old flatboat and unhooked it from the trailer. Jan was on the front porch as he paddled the boat around. There was no time to get anything. He held onto the banister to steady the boat while Jan climbed aboard. "The river bust through?" she asked, still not believing that could happen.

"It's not the river. The Gulf is flooding in!" Louis said.

The boat's five-gallon gas tank was nearly full, but the old-fashion Johnson Sea Horse motor had not run in a very long time. It had a rope pulley starter setup like a lawnmower, but the pull grip handle was missing. Louis wrapped the rope around his fingers and made a fist. He pulled and pulled. Sweat built up on his forehead. "Come on! Come on, baby!" He squeezed the rubber primer trying to pump more fuel into the carburetor. Louis pulled and pulled, and then pulled some more. The blood dripping onto the bottom of the boat was from his own hands as the starter rope cut deep into his flesh.

"You're not pulling hard enough!" Jan advised. Flood water was now at least eight feet deep. Neighbors in the area were climbing onto their roofs. The boat motor finally coughed to life.

WWL radio broadcasted from a tall building across from the Dome. This was the AM station where most local people in New Orleans got their news. There had been no recent alerts or updates from city hall. A small van was parked on the street near the stadium; it was clearly visible from the radio studio. The announcers commented on the rising water visible from their fifteenth story vantage point. "It is now up to the van's hubcaps. There must be a broken water main somewhere. I tell you, if they don't get this addressed soon we are going to have some real problems!"

The water continued to rise fast. Many climbed into their attics, but this would become a deadly decision if they had no sledge hammers or any other way to bust out onto the roof. Some swam outside and climbed on their roofs. There they sat and waited for help they were sure would be coming soon. Still others tried to walk through the rising flood waters to the Dome or Convention Center. Multiple fires were breaking out across the city ignited by broken gas lines. There were no firemen or firetrucks to respond.

The first major levee breach occurred at 9:00 a.m. on the industrial canal between Florida Avenue and Claiborne Avenue, almost the exact spot where Louis used to spend time fishing and daydreaming. A few minutes later, another industrial canal failure occurred at Tennessee Street. Then the 17TH Street levee collapsed in catastrophic fashion sending a wall of water through Lakeview like a tsunami. Homes were torn free of foundations and floated down city streets in ghostly single line formations resembling parades of Mardi Gras floats. The London Avenue canal failed on both the west side towards Robert E. Lee Blvd. and at Mirabeau Avenue on the east side, flooding everything from City Park to the University of New Orleans.

In all total, the levees failed in over fifty separate locations. Mr. Go failed in twenty places. By the time Louis and Jan got the boat going, 66% of the city was already deep under water. By noon 80% of New Orleans was inundated. Thousands of New Orleanians waited desperately on rooftops for the help they expected to arrive soon, but there was no one at city hall to issue warnings or direct rescue operations. Most gutless politicians, including the mayor, had already fled to Houston or Baton Rouge. This was the same bunch of political fools Louis encountered at the Marina Grill. At the time, Kathy jokingly said the city would be in trouble if these dimwits had to make real life and death decisions. She was so right. New Orleans was a sinking ship, abandoned and alone, deserted even by those elected to lead.

Louis steered the boat using a small handle attached to the top of the motor. Moving the handle from side to side pointed the boat in the desired direction, as there was no rudder. They headed south towards the high ground of the Mississippi River levees. Passing less than a block from the Bayou Contracting warehouse, Louis could see water reaching up to the soffits. All the equipment was completely submerged. He hoped William-Mark took care of the insurance as he was required to. Some of the roof tin was missing. Louis found humor in the situation, remembering William-Mark's concern about the small roof leaks.

Worried about the Bayou Contracting insurance, Louis also realized that he had no flood insurance on the Montegut Street house. He convinced himself that the flood was caused by the storm, therefore his regular homeowners' policy should cover things. By Louis's logic he saw no need for flood insurance. After all, the neighborhood was not even in a flood zone. On second thought, an inexpensive flood policy would not have been a bad idea.

With its misfiring motor, the boat struggled to cross Saint Claude Avenue, fighting against the powerful currents. The deluge rolled down the avenue towards the Central Business District like a whitewater river in the Smokey Mountains. Louis tried adjusting the choke to get more power, but the old motor just didn't have anything more to give.

A large black dog splashed in the water nearby. He had been swimming in the currents a long time and was growing weaker and weaker. He was barely able to keep his head above the water. Louis admired the dog's tenacious determination to survive and took a risky chance by turning the boat around.

"Come on, boy! Come on, boy! Swim a little harder." Louis splashed his hand in the water encouraging the dog to swim towards his direction.

"Are you crazy? You are risking my life to save a dumbass dog?" Louis ignored Jan and pulled the large dog into the boat. He was heavy and exhausted, too weak to climb in without help.

"You are going to capsize the boat! What is wrong with you?" Jan stood up and moved toward the dog, intending to push him out.

"Sit down. You're the one tipping the boat!"

Louis hugged the dog around his neck and petted his head. The dog wagged his tail and licked Louis's face enthusiastically. Jan complained when the dog got her wet.

"The entire city is under ten feet of water. Most likely you will get wet today!" Louis said.

The dog lay down on the floor of the boat and rested his head against Louis's leg.

"I'm going to call him Puncher. He didn't have a puncher's chance in hell fighting against those currents. He didn't let up."

Jan rolled her eyes, expressing annoyance. "He is just a dog!" she said. Louis admired Puncher's fearless tenaciousness.

"If he let up even for a moment he would not have gotten a second chance; he would have drowned. He's a fighter!"

Louis turned the boat back towards the higher ground near the Mississippi River, finally making it across Saint Claude Avenue. In this direction, flood water was gradually getting shallower and the currents were slower. Puncher tried to shake off the water, regaining some of his strength. He started at his head and wiggled aggressively, lastly shaking his tail in small circles. "You are going to be fine," Louis promised. The water droplets Puncher sprayed annoyed Jan further. She sat with her arms folded and an exasperated expression.

The old Bunny Friend playground was nearby. Louis spent many hot summer afternoons swimming in the public pool with childhood friends. He remembered how water droplets used to cover his chest and arms each time he exited the pool. Louis never dried off quickly with a towel. He enjoyed patiently allowing the sun to do that job. Everyone had a vigorous glow and sense of healthy body when swimming in the Bunny Friend pool. Somehow, he thought water always seemed to rejuvenate.

Louis could get the boat only so close to the high ground near the river. At this point the flood water was knee-deep, but he was concerned about damaging the boat's motor if he was to hit a submerged object. Hundreds of people were sitting on the levee or walking through flood water in that direction, carrying children on their shoulders or elderly relatives on their backs. Two small children were pulled through the flood on a floating mattress. Their father used an old piece of lumber as a paddle.

"You are lucky to reach this area. It never floods here. We call it the 'Sliver on the River'." A friendly neighbor helped pull the boat closer and assist Jan. He introduced himself as he handed out bottles of water. "I'm Clarence. My wife, Lesley, and I live right here in that beautiful Queen Anne home. From Poland Avenue, all the way to Franklin Avenue and a few blocks south of Claiborne should be high and dry."

'Lesley and Clarence, Lesley and Clarence,' Louis repeated the names to himself. "Does your wife operate a scholarship program at Tulane?" He realized why the names seemed so familiar. "My daughter, Willow, started Tulane this week. Your wife made that possible. She is remarkable." Louis commented on how small the world is.

"I know Willow! Lesley talks about her often." Clarence said he was looking forward to meeting her.

Many other people sat nearby waiting calmly for the help they expected to arrive very soon. A group of children played chase on a small patch of dry ground while more and more people made their way to the relative safety of the 'Sliver on the River'.

"You should get out of the boat here. The area looks safe and I think Clarence will look out for you. I am going back to find Willow!" Jan did not want to leave the boat. Louis planned to go back to Saint Claude towards North Rampart Street behind the French Quarter, then to South Claiborne. He could get to Willow's Butler House dorm easier from the north side of Tulane's campus near Audubon Street. It would be a very long and dangerous ride in a leaky old boat with a worn-out motor.

"Do you really expect me to actually walk through this filthy water?" Jan asked. Clarence offered his hand.

"I have to go all the way across town. You are safer here. I can try to get the boat a little closer."

Louis and Clarence helped Jan out of the boat, but she lost her balance anyway and fell over the side. Clarence quickly pulled her up. "Son of a bitch!" she repeated over and over. Clarence said Lesley had dry clothes that should fit. Louis thanked him and watched until he was sure Jan was safe on dry ground. "I will be back in a few hours," he said. Next, he tried to lift Puncher out of the boat. "Come on, boy! You're safe now." Puncher stiffened his body and refused to budge. He was not going to leave Louis's side.

"Go get Willow. Jan will be safe here. Hurry back," Clarence said. "He petted Puncher's back. You two be safe. Things could get dangerous."

Louis turned the boat around in a cloud of blue smoke from the tired motor as it struggled to speed up. He headed back towards Saint Claude Avenue with Puncher sitting proudly at the bow, reminding Louis of the hood ornaments found on classic cars like Packard and Cadillacs from the 1930s and 40s.

# 18

LATE MORNING SUNLIGHT SHINED
THROUGH a broken window frame and woke Willow first. She
reached for the ceiling, stretching as far as she could, trying to wake
up. It had been a long uncomfortable night with little rest. She had
maybe three or four hours of sleep. "That wasn't so bad after all. I was
expecting much worse!" Sloan said as she confidently collected some
things and splashed cold water on her face.

Willow clicked a light switch on and off, but everything stayed dark.
"Looks like the electricity is off." She explained that falling tree
branches always knocked out power lines. "The power company
should have things up and running soon. Besides, Tulane should have
emergency generators."

They decided to put all the pillows and cushions back where they
belong, change clothes, freshen up and go find something to eat. PJ's
coffee house was nearby and should reopen soon. "Looks like cell service is also out." Willow tried unsuccessfully to call her dad. "Due to
the hurricane this call cannot be completed." The same message was
repeated over and over.

"What are those strange popping sounds I keep hearing?" Sloan
asked. Then she answered her own questions. "Firecrackers or back-
firing cars, I guess."

"But why would anyone be using fireworks after a hurricane?" she wondered aloud.

"Somehow I don't think that's firecrackers. We need to see what's going on." Willow advised Sloan to stay away from the windows. "People in New Orleans like to fire their guns! On New Year's Eve bullets fall like rain everywhere. Innocent people always die."

Sloan forgot the electricity was out and impatiently pushed the elevator buttons multiple times. "I think we need to take the stairs, sweetheart," Willow said with a sarcastic smile. They opened a heavy door leading to the fire escape. With no lights or windows, it was all very dark and damp. Only one small emergency light was functioning on the top floor.

"Shouldn't there be some type of effective emergency lighting in here?"

Willowed agreed. "This is strange!" Sloan held Willow's arm as they cautiously navigated each step with just enough light to make out the next one. It was like walking into a long dark tunnel with no light at the end. They carefully made it down to the second floor, and midway to the first. "Almost there. One more floor to go." Willow was in front leading the way. "Something is wrong?" The next few steps seemed to disappear in total and complete blackness.

"Is that water?" Sloan asked.

"I think so."

Willow told Sloan to stay there on the dry higher steps for a few minutes while she looked around. "We can't stay in a flooded building forever. I'm going to try to open that exit door and see what's going on outside. Wait here."

The water was deep and cold. When Willow reached the last step water was already past her hips. She held her arms above the water to keep them dry. Willow found the exit door handle and pushed hard. It took all her strength. The entire campus was inundated, but the deepest water was on the Claiborne Avenue side of Tulane. Conditions improved somewhat towards Saint Charles where flooding was minimal. The avenue created a type of false levee, blocking the water. Willow saw dead-eyed young men holding shotguns and broken bottles moving from house to house. They were kicking in the front doors of uptown mansions and firing their guns at random. They laughed and joked, enjoying this new game. Willow tried to hide behind a tree.

"Knock-knock, motherfuckers!" the teenage thugs announced each time they kicked in another door. They were just as interested in vandalism and terrorizing homeowners as they were in looting. They always raided the medicine cabinets first, looking for prescription drugs, especially opioids. Willow could hear things smashing and glass breaking, women crying and the teenagers laughing. They took turns with the women while holding the men face down at gunpoint.

Use of illegal prescription anti-depressants and painkillers among the US population increased over 400% during the 1990s. The population of New Orleans reflected that dreadful trend as well, but the city had even higher addiction rates than national averages. The crack cocaine epidemic of the 1990s also devastated the city. The final destruction and total breakdown of civil order in New Orleans happened when all these addicts became desperate and violent, because Katrina made it impossible for them to get their drugs.

At the next house a man ran out with his young daughters and wife. He floored the S500 Mercedes sedan, smashed through iron gates and raced down the north side of Saint Charles. The looters fired shotguns at the car as it sped away. The New Orleans Police Department was nowhere in sight.

"Hello girlie! What's your name?" One of the vandals saw Willow and yelled at her from a porch on the far side of Saint Charles. He and another friend jumped off the porch and started to run in her direction. "Where are you going, girlie?" Willow moved through the water as fast as she could and hid behind a half-submerged car. She held her breath, then made her way back to the dorm.

"Where are you, girlie?" They were persistent and did not give up searching. Willow wished they would go back to smashing front doors.

"We need to move now! Get up, Sloan!"

Sloan was still waiting on the same step, but she was leaning against the wall, sleeping. "Okay, is PJs already reopened?" She rubbed her eyes trying to wake up.

"We have to get moving. Can't stay here. By-the-way, those sounds are not firecrackers, they're shotguns!"

"Some guys are out there yelling something. Are they looking for us? Maybe they're Tulane security? Are they cute?"

Willow grabbed her by the shoulders and shook hard. "Listen to me, Sloan! Do you want to stay alive? Get with it! We got to move now!" Willow grabbed a piece of paper and wrote one word: 'Paris.' She taped it to her dorm door.

"What is that for?" Sloan asked.

Willow knew her dad would come looking for her and he would remember their conversation about the Eiffel Restaurant. She pulled Sloan by the arms. "Let's go!"

"We know you're here, girlie! Come out, come out wherever you are." The two thugs were making their way to the second floor after ransacking everything not flooded on the first. "We just want to talk to you."

Willow and Sloan circled around and reached the first floor from the back-service stairs near an out-of-the-way exit. The flood waters warped the old wooden floors of the historic building. The spongy waterlogged planks bubbled up and sank back down with each step they took. "What is wrong with the floors?" Sloan said it was like trying to run inside one of those inflatable jumping houses parents rent for their children's parties. Willow thought it surreal, like a Salvador Dali painting.

Everything outside was completely quiet except for multiple gunshots echoing across the city. There were no birds or barking dogs. There were no traffic noises or police sirens, nothing making typical urban sounds. The air was thick with smoke from the raging fires left to burn out on their own. The peculiar silence was occasionally broken by desperate screams as the anarchy spreading across the city was taken as opportunity to settle old scores.

Most New Orleans police abandoned their positions and fled the city. Many went to Houston, Dallas or Baton Rouge. A few raided a Cadillac dealership and escaped in stolen SUVs. Fewer than seventy-five officers remained on-duty. Jefferson Parish deputies blocked the Mississippi River Bridge after looters from New Orleans burned a shopping center. Jefferson Parish also used horses and shotguns to close the River Road access into their parish, forcing those in New Orleans to fend for themselves.

A man was standing on his porch waving a white towel back and forth, trying to get someone's attention. "My mama is dying!" He begged Willow and Sloan for help. The water was just over four feet deep. The man's mother, extremely obese, was sitting on a plastic chair baking in the sun. "She is diabetic. The electricity has been out for a long time. Her insulin is warm. I can't move her." The woman was unresponsive and appeared to be unconscious. "She has been like this for a few hours."

Willow and Sloan helped raise one arm; the man lifted the other. They could move the helpless lady a few feet into shade.

"Sorry, but we need to go. We are being followed by two thugs. They are only a few blocks back." Willow promised to send help as soon as they found someone.

"I'll try to slow those knuckleheads down. Please hurry back. By the way, my name is Steve."

The thugs were falling further behind, but Willow could still hear them shooting their guns occasionally. She hoped they would get distracted by something else and lose interest in the chase.

The small area of land between the levee and the Mississippi River is called the batture. It changes with the ebb and flow of the river. This was the same hidden path Willow used to escape public transportation when she attended Warren Eastern High School. The storm's flood surge did not affect Mississippi River levels, so the batture was still high and dry. It is where the city's outcasts often hid off the grid in solitude, living in rundown shacks made from discarded materials and salvaged items. It was all hidden deep behind overgrown foliage and cypress trees. Locals know the only way around New Orleans without being seen was by using the old footpaths crisscrossing the batture. Sloan was worried about spiders and snakes. "Are we actually going down there?"

"Would you rather deal with insects or the armed gangs rampaging around the city?"

Getting across the batture was difficult, but not life-threatening. Willow used a stick to check the depth of standing water. Sloan lost a shoe in the soft muck and they saw a large snake slithering across their path. He was solid black and did not have a pattern on his skin. "I don't think he is poisonous," Willow said.

Sloan remembered a rhyme from preschool: "Red next to black, he's ok Jack." The snake was more afraid than they were, and he quickly disappeared in the tall weeds.

The girls soon realized that blackberry bushes were more dangerous than any snakes or insects they saw, and thorns cut like barbwire against their legs. The batture was the perfect habitat for the blackberry tangles of dense stems covered with curved sharp prickets. The plant's thorns could easily tear through denim and skin. They were difficult to avoid, because the arching tangled mass of dangerous stems grew across the footpaths. A machete would have been very helpful. When Willow and Sloan finally reached Washington Avenue their legs were bleeding and torn like they had escaped over a prison fence protected with razor wire. "If it was hard for us to get through, it will be hard for those punks, too." Willow told Sloan they had to keep moving.

The city streets were littered with piles of debris and trash carried by the flood waters. Sloan sat near the back wall of a looted Walgreens drugstore resting, while Willow searched through the store's debris looking for bottled drinking water, antibiotics cream for the cuts on their arms and legs, and shoes. Drug stores are always the first places looted. "Here is some water, right here!" Conveniently, Sloan saw two cases a few feet away. Debris piles can act like camouflage, hiding and concealing things. The bottled water was difficult to see at first, so was the body. Sloan saw an arm protruding out of the rubble and just assumed it was a mannequin from the store, until she got a closer look. She noticed the wedding ring first, and then touched the hand. "Oh God!" she screamed. "There is a dead person here!" Sloan threw up.

They would see many more dead bodies. Soon the heat caused the corpses to become bloated. The buttocks usually expanded first, busting out through pants. The decomposition process was strong enough to split jeans. The hotter it became, the easier it was to spot the cadavers. It is amazing the dreadful things they got used to.

Eventually, officials trained in these matters moved through the flooded areas looking for floating bodies. They photographed them, recorded their location and checked for identification. They also looked for a cause of death: drowning or gunshot. The remains were tied down where they were found, near trees, porches, stop signs or light poles, so that they could be collected later. Once the floods receded, the dead were left suspended and hanging in strange places throughout the city.

"Hey you! You see two girls pass here?" The man on his porch was still holding a wet towel on his mother's forehead. He was trying to keep her cool in the 98-degree afternoon temperatures.

"Yea, about twenty minutes ago. They were heading west. They said something about sneaking into Jefferson Parish from Freret Street." Sloan and Willow were heading south, then east.

"If you are lying, we'll come back here and kill you and that fat old woman," the thugs said.

# 19

SENTEX IS A POWERFUL AND deadly military explosive, but it could be stomped on, lit on fire or stacked and transported safely; you could even chew it. Unlike other explosives, it is perfectly safe until the proper detonator is applied, then it becomes extremely dangerous and volatile. Like a Sentex detonator, New Orleans seemed stable and safe until Katrina acted as the propellant that ignited a deadly chain of explosive events.

The old Johnson Sea Horse motor seemed to be running better as Louis made his way towards Tulane. Flood waters were very deep in some areas with only the roofs of homes visible. Louis turned west onto Claiborne Avenue.

"Don't come down here, bro!" A man standing on a second-story porch a block away aimed his loaded pistol at Louis as his boat rounded the corner.

"I said, don't come down here, bro! I warned you!" Louis heard the gunfire, and then he heard a bullet whiz over his head. It was a very long-distance shot with a pistol, but still Louis pulled Puncher down and laid flat on the bottom of the boat for a moment. This neighborhood had already been looted, and the remaining residents were not trusting or taking chances with anyone. He fired the pistol again. Louis reached for the motor and turned the boat around, heading back in the same direction as he came.

"You're going to get another." The man took aim again.

"Stop shooting. I'm turning around!"

When Louis approached each intersection, he slowed the Sea Horse motor down. The flood water was dirty and visibility was only a few feet, but the intense sunshine enhanced his ability to see the rows of vehicles submerged beneath him. They were lined up at each intersection as if they were waiting for the light to change, except they were eight feet under water. He could see Chevys and Fords, minivans and commercial trucks. The flood water came up very fast. Louis wondered how many people could escape safely and how many were still sitting in the cars beneath him. They were like the victims of Pompeii, frozen in time at the very moment of their death. Louis slowed the boat down out of respect, made the sign of the cross and said a short prayer. He felt like he was trampling on graves.

"Mister, I need help. Can I have a ride in dat boat?" A woman made her way through the water toward Louis's boat. Thin and missing most of her teeth, she was heading to the Convention Center. "I've heard the National Guard is there giving out food and water. They are going to move everyone to Houston. The governor is bringing in busses from all over the state." She held her hands up high indicating she was unarmed. Louis could see needle tracks up and down her arms. He was distracted by the woman long enough for her two junkie friends to quietly approach the boat from the other direction, unseen. It was a classic misdirection play.

"Sorry, I'm heading uptown. You're only a few blocks from the Convention Center. You're fine from here. Sorry I can't help," Louis told the woman.

Puncher reacted like a savage beast when threatened. He was lying quietly on the bottom of the boat, unseen by the men planning to steal it, until he sensed danger. They were just a few feet away when they found themselves face-to-face with a growling dog ready to tear them apart.

"Call off your fucking dog. We just want the boat."

The man near the boat's bow was foolish enough to try and grab hold. "Get him, Puncher!" On Louis's command, he ripped into the man's flesh. Puncher violently jerked his head back and forth, digging his teeth in deeper like a lion ripping apart a recent kill. The man's hand and arm was torn apart. Louis grabbed the other man by the front of his shirt and pulled him closer. His massive fist connected with the man's face like a hammer. Unconscious, the junkie slipped below the surface of the water.

"We just want the boat. You don't have to be such an ass about it!" the woman said while backing away, intending to help her injured friends.

"I warned you. I'm going to find my daughter. You just picked the wrong boat to screw with."

The man with the shredded and bleeding hand found his unconscious friend and pulled him out of the water. He gave Louis the finger while he tried to revive his knocked-out sidekick with slaps to his face. "Wake up, dude!"

Louis continued heading towards Canal Street with Puncher sitting at the front of the boat. "Good boy, Puncher. Good boy!"

By now large US Navy helicopters were active over the city. They flew from the Naval Air Station at Pensacola about a forty-five-minute flight away. Many were bringing medical supplies, MREs and drinking water. Still, others were hauling collapsible buckets used for fighting fires, each capable of carrying up to five thousand gallons of water. The buckets were lowered into the waters of Lake Pontchartrain, filled, and then carried over the city to battle the out-of-control fires raging across many neighborhoods.

Louis had to carefully maneuver his way around tree branches and power poles, slowing down his progress. The submerged power lines, although not under an electric load, were still dangerous because they could easily get wrapped around the boat's prop, destroying the motor. Trees were helpful, making it easy to camouflage the boat among the branches, protecting it from the desperate people likely to attempt stealing it. With the flood waters, high, the boat was even with the branches of trees, especially the live oaks with Spanish moss. Louis used the moss and branches to effectively conceal the boat from view. It also made him impossible to see by the Navy aircrews in the helicopters circling overhead.

Louis did not realize that the nearby raging fire had spread to three houses. He was close to the front porch of the second home when he first heard the giant CH 53 Super Stallion helicopters approaching. "They sure are flying low," he said to Puncher. Louis's small boat was completely hidden under a massive live oak, invisible to the Navy helicopters. They flew in a single-line formation, each carrying thousands of gallons of water. Realizing what was about to happen, Louis held tight to the sides of the boat with one arm over Puncher, protecting him.

"Hold on, boy. We are going to get wet!"

The concussion from the first bucket drop was like a massive bomb, causing the house to collapse inward upon itself and knocking it off its foundation. Louis looked up in time to see the exterior walls of the adjacent house pushed in and out as if they were made of rubber bands. Like an explosive concussion force, the impact caused entire walls to flex violently. Water weighs nearly eight pounds per gallon. The destructive power of five-thousand gallons dropped from five-hundred feet nearly on top of Louis should have been devastating, but the massive branches of the live oak disrupted the water's force, saving Louis and the boat.

"Hold on, Puncher, two more to go!"

The next water drop was on the fire furthest away, but still the impact nearly swamped the boat. Louis stabilized it by holding onto one of the massive oak branches and preventing the boat from capsizing. With the boat nearly filled with water and on the verge of sinking, and the next Navy helicopter only about thirty seconds away, Louis made a risky decision to leave the relative safety of the oak tree.

"Hold on, Puncher!" Louis gunned the motor, heading into the open while he brushed away the moss used as camouflage. He had no unrealistic expectations of out running a Navy helicopter with his tiny outboard motor and flooded boat still taking on water and listing badly. However, he was counting on the training and professionalism of the Navy air crew to spot him. Louis had moved only a few yards into the open and was still somewhat hidden by the tree when the third helicopter appeared nearly directly overhead.

"Abort, abort! Pull up!" The right seat pilot was the first to see the tiny boat with the big black dog barking at the chopper.

"Roger that." The right seat pilot reached out the window and gave the thumbs up signal. Louis returned the friendly jester with a salute and wave.

"You can always count on the US Navy," he said to Puncher. The helicopter pulled away, moving on to another nearby part of the city. Louis used a baseball cap he found floating in the water to bail out the boat.

The quickest way for him to reach Willow's dorm was by crossing directly to Tulane from the Loyola University campus next door. Louis thought it would be safer to stay off the main streets like Claiborne Avenue, avoiding much of the gunfire he was hearing. "Why would anyone want to loot a collage campus?" he said to himself. "What are they going to steal? Books?" The boat approaching ahead was new and powerful with an inboard motor, shiny blue paint and a center consol. It was at least fourteen feet long with a large aft deck area behind the consol. One man was on board maneuvering the boat around Loyola's buildings.

"Does that dog bite? He looks dangerous." The man was dressed in topsider deck shoes without socks, short pants and a blue Polo pullover shirt. "I'm Ray."

"If you don't bother the dog, he won't bother you," Louis replied.

Ray said he was a university official inspecting the campus for damage and photographing everything for insurance claims. He also explained to Louis that he was trespassing on private university property and should move on quickly. "You don't want to be mistaken for a looter," Ray advised sarcastically, perhaps not completely trusting Louis's story.

"Just passing through," Louis explained again before asking to borrow extra gas. "A gallon or two would be helpful."

Ray reluctantly shared a few gallons of fuel once Louis agreed to move on quickly. "Go between those two brick buildings, then head west for a block. You will end up close to Tulane's dorms." Ray stood at the front of his boat, pointing as he spoke. "It's just a warning, but you should know there are a lot of crazy folks running around here. I would be careful if I were you. For now, you are safe on a college campus. The looters want drugs, not books, although Xavier University was hit, but they have a College of Pharmacy. Tulane and Loyola do not."

"I can take care of myself. I do appreciate the heads-up. Thanks." Louis followed Ray's directions and headed towards Tulane.

Immediately, he realized that all the damage inside Willow's dorm building was not caused by the storm. It looked like everything was ransacked, doors were kicked open, furniture was ripped apart, smashed and broken into pieces, and windows were shattered. He ran up the steps to Willow's floor, skipping three at a time. Louis turned right into Willow's room. She was gone. He desperately looked around for clues to her whereabouts. The door was ripped off its hinges, but somehow a sheet of copy paper remained securely taped on front. Louis recognized Willow's handwriting: 'Paris'.

"That's my girl." Louis knew exactly where she had gone.

# 20

THE SHORT WALK FROM THE drug store to the Eiffel
Restaurant was uneventful compared to what Sloan and Willow had
experienced before. The middle of Napoleon Avenue was much
higher than the surrounding areas, designed to allow rain water to
drain off to the sides quickly under normal weather circumstances.
Locals called the land between the two sides of an avenue the 'neutral
ground.' Everywhere else in America it is called the median. Long
lines of people, mostly families, tried to make their way to the higher
dry ground near the river by walking along these neutral grounds of
main avenues. The higher elevation made maneuvering through the
flood waters on foot possible.

Hundreds were walking south; small children wore floats and swim
vests designed for pools, keeping them afloat as they were pulled
along by their parents. Some small children were carried, as were older
relatives, too weak to make it on their own. One middle-aged man
carried his elderly grandmother on his back for ten city blocks. He
passed out from exhaustion and dehydration just as he reached Saint
Charles.

Another family of three generations was standing in one area for a
long period. Upset and crying, they refused to move on, slowing
down everyone else that was trying to reach dry ground. "Let's go! Get
moving! What's your damn problem?" It was walker road rage. A six-
teen-year-old boy from this family's group had wandered further out

into deeper water of the street, trying to find a way to move everyone faster. He disappeared after stepping into an open manhole and had not been seen for thirty-five minutes. Still the family waited, heart-broken, refusing to give up hope and move on. Still they waited. These massive waves of desperate families were like WWII refugees fleeing a war zone.

"They all look so pathetic, and why are they still walking in that filthy water?" Sloan commented.

"You know, we don't look much better!" Willow was growing tired of Sloan's cavalier attitude.

"Whatever!"

Sloan was confident her father would show up soon to rescue her from this despair, returning her to a life of comfort and privilege.

"I am sure your dad is coming for you, but until then you still need to survive." Willow said it was time to get moving.

Jeff Krueger left no stone unturned trying to locate and rescue Sloan. VistaFlight said there was no way to get any unauthorized aircraft into New Orleans. Jeff already had his legal team draw up the lawsuit paperwork. VistaFlight's lawyers said the company's advertisements were an illusory promise containing no commitment by the company. The promise to rescue, 'anyone-anywhere-anytime' seemed cloaked in promissory language, but contained no enforceable commitment by the company. "It is no different than a local coffee shop claiming to have the world's best espresso or a neighborhood grill offering a healthy menu. It is all just advertising talk, and ads are not contracts. Sorry we can't help."

"I am going to own this chicken shit company, sell the airplanes to some bush-league dictator in South America and fire all you bastards. Then you can take your promissory estoppel and shove it up your ass!" Krueger slammed his desk phone down, ripped the wire from the wall and flung the phone across his office, just missing surprised staff members.

"Find a way to reach my daughter!" He demanded that his employees accomplish the impossible.

A young intern on his staff informed Jeff that because of the gunfire only military aircraft were flying over the city. "Even the military is not authorized to return fire. There is confusion involving the New Orleans Police Department. A drug gang has taken over a Coast Guard station on the lakefront. Most relief helicopters can't fly because they are taking incoming gunfire from the ground. There are shootouts everywhere. There was a gunfight on a bridge. Five people died. Killing, raping and looting are rampant. Its total anarchy, a reign of terror, a real shit sandwich down there."

"Pack your crap and leave. You are fired. Does anyone else have anything negative to add to that?" Jeff paced back and forth with his hand on his forehead, unsure what to do next.

Everything in the Eiffel Restaurant was ransacked. Picasso's favorite booth was smashed into a million pieces and most of the windows were busted out. The looters had a great time destroying everything and drinking the alcohol. They even took the time to spray-paint gang tags. Most likely they would be back looking for more booze. Unable to push the front door open, Willow and Sloan had to climb through a broken window and over piles of debris just to get inside.

"Sooooo, why are we here? How will your father know where to find us, anyway?" Sloan dragged out the pronunciation of 'so' to emphasize her smart-alecky attitude.

"Don't worry. He will know."

Willow grabbed hold of Sloan's hand and pulled her toward the back of the restaurant, climbing over mountains of debris and smashed furniture. "We need to find the garbage room. Every New Orleans restaurant has one. It is usually near the dishwashing area." Willow explained that leftover food is scraped into trashcans before the dishes are washed. The trashcans are not emptied in the outside dumpsters until the end of the night. Clearly, Sloan had never worked in a restaurant before.

"Do all restaurants do this? How can this be hygienic?"

"It's not hygienic. It's New Orleans! No one worries about stuff like that here."

"My God, it stinks! It's a whiff of hell!" Sloan said she was going to throw up again. The decomposing seafood and other trash created a rancid, rotten and pungent smell that was overpowering. The 100-degree heat did not help the situation.

Willow dragged and pushed four full garbage cans into a semi-circle against the corner of a back wall. "We will be safe here. If we can't stand this smell, thugs can't either. Looters won't come in here." The girls hid in the small cavity Willow created between the trash cans. "Don't worry, your dad is moving heaven and hell to find you," Willow said.

"He will find me, but the truth is he doesn't love me. He only treats me like a princess because he feels guilty. He divorced my mother when I was three, and he has been married four times since then. He got sole custody because he paid off the family court judge. He loves his money, not me. That's why I milk it for all its worth," Sloan said as she rested her head against Willow, the exhaustion wearing down her carefree veneer.

Not realizing how tired they both were, it was easy to doze off. They may have been asleep for a few minutes or an hour, or perhaps longer.

"Quiet," Willow said in a very soft voice, placing her hand over Sloan's mouth. "Someone is in the restaurant! Shhhh!"

Louis was strong enough to push the front door open despite the rubble blocking his way. He picked up a wooden table leg and held it like a baseball bat, listening for signs of movement before inching deeper inside. He let Puncher go in first. "Go see, boy. Anybody hiding in here?" The booth where he'd sat with Kathy was destroyed and tagged by the gangs. Louis rubbed his hand over the broken remains. For a moment, his thoughts wandered back to that evening with Kathy. He could never forget that night; even if Picasso's table was gone, his feelings for Kathy were not.

Louis moved around cautiously and once he was convinced the dining room was empty, he pushed toward the kitchen area. Willow kept her hand over Sloan's mouth as the trash room door eased open and their hearts raced. "Don't make a sound," she whispered.

Louis pulled Puncher away and moved on. "Nothing in there," he said after a quick glance around. Disappointed, he planned to back track to Tulane.

Puncher pulled free and ran back to the kitchen area. Reluctantly, Louis went after him. "We don't have time for this, boy!" Puncher was at the trash room door trying to dig under it. "What is it, boy? Is someone in there?" Louis held the table leg high above his head with his right hand and pushed the door wide open with his left. Puncher was wagging his tail.

"Willow, are you in here?"

"Daddy!"

Willow jumped out from her hiding place. "I knew you would come for me. I knew you would."

They embraced for a long time. "Everything is going to be okay, but we do need to get moving. Looters can be back any time." Louis helped the girls step over the debris. "I love you, Daddy!" Willow said again. "By the way, when did we get a dog?"

"It is a long story, but he is our pet now."

"Welcome to the family, Puncher!" Willow hugged Puncher and rubbed her nose against his.

"He smells!" Sloan said.

"Actually, he might be thinking the same thing about you!" Willow had endured enough of Sloan's attitude.

Louis helped the girls climb into the boat. He gave Puncher a pat on the head. "Good boy," and lifted him into the boat as well. Puncher licked his face. Louis kept the table leg at his side. The motor started with its typical cloud of blue smoke.

"Before we head back, I promised to help someone! I gave my word." Willow told her dad about Steve and his very sick mother stuck on the porch of their flooded home.

"You gave your word and he helped you and Sloan. Let's return the favor and go get em. We used to call that neighborhood the 'Black Pearl.' I know exactly where we are heading."

Louis and Willow sat together at the back of the boat. Puncher took a liking to her and rested his head on Willow's lap. Sloan sat alone further up. Louis kept the table leg at his side. The Black Pearl neighborhood was originally home to many of the people that worked as domestic help, nannies or lawn maintenance folks for the mansions lining Saint Charles Avenue. The Black Pearl houses were small, shotgun designs built on tiny lots, but the community was strong with hardworking families, churches and schools.

Louis slowed the boat down to a crawl and listened for a minute. He put his finger to his lips asking everyone to quiet down. They were still a block away, but could easily hear angry voices.

"That's him! That's the guy that was chasing us!" Willow said in a whisper. She could not forget that voice.

"I can't be lied to! No girls went to Freret Street. I told you I would be back if you lied. You lied to me, and I can't be lied to! I warned you!" The yelling was growing louder and more aggressive. The thug held a shotgun pointed at Steve's chest. His elderly mother was still in the same position, not moving, but sweating and breathing heavily. "This old bitch has got to have some good drugs. Go find them." The other junkie went inside searching for the medicine cabinet.

Louis stopped the boat just out of sight. "Everyone out. I will be back in a few minutes." He told Willow to keep Puncher close by her side. "He will protect you. I promise I'll be back." He kissed Willow's forehead and headed to the house.

"Hello there. Do you two fellows have any water to share? It is hot as hell out here!" Louis acted overly friendly and defenseless. He clumsily guided the boat close to the porch.

"We ain't got no water. Get the fuck out of here!"

Louis acted like he was having trouble handling the boat. "I'm leaving. Just give me a second here. Having a little trouble driving this thing." All the while he was working closer into position.

"I told you to get the fuck out of here! What the matter with you?" The punk stepped toward the edge of the porch intending to push the boat away. It was the opportunity Louis needed. He swung the table leg like a baseball bat. The swing was so hard it could have been a Yankee stadium homerun. The blow against the man's head even sounded like the crack of a major-league hit. Face first; the gangbanger fell onto the porch in a pool of his own blood. Four of his front teeth splashed into the water.

Louis picked up the shotgun and opened the front door. The other punk was running toward him from the back of the house carrying a broken bottle and yelling like a crazy person. "I'm going to cut you up, man!" Louis calmly cocked the gun with a one-hand up and down motion, and leveled the gun's barrel at the fool's chest. Everyone respects the sounds made by a large gauge shotgun. The junkie dropped the broken bottle, ran out the back door, jumped into the water and started swimming away.

"That's exactly what I expected," Louis said.

"I appreciate your help with those guys. My name is Steve, but I ain't got no water or food, and certainly ain't got no money."

"I'm Louis." They shook hands. "The first thing we need to do is get your mother out of this sun." Louis easily picked her up and carried her into the front room, and gently placed her on a couch. He wet some towels in the flood water and placed them on her forehead. "We need to keep her cool. This should help."

Willow walked through the water carrying Puncher; Sloan was close behind. "I see you already met my dad." She was happy to see Steve survived the dangerous encounter with the thugs.

"I am really glad to see you again," Steve said. "I would not have blamed you if you never came back. It is very dangerous around here. But I sure am glad you did!"

The gangbanger was still knocked out. Sloan asked if he was dead. "No, he is not dead. He is going to eat his meals through a straw for the next six months." Louis said healing a broken jaw is a long painful process. "On the other hand, if he somehow rolled off this porch and drowned I don't think anyone would care."

"We don't have much time before the other gang members return looking for their pal. We got to move. Unfortunately, we can't all fit in this small boat." Louis gave the table leg to Steve and told everyone else to stay inside with Puncher. He tied up the knocked-out junkie just for good measure. "Give me twenty minutes." Louis climbed into the boat with the shotgun, pushed away from the porch and headed north.

# 21

**THOUSANDS OF DESPERATE PEOPLE WERE**
herded into the Dome and Convention Center with no food, water or
electric power. They were expected to be safe there. Most NOPD officers failed to report for duty or ran away. Intense gun battles broke
out across the city between armed gangs fighting for territory. Search
and rescue teams arrived from Florida, Indiana, Ohio, Maryland,
Missouri, Tennessee and Texas, but were kept out as gangs and looters shot at them. Over 4,000 Louisiana National Guard were sent to
the city by the governor to restore order. They were soon over-
whelmed, and then she had to request federal troops. "It's a very, very
desperate situation. It's imperative that we get everyone out. The situation is degenerating rapidly." Governor Blanco called for the total
evacuation of the city.

The government's ambitious but poorly carried out game plan called
for the National Guard to evacuate all remaining storm victims from
throughout the city and move them to the Convention Center where
they could be protected, cared for and eventually transported out of
the area. Then federal troops, many coming directly from combat
tours in Afghanistan and Iraq, would move in and restore order.

Civilians by the thousands were herded into the Convention Center
from all areas, including the 'Sliver on the River.' Thousands waited
on the sidewalks in front of the building. It was too dark, hot and
dangerous inside. They were like Vladimir and Estragon, the main

charters in Samuel Beckett's classic play "Waiting for Godot." The two characters waited endlessly and in vain for the coming of someone named Godot. As Vladimir and Estragon waited forever, so did the Convention Center refugees. Where was the promised food that never arrived? Where was the drinking water and medicine? Where was the sanitation and safe shelter they waited for but never came? What about the police protection that never arrived? Everyone just waited.

Clarence was in the front room of his home when the National Guard began evacuating the Sliver. Troops knocked heavily on his front door. "Sorry sir, but it is time to go. Everyone is being moved to the Convention Center. How many people are in the house?"

Clarence said it was just his wife and another friend. "I have three here!"

On que, a green Humvee pulled onto the front lawn. A polite young private held the door open for Jan and Lesley, his M-4 Commando rifle at his side. "Please watch your step."

Jan complained about the uncomfortable canvas seats. "It's a combat vehicle, not a Cadillac for Christ's sake!" Lesley was growing very tired of Jan's annoying tenor. Clarence locked the front door to the house and jiggled the knob to make sure it was secure. "That is probably not going to do much good, sir," the soldier said.

Clarence asked about the age of the beat-up Humvee. "It's a hand-me-down from the first Gulf War. She has never let me down." The soldier caressed the vehicle's hood like a familiar lover.

The convoy of old Humvees made their way to the Convention Center from the east, traveling as close to the river levee as possible. The first and last vehicles in the group were armed with fifty caliber machine guns mounted on their roofs, and each driver carried a loaded M-4 commando rifle. "Is all this fire power really necessary?" Clarence asked.

"Yes sir. It is. Actually, I wish we had more."

As they passed Elysian Fields and Esplanade Avenue, the convoy picked up speed while avoiding the heavy gun fire in the area. Approaching the foot of Canal Street near the Convention Center, the stench from human feces and death became overwhelming. It smelled worse than a rotting landfill. Lesley had her shirt collar pulled high over her nose. A banner was still hanging on the Convention Center's wall near the main entrance. It was left there from a recent event or convention. 'Life is like a po-boy! Fill it with good stuff!'

"Why are all those dead bodies just heaped over there?" Lesley asked.

The Humvee driver did not even seem to notice them at first, at least until Lesley spoke up. "Do you have any better suggestions, ma'am?" he asked politely. Some of the bodies died in the flood, some looked like gunshot victims, and still others looked as if they had been beat to death.

Helicopters hovered at twenty feet and pushed pallets of water and supplies out to the waiting crowds below them. "Why don't they land and unload? Wouldn't that be more efficient?" Clarence asked.

"They can't land because the aircraft would be stormed by these distraught people. That is one reason supplies are so limited."

Clarence was quiet for a minute. "Are we really going to be safe here?"

"We have 250 armed soldiers. It is the safest place in town." The young guardsman failed to mention that at night all the troops retreated to a separate room in the exhibition hall protected behind a reinforced firewall. They parked trucks against the doors, using them as barricades. The driver said the National Guard was just not trained for crowd control, but there was nothing to worry about because night duty was the responsibility of the NOPD. "They are great at crowd control. Mardi Gras is good training for this."

Yet, the NOPD abandoned most positions as well. Their blue uniforms and shiny badges were lying here and there, exchanged for civilian clothes. The police officers were afraid they would be targeted by the angry mobs. They ditched their uniforms before running away and abandoning their positions. Who could blame them? The police had no water, communications or ammunition.

Just before Clarence, Lesley and Jan arrived, someone began screaming that the river levee collapsed and the Center was about to flood. The widespread panic raged for nearly an hour with gunfire, fighting and people throwing chairs. An infant was killed after she was crushed by stampeding refugees. The situation was aggravated once two-hundred cases of hard liquor were discovered in a storage room.

Clarence found an isolated corner against an outside wall of the complex. The 'Life is Like a Po-Boy! Fill it with Good Stuff!' banner was visible hanging on an adjacent wall. Clarence did not want to be inside the Center after nightfall, as all lights were out, even the emergency lights. "It's a death sentence in that godforsaken place," he told Jan and Lesley. Clarence told them to sit back to back against the corner. He found a long piece of razor-sharp broken glass and wrapped one end with a sleeve he tore off an NOPD shirt, making an effective hand grip. It was an extremely deadly weapon that would slice through flesh easily. Clarence stood defiant. "No one is going to hurt anybody without getting past me first."

A troublemaker walked harmlessly by until he noticed Jan and Lesley sitting against the wall. He returned with another punk a few minutes later. They held their crouches and called Lesley and Jan bitches.

"We claimed these bitches first. Get the fuck out of here. They ours."

Clarence was not going anywhere. He side-kicked one on the right knee. He fell to the ground in agony, his leg bent in an unnatural way. With torn ligaments, he was unlikely to get up anytime soon. He cried like a little girl. Late-day sunlight reflected off Clarence's long glass blade. "I will kill you in a second if I have to!" Clarence wasn't joking, but the remaining punk was still standing and acted like he wanted to hold his ground. "You sure about this?" Clarence asked him once more.

Clarence stomped again with all his strength on the injured fool's already torn-up knee. Then he picked him up by the front of his shirt and placed the glass blade against the side of his head below his left ear. "You can leave now with your friend still in one piece or you can both die here. It makes no difference whatsoever to me!"

The other delinquent continued to advance toward Clarence threatening to finish it. "I'm going to fuck you up, bro!" He failed to realize just how precarious the situation was. Clarence was no push-over.

To survive, Clarence knew he had to be meaner and crazier than all the other mean and crazy people around there. He had to make them afraid to mess with him. With a quick flick of his wrist, the razor-sharp glass sliced off the punk's ear with ease. It was like a butcher knife. "What's next? How about his nose? It's your call! When I finish with him, I am going to cut you up next!" The second fool began to reconsider his plan. He looked at the women, then back and forth at his impaired friend.

"Damn, that ear is bleeding a lot. It stained my favorite shirt," Clarence said as he wiped the glass knife on his pants. "He lost just an ear and a knee. Under the circumstances, he got off easy. Now it's your turn. I am going to dissect you from your neck to your dick!"

"You are a crazy fuck!" Both delinquents withdrew, picked up the ear and didn't look back as they hobbled away while trying to stop the bleeding with a filthy cloth they picked up off the sidewalk.

"If I see you back here I will kill both of you."

Although Clarence did not show fear during the fight, his hands were shaking uncontrollably after the encounter ended. Lesley hugged him around his neck. "I love you!"

"This is not my thing," Clarence admitted. "I don't like to see blood." He had been involved in many scrapes over the years, although he never actually enjoyed it. Fighting was just a fact of life growing up in New Orleans.

"Fighting may not be your thing, but you seem to be very good at it." Jan was thankful for Clarence's protection, but thought cutting off the ear was unnecessary, and "over the top."

Being surrounded by so much human suffering, Lesley thought about those unfortunate kids condemned to attend the horrible Orleans Parish Public Schools. Some schools offered conditions not much better than the circumstances at the Convention Center. As Clarence had to fight, how many good kids were forced into daily violence just to survive?

"I thought I knew, but really I could not imagine what children endured in those rat holes we call schools! That was, until I spent time here. Now I understand better what their lives are really like." Lesley was heartbroken, but also determined to do more to improve things.

Meanwhile, three hundred miles north and safe in Greenville after a long night of worry and concern, Kathy finally fell asleep once it became clear that New Orleans was spared the worst of it. She nodded off after Katrina took that last-minute turn toward Mississippi. Late the next morning she made coffee and turned on CNN just as the first reports of the New Orleans devastation hit the news. Kathy cried uncontrollably.

Flood levels in the city dropped nearly a foot. It was not because the levees were repaired; the water levels fell because New Orleans had a tide.

# 22

LOUIS REACHED LOYOLA'S CAMPUS IN a few uneventful minutes. He did hear screams and gunshots, but the sounds were off in another direction, mostly towards Central City. A woman asked for help reaching dry ground, but the old Johnson Sea Horse motor was on its last leg and Louis did not have time to help her. He worried the motor would conk out before he found the Loyola insurance official again.

The shiny blue boat was easy to spot. It was leisurely moving from building to building. Louis could see Ray was still photographing damage, measuring flood levels and making notes on a laptop. Still wearing shorts and a Polo shirt, Ray was surprised to see Louis again. "Did you find your daughter? Where is that menacing dog of yours? What do you call him? Puncher? Right?"

"People need help!" Louis had no time for small-talk. "Ray, while you are writing insurance claims, people are dying. Do you understand that?"

"I have a job to do. I can't be worried about everyone else's problems."

Beginning to sense danger, Ray reached for his throttle controls, planning a fast getaway. Louis gunned the old Sea Horse motor, hoping for enough power one more time. He sacrificed his small boat, blocking the larger boat's escape path. "I don't want to hurt you!" Louis reached for the shotgun and aimed it directly at Ray's head. "I am taking that boat. No two ways about it. Back off that throttle!" Louis cocked the shotgun.

"You are no different than all the other crazies around here. You are a looter, too!"

Hearing an approaching boat, Puncher became excited and began jumping up and down, wagging his tail and barking. Willow tried to quiet him down while she looked through a small opening in the window blinds. "Quiet, Puncher. Quiet down, boy." She did not recognize the blue boat approaching at high speed. "He is coming in this direction! Somebody please quiet down Puncher." Steve picked up the table leg, he did not want to hit anyone with it but he would do his best to defend the girls. "Is it those punks coming back?" Then Willow realized who it was.

"No, it's not punks! It is my dad!"

Louis tied the boat to the porch railings. Puncher jumped up and licked his face. "Where did you find this boat?" Willow asked. Louis said he would explain later, but right now there was no time. He asked Steve to get some cushions off the couch and lay them on the bottom of the boat. "I will go get your mother. Everyone else get in." Louis carefully placed Steve's mother on the cushions, making sure she was as comfortable as possible. "I noticed some military helicopters operating from that direction. They should have medical help available." Puncher went right to his favorite spot at the front. He seemed to like this new boat.

Louis followed the sound of the helicopters and could get the boat within a block of the makeshift military base. Armed guardsmen protected the small area of high ground. "We need medical help over here."

Three young soldiers ran in his direction. "You are in the right place. We are setting up a field hospital." Steve said his mother was diabetic and needed insulin. "No worries, sir. We will take care of her from here."

New Orleans has very strict gun control laws. Louis did not want any more trouble and told the guardsmen that he had a firearm. "That is okay, sir. So do we!"

Helicopters were landing one after another, delivering supplies and then taking off again. "How can I get seats on one of those helicopters? We need to get these girls to a safe place." Louis explained Sloan's situation and the fact that she was from New York and had only been in New Orleans for a few days. "I know her father must be going crazy trying to reach her. We need to get her out of here." Willow refused to leave her dad.

"I'm staying with you," Willow said, holding on tight to Louis's arm.

Steve thanked Louis for saving their lives and he agreed with Willow. "You are always safe with this guy; he is super-human!" Steve wasn't shy about hugging Louis, but Puncher seemed to get a little jealous. "You too, buddy. I love you, too! You're a super canine." Steve bent down low and placed Puncher's front paws on his shoulders. He rubbed his head and ruffled his ears. Puncher loved the attention.

Louis suggested that Steve go look after his mother while he tried to hide the emotion overcoming him. During the goodbyes, Sloan wandered off and found a seat on a Navy helicopter heading to Pensacola. Her eyes met Willow's. She mouthed two words. "Thank you." It did not take Sloan long to start flirting with the aircrew.

Sloan's helicopter would reach the Pensacola Naval Air Station in about an hour. VistaFlight's jet was already inflight and would land at Pensacola in forty-five minutes. By tomorrow Sloan would be back in New York City having lunch at the Four Seasons restaurant on 52nd Avenue. Most likely she would order her favorite: duck chestnut ravioli and a strawberry cream roll for dessert.

Louis asked the young soldier about getting to the east side of town. "You could make it to the Sliver area, but there is no reason to. The entire city has been evacuated, sir. Everyone has been moved to the Convention Center." Louis wondered if that was a good idea.

"Sir, we have two-hundred and fifty armed troops keeping a tight lid on things. The NOPD also has a command center set up there. The Convention Center is probably the safest place in town these days." The young guardsmen believed the honeyed lies he had been told. Nevertheless, the reality of the situation was something very different. "Supply helicopters have delivered plenty of water, food and medicine. If your wife and friends are at the Center, they are in good hands, sir," the young soldier said.

Still Louis wondered how packing thousands upon thousands of desperate, sick and scared people into one hopeless place was a good idea. The guardsman was optimistic, but to Louis it sounded as if the Center was more like a refugee camp in a third-world war-torn nation. A convoy of three Humvees was heading in that direction, but Louis knew he could reach the Convention Center quicker in the high-powered speedboat.

Down Claiborne Avenue to Clio Street to Loyola Avenue, then south on Poydras Street to the Convention Center, Louis expected the trip to take about twenty minutes. "Let's go find your mother."

Willow and Puncher climbed aboard and the guardsman gave them a case of water and a leash for Puncher. "You may need this." Louis quickly got it up to about twenty knots. This boat could easily go much faster, but Louis was worried about hitting submerged obstacles. Twenty knots were just about right; any slower and people could climb on; any faster and they could hit unseen objects in the water, destroying the boat. Puncher's ears flapped in the wind.

"We need that boat! Slow it down!" Louis ignored everyone trying to flag him down. He sped up when he heard random gunshots.

Willow reminded her dad that she knew the Convention Center like, "the back of my hand. We should find mom quickly," she said. They both assumed the military would have some type of roster system.

"Everyone there is probably identified and accounted for. The army is very efficient," Louis added with confidence.

The area around the Convention Center was beginning to resemble a combat zone with damaged buildings, total darkness, and the few unflooded streets were blocked off by armed military checkpoints. Louis and Willow counted six bodies floating in the water, and one was a child. Others were in water up to their necks, pulling their last belongings toward the Convention Center. Louis carefully slowed the boat and inched up to an Army roadblock. The floodwater became shallow as they got closer.

These were battle-hardened troops from Iraq, not the polite young guardsmen from Shreveport that Louis had encountered earlier. They fired weapons over Louis and Willow's heads. "Stop that fucking boat!" Louis shoved the throttle into reverse and apologized for approaching the checkpoint too quickly. Their ammunition was live, their bayonets fixed, and their faces were covered by masks designed for biological warfare. "The Convention Center is full. It is closed. Turn that boat around." The soldiers said everyone was on their own now. "Nothing more anyone can do. Besides, you haven't been medically screened for communicable diseases. This entire city is an open sewer infested with cholera, typhoid and hepatitis. Get the fuck out of here!"

Louis had one response: "Roger that!" Cities like to publicize their tourist areas, fine homes, neatly swept streets and handsome shops. They entomb the filth and sewer underground in hidden pipes where it is expected to be carried away unnoticed. Unfortunately for New Orleans, Katrina exposed everything that was supposed to remain hidden.

# 23

**WILLIAM-MARK'S HOME ON JEWEL STREET** in the Lakeshore area did not flood. These few residential streets along the lakefront had much higher elevation than the rest of New Orleans. The ground here was built up somewhat like the 'Sliver on the River.' Jewel Street was also close to the Jefferson Parish line. The Seventeenth Street canal levees collapsed on the Orleans Parish side, but Jefferson Parish was fine, comparatively speaking. Once electric power was restored to the pumping stations, Jefferson Parish pumped out the standing water and worked quickly to get things back to normal.

William-Mark and his wife could easily make their way to Metairie for food, water and shopping. They walked along the levee past West End to the Robert E. Lee Blvd bridge over the Seventeenth Street canal and into Jefferson Parish. They planned to have a seafood dinner in Buck Town later that evening. Lucky for William-Mark and his wife, they could avoid the Superdome and Convention Center completely, and because they were close to Jefferson Parish their cell phone service was restored shortly after the storm passed. William-Mark spent the morning raking the yard and sweeping his sidewalks. He checked the roof, cleared his storm drains and had another beer.

He did not care at all about Bayou Contracting's flooded warehouse and submerged equipment. William-Mark just planned to stop paying the mortgage notes, collect on insurance policies and screw Louis.

A ringing cell phone had annoyed him all afternoon. "Why da fuck do these people keep calling me?" He did not answer the persistent calls because he did not recognize the long-distance number, and he did not want to put down the cold beer he was always drinking. "I don't buy anything from da fucking telemarketers. Stop calling me. Why don't these fuckers find an honest way to earn a living?" William-Mark said out of frustration. He would have blocked the incoming number, but he did not know how to do that, so he just turned off the phone. By the next morning he had twenty unread messages from the same out-of-town number.

"Perhaps you should listen to those messages. That does not sound like normal behavior for a telemarketer. Why would they call you so many times?" William-Mark's wife offered to listen to the messages if he would not. "Do you owe someone money?"

"I'll listen to it. Don't worry 'bout it." He turned the phone back on.

"Who da hell is da Level Lock Foundation Repair Company?" William-Mark asked his wife.

"Apparently, they are going to expand operations in dis area, expecting much more business because of da storm. The message says they are sending fifteen new crews and trucks to New Orleans dis week with more on da way. They are staging everything from Baton Rouge until da water is drained. Da message says dis is the biggest opportunity da company has ever had, and they are moving resources from as far away as California. They are happy to work with me and asked if I would accept $550,000 as an initial payment on their proposed franchise agreement expansion considering my exclusive territory contract." William-Mark looked at his wife with a puzzled expression. "What da fuck?" he said.

"Isn't Level Lock Foundation Repair Company part of Bayou Contracting? I think you own that franchise agreement now!" she said. "That's why they are calling you!"

"No shit?" William-Mark sat on his sofa and opened another beer.

# 24

THE CONVENTION CENTER STARTED LIFE as part of the 1984 World's Fair International Pavilion and Great Hall. The old Poydras and Julia Street wharfs were demolished, making way for the fair's exhibition halls. Louisiana's Pavilion became the Convention Center's main conference area. The US Pavilion was located at the very end of the giant building near the Mississippi River bridges and Tchoupitoulas Street. A multilevel employee parking lot was located just outside the fair's exterior fence near the US Pavilion under the Mississippi River Bridge. NASA's Enterprise space shuttle was displayed on the other side of the US pavilion.

Everyone loved the fair, but attendance numbers fell well below expectations, it closed early and ended up in bankruptcy court. One reason for the disappointing financial failure was the high cost overruns and expensive ticket prices. The construction was more expensive than originally planned because buildings were built as permanent structures, not temporary fabrication. In 1984, Louis was a teenager eager to enjoy the fair, but unable to afford the high cost of admission. After persistent searching, Louis and his group of fearless friends discovered an unlocked employee entrance leading into the fair's Great Hall from the Tchoupitoulas Street employee parking lot. They slipped into the fair from this garage entrance every Saturday night until the fair closed.

"I have an idea," Louis said to Willow as he wondered if his old World's Fair secret entrance still existed. "Sorry gentlemen. We are leaving right away. We are very sorry if we caused trouble for anyone." Louis was not afraid of the Army with their bayonets and biological warfare suits, but he did not want to face any additional delays. He apologized to the soldiers manning the check point and promised to get the biomedical screening done real soon. Louis quickly turned the boat around. Willow knew he would not just leave like that unless he had a better plan to reach the Convention Center.

Louis drifted slowly with the engine at idle speed, but once he was a safe distance from the military checkpoint he jammed the throttles forward. The powerful engine redlined and raised the boat's bow straight out of the water like the nose of a jetliner on takeoff. "Hold on, everyone! Let's see what this pretty little boat can really do!"

The soldiers had other more important things to worry about. "Where the fuck does he think he's going? This whole town is a shit shower! What's he in such a hurry for?" The soldiers just figured Louis was crazy like so many other people moving around in the flooded streets.

Eventually, Louis got the boat as close as possible to the World Fair's old parking area. He tied it off to a light pole near Tchoupitoulas Street and opened the engine compartment. Louis pulled wires off the distributer. "Hopefully the boat will still be here when we return." He hid the ignition wires under a nearby pile of debris. "She will never start without these." Willow carried the table leg; Louis made sure the shotgun was loaded and rested it over his shoulder.

The parking area was full of cars left on the second level. They were parked there to save them from the flood, but the owners were long gone. The old parking lot entrance door was still in place. It had been upgraded and reinforced for security reasons sometime over the last thirty years. Louis pushed and kicked the heavy steel door. He rammed his shoulder against it. "This thing is built like a bank vault. It won't budge!"

"Why don't we try my keys? They are supposed to open all employee areas," Willow said, reminding Louis that her job at the Hilton Riverview required access to the Convention Center.

"It's a longshot, but let's give it a try." She handed her ring with five keys to Louis. On the third try the door opened.

"Well, I'll be darned!" Louis said, surprised the old door opened.

Puncher went into the darkened hall first. Louis told Willow to stay close behind him. On the inside it looked like evacuees had tried to claw their way out. Blood, scratches and damage from hammers and crowbars indicated people were desperate to get out. An old woman was dead in a wheelchair. Someone had wrapped her in a blanket and left her there. The floors near the bathrooms were covered with shit. The smell of death and feces fouled the air with a putrid stench.

Only one other person was visible in the hall. He was sitting slumped over against a wall. "Where is everybody?" Willow asked.

"I don't know. Stay close." Louis approached the man that from far off appeared to be resting. His unresponsive head hung down low. "Hello," Louis called out from a safe distance. Puncher approached him first.

"Is that brass knuckles?" It was Willow who noticed the bloody pair of brass knuckles lying on the ground a few feet away. Louis lowered his shotgun and released the safety. His finger rested on the trigger.

Carefully, Louis lifted the man's head for a closer look. Every bone in his painfully distorted face appeared to be broken. "Someone beat him to death! Perhaps everyone left because of murders and smells!" he said.

"Where are the two-hundred and fifty soldiers that are supposed to be here protecting these people?" Willow asked.

"I don't know. It is getting late and I don't think we want to be in this building after dark." Louis picked up the brass knuckles and put them in his pocket.

An oil storage facility in the 9th Ward exploded. Everyone panicked and believed the government was blowing the levees to save other areas. They believed it was safer to be outside on Convention Center

Boulevard. From the windows, Louis saw twenty-thousand desperate people down on the street below. "They are tired, hungry, thirsty and sick. I don't think we have much to worry about. Most of these poor folks look so weak they can barely stand up."

Willow suggested they use the employee service passageways. "We should be able to get around faster. These secret tunnels connect the Hilton, the Riverview Mall, Food Court and the Convention Center. It's like catacombs. I know the way!" A few battery-powered emergency lights were still working. Louis, Willow and Puncher ran for nearly two blocks before reaching the main convention areas.

"What is all this water and food doing back here?" Louis asked after they stopped to rest near pallets full of water.

Willow explained that the Hilton and Convention Center hosted over two-hundred large and medium-sized conferences each year. "Stuff like this is stored everywhere back here. It is enough to feed thousands."

Louis cautiously opened the door. The main room was empty except for a group of tough-looking young men eyeing him suspiciously. "Don't point that shotgun at us. We don't want no more trouble today, mister."

"I don't want trouble either. We need help distributing this food and water," Louis said.

The men walked over to have a look. "Old people are dying on the streets and all this stuff is sitting right here under our noses?" Soon, two to three hundred healthy men were chipping in to help bring water and food out to the old, sick and weak still living on Convention Center Boulevard. The leader of the group thanked Louis and Willow. He said his grandmother would die without this water. "Is there anything we can do for you?" he asked.

"As a matter of fact, there is." Louis described Jan, Lesley and Clarence.

"Ain't many white folks around here, but I did hear about a crazy white dude cutting off a brother's ear!" He told Louis where the fight took place. "Don't worry about anything. We got your back."

Louis, Willow and Puncher cautiously approached the area where Jan was supposed to be hiding with Lesley and Clarence. With no electricity, the only light was from fires lit in metal trashcans. A group of men carrying sticks were standing in a semicircle blocking Louis's view. They were facing out as if they were protecting whoever was at the group's center. The scene looked medieval, like a Templar gathering of knights preparing to settle a feud. The 'Life is Like a Po-Boy!' banner seemed surreal under the circumstances. "We been expecting you." The group's leader pounded fists with Louis and Willow. "Your friends are safe."

Clarence saw Louis first. "I don't know where these guardian angles came from. Their timing could not have been better. Did you have something to do with that?"

Jan and Lesley were still safe inside the protective circle, but were sure happy to see Louis and Willow arrive. Jan hugged Willow and kissed Louis. The embrace seemed heartfelt. "I missed you so much," Louis said.

"I'm sorry your first Tulane experience has turned out this way." Lesley explained to Willow that life can be troublesome like this sometimes.

"Ah! Tulane again!" Jan rolled her eyes.

"Let's get the hell out of here!" Louis said as he handed Clarence the brass knuckles. "Just in case."

"Yea, good idea!"

They made their way back to the parking garage and broke into all unflooded cars until they found one with the keys hidden under the front floor mat. It was a newer model Ford Crown Victoria sedan with US Government plates. "I found keys!" Willow waved them in the air. Everyone else ran in her direction. Puncher insisted on sitting in the front next to Louis. They drove onto the old Mississippi River bridge approach by heading backwards from the Saint Charles Avenue onramp. Louis drove slowly, weaving his way through the groups of people camped on the bridge, and into Gretna where Jefferson deputies moved the road barricades aside and allowed them to pass.

"They think this is an unmarked police car! Puncher must look like a police dog!" Clarence determined.

"Well, we are due for some good luck for a change," Louis said.

It was a relatively short drive to the Huey P. Long Bridge and back over the Mississippi River into Harahan, and from there to the I-10 heading north was an easy five-minute drive. They were only twenty minutes outside New Orleans, but things here seemed ordinary; streetlights worked, police were on duty, fast-food restaurants were open as normal, and people were going about their daily routines while young boys crossed at a red light riding bikes and laughing. For Louis, Jan, Clarence, Lesley and Willow it was a surreal feeling almost like they had lived through an episode of the Twilight-Zone. It would not have been surprising to them if Rod Serling appeared explaining the horror they experienced as some type of science-fiction drama.

"I would sure love a Quarter Pounder with cheese!" Lesley said as they drove past a McDonalds.

Out of the blue, Jan asked Louis if William-Mark was alright.

"Bayou Contracting is completely flooded. I haven't seen him or heard anything from him," Louis said.

# 25

ONCE STATE AND FEDERAL GOVERNMENT
agencies got organized, things moved quickly. Hundreds of busses
headed to New Orleans, some from the direction of I-10 and others
from the Huey P. Long Bridge. Within a day or two everyone at the
Convention Center and the Dome were on their way to Baton Rouge,
Houston or Lake Charles.

The Army Corps of Engineers managed to fix the levee breaches with
temporary patches made of rocks and sand, dropped in place by heavy-
lift helicopters. Once the surge was inside the city, repaired levees acted
to trap water inside like a giant bowl. Prolonged flooding was an unin-
tended consequence of a failed, poorly engineered system. The city had
to be siphoned dry with powerful pumps lined up on the levees. They
sucked the water out through pipes resembling the mouths of thirsty
mosquitos. Still, it was a month before the city was dry.

Overwhelming problems were just starting for New Orleans. The city
was left with no infrastructure, no police protection, no fire department, no court system, no water or sewer, no electricity, public transportation or trash collection, and no schools. Packs of wild dogs
roamed the desolate streets. Criminals took advantage of the mayhem
and claimed control of entire neighborhoods. Most homeowners who
attempted to return too early could not clean their property, make
outside repairs or use flashlights at night. Lawbreakers scouted for
these clues, targeting helpless people trying to live there.

Over two-hundred thousand abandoned cars and trucks had to be removed. They sat under ten feet of filthy water for nearly a month. Then they baked in the hot sun with the windows up until they were eventually towed months later. The vehicles became mold and mildew-infested petri dishes presenting alarming health issues.

Tulane's president sent the sad news in an email. "As you all know by now, New Orleans and the surrounding parishes were severely damaged by Hurricane Katrina. The physical damage to the area and Tulane's campuses was extensive." He canceled classes for the fall semester and encouraged students to take classes at new schools. The president said other universities would accept Tulane students as visitors, not transfer students. Tulane's students would not be charged tuition at their temporary schools.

Clarence and Lesley's home was not flooded. They were encouraged when they did not see a water line halfway up the outside of the first floor. The front door was wide open.

"At least we didn't flood. Maybe we are going to be alright," Lesley said hopefully.

"We'll see."

"Don't you think it could just be poor families seeking shelter in there? We don't have to assume its looters, do we?" Lesley asked.

Clarence told her to wait on the front porch while he made sure no one was still inside. He wrapped his fist tight around the brass knuckles in his pocket that he always carried now and cautiously entered the front room. He turned around and signaled for Lesley to back away from the door in case there was trouble.

Their home was more than just looted; everything not stolen was smashed and destroyed. The marble tops of the Empire period furniture they had so carefully collected and loved were broken or missing. The Victorian stained glass above the landing was smashed with a piece of that marble. Their cherished mantels were ripped from the walls. This was not just looting, it was hatefulness.

During the restoration, Clarence had carefully hand-painted the decorative and ornate plaster crown molding and ceiling medallions with a paint resembling gold leaf. The plaster work was originally applied with remarkable craftsmanship, impossible to duplicate today. Many historians considered this to be the home's finest feature. The looters saw the gold color and assumed the plaster was real gold. They chipped all of it off and hauled most of it away. Clarence did not go in past the front room, but he did wonder how things went down when these fools tried to sell their wheelbarrows full of 'gold.'

"That would be funny. These knuckleheads could have stolen Faberge eggs from the Museum of Art, but instead they took flat-screen TVs, beer and our plaster. Good thing they are so dumb!" Clarence hugged Lesley.

"Everything is insured. Let's get out of here and take a vacation." He did not want Lesley to see her beloved home in this condition.

It would be a long time before New Orleans was a livable city again. Some people believed it would never recover. Louis stopped by Tulane to see Wilson and discuss his employment prospects. "I don't know anything for sure at this point. Classes are canceled for the fall semester and spring is not looking good either. Even if the campus recovers, no parents are going to send their kids down here with the city in chaos. In case you were wondering, the Tulane mummies, Newcomb pottery, civil rights documents and Tiffany windows all survived. You did good." Wilson said Louis would have a job at Tulane when the time arrived, perhaps in a few months. He also asked Louis if he and his family had a safe place to live in the meantime.

"I hear a lot of folks are heading over to Houston." Louis said.

"Have you thought about South Alabama? My mother's old house is down there in a community called Mon Luis Island just south of Mobile. It is only two hours or so from here. The home is not much to look at and it has been vacant for a few years, but it is in a wonderful old area and a great place for relaxing and fishing. It's yours if you need it." Wilson's generous offer came at the right time, since

Louis was nearly broke and had planned to ask the Red Cross for assistance.

"You know, Spring Hill College is nearby in Mobile. A lot of Tulane students are enrolling there." Wilson said Willow would love Spring Hill. "It is one of the oldest Jesuit colleges in the country, and like Tulane it has a beautiful and historic campus. The college is not far from the old Mon Luis house. You know, some people even think the pirate Jean Lafitte hid treasure somewhere back there!" Wilson said as a kid he used to hunt Lafitte's treasure all summer long. "All I ever found was an old, Spanish 8, Reales silver coin." Wilson laughed and said he still had it. "The coin is good luck."

Willow called Lesley to discuss Spring Hill. Cell service was working again, somewhat. Lesley agreed, and thought Spring Hill was a wonderful choice. "Spring Hill College has Southern Association accreditation just like Tulane does, except Tulane has a Level VI accreditation allowing for PhD programs. All your undergrad credits taken at Spring Hill will transfer back to Tulane with no problems. I think it's a great southern college like Sewanee and its run by the Jesuits!"

Mon Luis Island is only two miles wide and about six miles long. The area is so small that it does not appear on most maps. Home to an old French Creole settlement on the western side of Mobile Bay, it was first settled in 1710. The ancestors of some original French settlers still live in the area. Orrell, Boudan and Durrette are some common family names of the original Creole descendants. The Mississippi Sound is to Mon Luis's south, Mobile Bay is to the east, and Fowl River is to the north and west. Fowl River is wide with slow-moving dark water. It was like the bayous of south Louisiana's Creole country so familiar to Louis. Many of the Mon Luis' historic structures survived, especially the old creole cottages.

"This looks just like the Rigolets and Lake Catherine. I like this area." Louis stood where the Fowl River flows into Mobile Bay. "Wilson says the fishing here is great!" Willow had not seen her dad this relaxed in a long time.

"That is just wonderful, but can we please go see the house now?" Jan was not into fishing.

Louis followed the map Wilson gave him on which he identified the Mon Luis church, school, hardware store, gas station and the house. Following Wilson's handwritten directions, Louis drove along Durette Avenue enjoying bay breezes and cool shade from the canopy of oak branches overhanging the road, Saint Rose of Lima was the prettiest little Catholic Church Louis had ever seen. Even though it was not a prestigious structure like Saint Peter's Basilica in Rome or Notre Dame in Paris, it was magnificent in its own unique way. The unassuming hundred-year-old wood frame Saint Rose chapel was surrounded by massive live oaks, history and rich traditions. It was an important part of this small community.

A one-room schoolhouse called the 'Creole School' survived nearby. It was in a state of disrepair, but still added to the area's historic charm. Across the street was the Catholic cemetery with two-hundred-year-old grave markers. "Imagine all the weddings, first communions, funerals and baptisms that have taken place in this church." Louis said he already felt like he belonged in this captivating community.

Wilson's family home was a Creole type cottage built in the 1800s with a long and deep front porch, a rusty tin roof covered with oak tree leaves and pine needles, and a backyard enclosed with a simple wooden fence. The Fowl River flowed near the back of the property. "Puncher will love chasing squirrels back there," Willow said. The windows were boarded up, but Louis could pry the boards off easily with a crowbar.

"This is a very strong, well-built solid house," he said while exiting the car.

"Really, you have been here five minutes and you already know how the house is built?" Jan asked, deliberately needling him.

"Actually, I do. It has been here since the Civil War. If it wasn't sturdy and vigorous, the hurricanes would have wiped it out years ago," Louis said.

"Whatever. It just looks like an old shack to me!"

Wilson promised the front door key would be under a flower pot near the steps. It was right where he said it would be. Before opening the door, Louis took a minute to relax in one of the four rocking chairs, and Willow joined him. Impatient, Jan took the key and went inside.

"There's a rat in here!" Jan yelled while chasing it around the kitchen with a broom.

"You will never get him. He's way too fast. Besides, it is just a little ole house mouse, not a rat. He is harmless." Louis said the mouse would leave once they moved in. "You don't need to hurt the little fellow."

A few light bulbs were out, some fuses were missing and the place needed a good cleaning, but was otherwise it was in great shape. Louis admired the home's sturdy construction and the remarkable crafts-manship of the skilled carpenters that built it. Original wide-board heart pine floors displayed a hard-earned patina achieved over the past hundred years. The mantles were made with hand-hewn lumber and wooden pegs. Louis could imagine the memories of past generations collected here as he traced his fingers across a dusty threshold.

"These walls must be a foot thick. This is original horse-hair plaster! These high ceilings and center hallway design should keep the place nice and cool," Louis said.

"What!? No central AC!?" Jan asked. She opened a kitchen window begging for a cool bay breeze.

The hardware store was only a few blocks away. Louis expected to spend a lot of time there while he got the house back in good condi-tion. He also thought it would be a great place to work part-time while he waited to return to New Orleans. Louis was gone longer than expected because he spent time getting to know the store's owner, Heather. She grew up in the Mon Luis area and was a Spring Hill College graduate many years ago. Her family had owned the local hardware store for three generations and she has run it since the

1970s. Heather's grandchildren helped on Saturdays and some afternoons during the summer.

"I think your daughter will love Spring Hill. The Jesuits have been running colleges for a long time. They know what they're doing. It's a wonderful school. And yes, I can always use some part-time help around here," Heather said.

When Louis returned, Jan was standing on the porch with her arms folded and an irate expression across her angry face. "Where the hell have you been?"

He set the bulbs, bleach, mops and fuses down on the steps and approached Jan. "What's wrong?" Louis asked.

"It stinks like something's dead in there!"

Louis cautiously entered the front room and looked around. "It's nothing to worry about, just a skunk!" The raised foundation was built on brick pillars creating a three-foot crawlspace underneath. "A skunk sprayed his territory. That's all! Don't worry; Puncher will chase all these critters away in no time."

Louis recognized the '212' Manhattan area code. He knew only one person in New York City.

"Hello, Mr. Krueger. How are you, sir?" Louis stepped out onto the back porch to take the call.

"Sloan tells me you and Willow took her on quite an adventure down there. I appreciate the fact that you looked after my little girl. New Orleans was all over the news. What a mess, total mayhem and chaos. I know I haven't sent you that autographed photo yet. It is in the mail as we speak. I have another call coming in and my helicopter is waiting to take me to Shinnecock. Today is a great day for some golf. I've got to run. Thanks for everything, buddy!"

Mr. Krueger's assistant came on the line and requested Louis's current mailing address. Louis had to think before answering that question. "What's the problem, dude? Don't you know your own address?"

The Mon Luis Island house was the only address Louis could give.

"That's Alabama. Mr. Krueger said you lived in New Orleans."

"No one lives in New Orleans anymore." Louis hung up the call. He sat on the back steps and dropped his forehead into his hands, realizing for the first time how it must feel to be homeless.

# 26

WILLOW HAD NOTHING FROM TULANE to verify her attendance there except a water-damaged student ID and copies of recent emails from Tulane's president. The university was unable to provide verification confirming admission, tuition paid, enrollment status or selected majors. In fact, it was impossible to reach anyone affiliated with Tulane's admissions office. Willow had no way to pay new registration fees or additional tuition, even if it would be reimbursed later. Fortunately for her, the Mon Luis Island home was a short drive away, so she would not need a dorm room on Spring Hill's campus.

The fall semester at Spring Hill was well underway, so earliest registration issues had been resolved weeks ago. The admissions office was quiet when Willow approached the front desk and presented her Tulane ID.

"Oh, my dear!" The admissions director came around the counter and put her arm around Willow. "I am so sorry about what happened to your beautiful city and Tulane's campus. We are all heartbroken." She assured Willow that everything would be taken care of. "I can't imagine what you must have gone through."

Willow said her family was living nearby in a borrowed home.

"Not to worry. You came to the right school. This is a Jesuit college, after all. Our doors are open to everyone, especially during difficult times like this. By the way, Spring Hill and Tulane have a lot in common. Did you know they were both founded in the 1830s? Like Tulane, we also offer strong academic programs." The admissions director said Spring Hill expected to enroll over one hundred students from New Orleans. "Most are from Loyola New Orleans, another Jesuit college, of course, but we also expect a fair number of new students to show up from Tulane. We will enroll everyone. You may see old friends here."

Willow filled out some routine forms and completed a new admissions application. She never saw a bill or invoice. The admissions director looked over the paperwork.

"Welcome to Spring Hill College. We are pleased to have you as a new Badger." She shook Willow's hand and presented her with a school baseball cap, t-shirt and meal pass for the cafeteria. She explained that the school's mascot is a purple Badger.

"Now, let's go see the campus."

She showed Willow the important college buildings, introduced faculty and asked Willow if she was spiritual. "I would like to show you our Saint Joseph Chapel. It is the center of campus life here at Spring Hill, truly beautiful. It is a sacred place where people of all faiths are welcome. The doors are open 24-7."

"I would love to see it," Willow said.

Saint Joseph Chapel was peaceful. Willow cherished the serenity of old churches and appreciated the quiet sanctuary. "I think I will spend a lot of time here. The tranquility is a welcome change."

The admissions director used the quiet time to bring up course selections and discussed the importance of doing things in moderation. "I suggest that you register for some general freshman electives at Spring Hill, saving the more difficult course work for when you return to Tulane and things get back to normal. You can still expect to graduate on time in four years, but this may save some stress as you and your family work to move back home. I would not recommend taking on a full academic load under the circumstances. By the way, Spring Hill is wonderful, but the only way to get that beautiful acorn ring is by graduating from Tulane/Newcomb. That is something really special." The admission director winked at Willow as if they shared some important secret. Willow took her advice and registered for basic freshman composition, math, a history class, introduction to music appreciation and art study.

"Well, you are all set. You can start class tomorrow. If you need anything just stop by my office"

Puncher was having a great time at the Mon Luis house. He chased squirrels up oak trees and found a favorite cool spot under the house for those few occasions when he was not sleeping on the front porch. Louis pried the boards off the windows, removed the leaves from the roof and mowed the lawn. He used an old push mower he found in a shed. Louis enjoyed the physical challenge of cutting the lawn by hand. Earlier that morning, he'd set crab traps in the Fowl River, hoping to have a few dozen, fat blue crabs to boil for dinner. He was painting the front door when Willow returned.

"Everyone was so helpful! I love Spring Hill! It's perfect!" she said.

# 27

**THE MONTEGUT STREET HOME WAS** in an area that was not supposed to flood, ever. A few years back, Louis's insurance agent said flood insurance was not necessary and certainly not required. He showed Louis a 'Federal Flood Zone Map' prepared by the US Corps of Engineers. "Let me show you this. You are in flood Zone D. It would be a waste of money to purchase unnecessary coverage. Even the Federal Government says so." The agent convinced Louis the money would be better spent elsewhere. "Put it toward renovations," the agent suggested.

"I will trust your advice. If you don't think I need flood insurance, then I will save the money and not buy something that's unnecessary," Louis agreed.

Louis would have gladly paid the one hundred and twenty-five-dollar premium if he had understood the risk. "I have called you a least ten times. Please return my call." Louis sat on the back steps of the Mon Luis home and called his insurance agent repeatedly. "I think he is avoiding me," Louis said.

"It was your decision to waive flood coverage. I explained everything to you and you decided to save money. I have notes on all our conversations in case your memory needs help. Insurance companies don't pay on policies that were never purchased or issued. That is not insurance; it's welfare!" The agent left a message and said he was extremely busy and did not have time to sugarcoat anything. "Sorry, you made a bad bet and lost."

Louis did not realize that paperwork for the Federal flood insurance coverage was complicated and premiums were inexpensive, so agents made very small commissions. Consequently, some insurance professionals did not want to bother with the added headache.

On the other hand, Clarence and Lesley called their insurance agent to confirm if everything would be covered as they hoped. The 'Sliver on the River' home had no real storm or flood damage, but was torn apart by looters and vandals. They had never filed a claim for vandalism, and were not completely sure how the insurance company would handle the loss. Frankly, they expected to get the run-around. "Do you remember back when you first signed this policy? I suggested at the time that you should purchase the Civil Unrest rider. For $39 dollars a year it was a good value. Well, don't worry, everything is covered. That $39 dollar per year turned out to be a great investment," their insurance agent said.

With their home covered by insurance, Lesley and Clarence began looking for some place relaxing to spend a few months. It had to be close enough so they could return to New Orleans as necessary, but far enough away to escape all the problems. Lesley suggested Callaway Gardens in Georgia. She went to summer camp there when she was six years old. "They have a beautiful lake for swimming, with a beach, miles of hiking trails and bike paths. Some of the best golf courses in Georgia are there. Callaway Gardens has a strong connection to Callaway Golf, and it is only about seven hours from New Orleans," Lesley said.

"Let's have a look." Clarence pulled up Callaway's homepage. "What a beautiful place! It's in the foothills of the Blue Ridge Mountains. Wow! They even have a glass-enclosed butterfly pavilion with fifty different species, and look at this restaurant. It is called the Country Store! The Lodge and Spa is also very cool looking, but we can rent a private villa in the woods. They have wood-burning fireplaces!" Clarence said in a flirtatious manner. "And they have vacancies!"

He pulled up attractions in the nearby town of Pine Mountain. "Check out these restaurants! This one is called Eatz Grill. Look at this shrimp special. I want to eat here first! The Aspen Café also looks great. They have an old wooden canoe over the bar and black bear skins hanging on the walls. It looks like the place on that old TV show, 'Northern Exposure.' The Oyster House has a great bar with live music provided by local artist. The town also has antique shops galore, and even a wax museum nearby. The museum claims to have a Rolls Royce used by Winston Churchill!"

Lesley and Clarence rented 1121 Duck Pine Branch in the Mountain Creek Villas. It was a secluded and private villa located on an out-of-the-way cul-de-sac. It backed up to the FDR State Park. An abandoned railroad bed ran nearby with a mountain stream flowing adjacent to it. The old railroad track was great for historic mountain bike adventures. "Let's stop at Dick's Sporting Goods and pick up a couple of inexpensive mountain bikes," Clarence suggested. The Ferdinand Magellan, FDR's train, used this track on his visits to the area.

The Duck Pond Branch villa was over 2,500 square feet with two stone fireplaces and three bedrooms designed with a midcentury modern look. Each room had a wall of heavy, sliding glass doors providing private views of the dense woods. The master bedroom had a mirrored wall and a king-sized bed.

"This place is remarkable!" Clarence said.

"I know, right?"

Clarence loved Eatz Grill and ordered the Caribbean shrimp special twice. "This is incredible. It is the best shrimp I've ever had, and I love the unique spices and touch of coconut." The restaurant had a cool Caribbean ambiance with a southern home-cooking family atmosphere. The menu specials were like spicy Creole recipes found in New Orleans, but with a unique Caribbean twist. Eatz was family owned. The father and head cook was from Jamaica, and created many of the unique recipes himself.

"I feel like I'm in a Caribbean-Creole restaurant in the islands. I love this place. Hard to believe we are in west Georgia," Lesley said.

"Why don't we give Louis and Jan a call? They would love to visit Callaway." Clarence told Lesley that it was only a four-hour drive from Mobile.

"It is great to hear from you. How are things going?" Louis said he loved Mon Luis and enjoyed working on the old house.

"We have a six-month rental agreement on a Callaway villa with three bedrooms and two fireplaces. Why not come up and spend a few days with us? We would love to see everyone." Lesley told Louis about Eatz Grill.

"Callaway Gardens in Georgia? Isn't that near Warm Springs? I had a financial advisor that spent time at Georgia Hall, the old polio treatment center founded by FDR, and my friend Kathy loved talking about the Little Whitehouse. When she was a child, her family spent summer vacations in Warm Springs. Yes, I would love to visit Callaway. Jan is anxious to get back to New Orleans, so I plan to start gutting the house soon, and Willow has a full class schedule at Spring Hill. We will get together soon, I promise. Great to hear from you." Louis did not want to admit that things were very tight financially and he could not spend anything on a vacation. He did believe things would be fine once he received the check from FEMA. Clarence and Lesley both offered to help, however Louis was proud and would never accept anything from friends.

"This new FEMA Road Home program I read about is designed to help homeowners without flood insurance. Montegut Street will qualify no problem. Everything is going to be fine," Louis explained to Jan confidently.

Callaway was awesome, but still Lesley had trouble sleeping. Her insomnia-ridden nights were haunted by memories of the hurricane and the destruction of New Orleans. She relived the Convention Center nightmare repeatedly, every night. Lesley could not escape the images in her head of so many desperate people left to rot by corrupt officials and sweeping incompetence. The rampant violence and senseless looting ran over and over again in her thoughts.

"It is the education system. Those poor kids never had a fair chance." Lesley spent a lot of time in the Orleans Parish public schools working on her scholarship and other reform programs. She saw firsthand how terrible things were in those dangerous schools. She once saw a school principal hide a dead rat under her desk. Lesley understood how hopeless the Orleans Parish school system was.

"Orleans Parish public school kids have been condemned to failure for generations. There must be a way to use this rotten school system against itself. If we are going to rebuild the city, it is going to start with the public schools first," Lesley said.

She enjoyed relaxing at Callaway Gardens at first, but she soon grew antsy. Lesley did not know when she would return to New Orleans and wanted to be productive in the meantime, so she volunteered at the nearby Harris County High School. Built in the late 1990s, it was in Hamilton, just a short drive from Callaway. They had a remarkable industrial arts program for non-college-bound students. "Not everyone needs to go to college. There is dignity in all work," Lesley agreed with the school's message. The industrial students worked on airplanes and a classic, 1964 Chevy Corvair convertible they were restoring. Welding, electrical and carpentry programs were also offered through the Columbus Technical College. Students interested in automobile manufacturing worked at the new KIA assembly plant while earning high school credits.

The school was ranked near the very top for literature, and had a recognized drama and preforming arts program as well. ACT scores were always high, as was the advanced placement test results, especially for AP Economics and US History. The AP History class taught by Ms. Gates was one of the best. Academically gifted students were also eligible to cross enroll at Columbus State University, taking a wide range of courses and earning college credit. They could take Biology, French, Latin, Statistics, Middle Eastern Studies and Global Politics.

The NJROTC programs worked closely with nearby Fort Benning, offering opportunity for those students seeking a career in the military. Harris County High School seemed to be multiple successful schools rolled into one. They did not have a drop-out problem. Lesley tried to spend time in as many different classrooms and programs as possible. The school offered something for everybody.

Harris County students overall were happy and well adjusted. For an extra $1.00 they could buy sweet tea with lunch. They also loved peanuts and coke. Coca Cola was developed in Columbus before moving to Atlanta, and peanuts were an important area crop. The students poured packets of peanuts into their coke bottles and drank it fast before the peanuts got too soft. Then they ate the Coca Cola flavored peanuts like other kids eat chocolate candies. It's a Georgia thing! The student body enjoyed school. This Harris County experience changed the way Lesley thought about public education.

"Louisiana has the oil and gas industry, seafood, tourism, the port and great universities, but we have never had any type of collaboration with the public schools. Why can't we offer programs of unique study just as diverse as student interests? The Harris County community partnerships are a remarkable model for public education. Why can't we do something like this in Louisiana?" she pondered.

Lesley believed many of the ideas she learned from Harris County High School could be adapted for New Orleans. Clarence supported her but he was realistic. "One of the things I love most about you is your determination. How can you change an entrenched system like the Orleans Parish Public Schools? I know if anyone can find a way, you can!" He encouraged Lesley to get some sleep. "Tomorrow is a new day," he said. Clarence played a version of 'Favorite Things' by John Coltrane on his iPad. Jazz music always relaxed Lesley. She said Coltrane music was "nourishment for the soul."

Lesley slept for a short time, then shot straight up in bed. "We need to get to Baton Rouge now! When is the next State Board of Education meeting?"

"I don't know! It is 2:00 a.m. The Louisiana State Board of Elementary and Secondary Education? Didn't the newspaper say that was a den of political snakes that cheated poor kids out of scholarships? Do we really need to go to Baton Rouge tonight?"

"Yes! We need to go now," Lesley insisted.

"Okay then, let's go."

"October 19th! It's right here in the MFP funding rules." Lesley pulled up the Louisiana Constitution and the MFP statutes established by the Department of Education and BESE. She showed her laptop to Clarence.

"I can't look now, I'm driving. What is the big deal about MFP funding and October?" Clarence asked.

"Don't you see? If Orleans Parish public school students don't return home and enroll in school by October 19th, then they can't be counted for MFP funding purposes. If students can't return, most likely the corrupt political leaders and incompetent administrators, teachers and staff are displaced as well. No enrollment means no funding, and no one will be around to fight for the old dysfunctional system. We have a chance to totally defund the entire Orleans Parish public school system and start over!" Lesley checked and double-checked her information.

"Can you drive faster please?"

"We should arrive in Baton Rouge at 9:30," Clarence said.

# 28

**LOUIS DROVE BACK AND FORTH** daily between Mon Luis Island and New Orleans for two weeks. He left at 3:30 a.m., stopped for gas at the I-10 Shell station and bought a 32-ounce coffee every day. Jan liked to sleep in, and Louis did not want to disturb her, so he placed his clothes and shoes in the front room the night before, getting dressed quietly before dawn.

The total devastation he saw was beyond anything Louis could ever imagine. Streets were littered with trash and debris making it nearly impossible to get around. His catholic elementary school was destroyed beyond repair. The old drycleaners where his father worked was destroyed. The church where Louis served as an altar boy was in a low area and had eleven feet of water. Packs of wild dogs roamed the neighborhoods. People were gone; his community was devastated. *Is this what it is like to be an impoverished war refugee returning to a bombed-out city?*

The FEMA qualifying process for a temporary trailer and Road Home rebuilding funds was ridiculously complicated with multiple forms and applications. Louis went to the upper 9th Ward FEMA office every morning and took a number. No matter how early he arrived, there were always hundreds of desperate people already waiting. Everyone was tired, frustrated and short-tempered. They had been fighting over Meals Ready to Eat (MREs) and bottled water brought in by the National Guard, sleeping in cars and standing in long lines for tetanus and hepatitis vaccines.

Even if Louis eventually received approval for a FEMA trailer, it would not be delivered and set up until water, sewer and electric service was first restored by the city. After utilities were reestablished and available, then approved FEMA contractors had to build steps and cinderblock footings for each trailer. The total wait could be a few weeks or a few months, depending on work schedules. Louis was okay with the fact that the elderly and those with special needs were moved to the front of the work list.

Louis would have been happy to stay at Mon Luis until the Montegut house was restored and forget about living in a cramped FEMA trailer, but for some reason Jan was impatient and eager to return to New Orleans.

"I want air conditioning. Even if it is in a shitty trailer!" she said.

Louis wondered if Jan realized just how small these trailers were. "They are only 300 square feet; that's smaller than a tow-behind camper. It's very close quarters. All the furniture is nailed down, there is no storage or closet space for clothes, and it is illegal to repaint the inside."

Finally, one hopeful morning his number was called by the FEMA adjuster. Louis filled out the Road Home application and promised to restore the Montegut Street home and move back in within three years. Louis proved that he did not have flood coverage and verified his fragile financial situation. The FEMA adjuster asked for property tax records and mortgage records, none of which Louis could produce. "Everything was lost in the flood."

"Not a problem. We will determine if you qualify for short-term living expenses and temporary housing until your home is repaired. We should be able to verify everything, especially if you don't have a mortgage. You are lucky; we won't need to do a forced mortgage payoff with your lender. If this paperwork is all in order, your Road Home check will arrive in a few short weeks at the Mon Luis address and you will be placed on our waiting list for the trailer set up. You are all set." The FEMA adjuster also explained that Road Home grants for rebuilding were based on pre-storm home values.

"Pre-storm? It is not going to cost me less to rebuild my Montegut Street house simply because I live in a poorer neighborhood. A 2x4 costs the same whether it is going to a Lakefront mansion or a 9th Ward double. I feel like I am being cheated," Louis said.

The FEMA adjuster moved Louis's file to another larger pile of files on the other side of his desk "I just work here, fella. You don't have to accept the damn check. If you feel that strongly about it, just decline the money." He shook Louis's hand, then yelled, "Next!"

It was impossible to buy building materials anywhere around New Orleans. Luckily, Louis could find almost everything he needed at the Mon Luis Hardware store, and Heather said if he worked a few hours here and there she would subtract his wages from his purchases or pay him cash. Heather warned Louis that earned income could affect his FEMA eligibility status.

"The eye of Katrina hit Mississippi, but many of the waterfront homes around here also received damage. The store hasn't been this busy since Hurricane Fredrick." Heather said she'd ordered extra cases of bleach, plastic bags and full-face breathing masks. "You are going to need this more than anything else. You should use special masks, especially if you smell a strong musty odor. Breathing mold spores and mildew will kill you, especially the black mold. Remember, mold is more aggressive in the damp conditions present after the flood water recedes." She said paper masks with the tiny metal nose clips are for sanding sheetrock, not for mold eradication. "Take this case of military grade masks with you. I am sure the folks in New Orleans can put them to good use."

Heather gave Louis a printed guide to removing mildew:

1) Repair water problem.

2) Isolate contaminated area.

3) Suppress dust.

4) Remove and place contaminated materials in plastic bags.

5) Clean area with bleach.

6) Dry

"Sounds easy enough," Louis said.

The Bayou Contracting warehouse was not the devastated sight Louis expected. The building was already cleaned out and repaired. A large portable generator sat on a trailer providing reliable electricity. The flooded-out equipment Louis had leased was all pushed to the back of the yard. His old dump trucks had water lines near the top of the cabs, indicating they were nearly completely submerged and were now total loses.

Most surprising to Louis was all the work crews and new equipment present. He counted fifteen new trucks all with 'Level Lock Foundation Repair' painted on the sides. The place was a beehive of activity. William-Mark was driving a new black Lincoln Navigator with tan leather interior. He was dressed in a dark suitcoat and pants with a black t-shirt, and said he preferred a high-performance Jaguar sedan, but settled for the Navigator because the New Orleans roads are terrible.

"Did you file insurance claims for the flooded equipment yet?" Louis asked.

"Things are really rocking here, bro! Dis whole Bayou Contracting thing has turned out to be a sweet deal." William-Mark ignored the insurance question. "By da way, I know how much you love old run-down houses, but no AC!? Really, do you expect Jan to just sit around and roast in some crumbling creole ruins until winter?" William-Mark asked.

"Why do you care if we have AC or not?" Louis wondered.

"Not to worry. I'm just a concerned friend putting in his two cents, for what it's worth. After you check on Montegut Street, let's go have a beer." William-Mark put his arm around Louis's shoulder. "We're good? Right!?"

Louis unloaded three cases of bleach, masks and other material, and placed them under the carport. He took one mask, still in its unopened package, and carried it with him. The Montegut Street front door was warped by the flood water. Louis tried to push it open, but it would not budge.

The air-conditioning comments were eating at Louis, so he decided to call Jan and get to the bottom of it before dealing with the house. The call was brief, because cell service was unreliable at best. He stood in the front yard, held the phone up high and turned in circles, trying to find a signal.

"Don't be ridiculous! What exactly are you implying?" Jan's anger did not seem completely authentic somehow. "Oh, and one more thing. I saw your cell phone. Who is Kathy and why does she call so much?" Jan asked.

"Has Kathy called? She is a friend from Tulane probably trying to check on things." Louis apologized to Jan about the inappropriate William-Mark questions and went back to work. He wanted to finish up at the house and then find a strong cell signal.

Kathy's messages said that she would stay with family in Greenville until things in New Orleans settled down. "I am worried sick about you! Are you okay? Please call me!"

Louis's heart raced as he anticipated hearing Kathy's sweet voice again. Phone service was still erratic in New Orleans. Weeks' worth of messages would appear suddenly out of nowhere, then nothing new for another week. It was not uncommon for messages to appear and then disappear completely. Louis planned to call Kathy, but his service stopped again. He had full bars for only a few seconds.

Louis stepped back about two feet, planted his left foot firmly on the porch and kicked like Bruce Lee. After three or four powerful hits the door and frame gave way. He walked into the living room expecting to find the green algae, but everything below the waterline had turned black with an iridescent shade of blue highlights. Above the flood line everything was covered with a thick green mold. It reminded Louis of the green shag carpet from the 1970s that he hated. His throat burned like strep and the poignant smell was overwhelming. Louis took the breathing mast out of its packaging, tightened the straps and pulled it down over his face. The sponginess he felt with each step was caused by the thick layer of mud and raw sewage covering the floors. Sewers backed up after the city tried unsuccessfully to restart the system. At first, Louis thought Heather's full-face breathing masks were a little excessive, but not now.

Louis pulled the mask's straps even tighter. He looked like a soldier in a WWI trench facing a mustard gas attack. Carefully, he moved deeper into the house. The mask magnified the sound of his own breathing; he was panting. The living room was unrecognizable. He might as well had been walking on the surface of the moon. Black mold was growing on everything, covering the TV, stove, bookcases and dining table.

Louis walked into the kitchen. Something had been bugging him since he left in great haste ahead of the flood waters. The coffee machine was still on the stove exactly where he'd left it. He eyeballed the on-off control. Mystery solved; he did turn it off!

Louis's exposed skin began to itch and burn. He had one more thing to do and carefully made his way upstairs. There was one important item he wanted to retrieve. When he sold, Bayou Contracting Louis took his Tulane pendent off his office wall and brought it home. It was the same one his dad had given him many years ago after the 1973 Tulane-LSU game. Jan did not want it hanging on their bedroom wall, so Louis had carefully stored it in a Ziploc bag and tucked it away in the back of his dresser. It was still there, just as he'd left it. Louis carefully descended the stairs one at a time, being extremely careful with each cautious step.

Where possible, he opened windows to encourage air circulation and got outside quickly. He did not bother to secure the front door. *Ain't nobody crazy enough to go back in there! Certainty ain't anything worth stealing anyway.* Louis soaked a cloth with bleach and wiped down his exposed skin. He poured bleach over the soles of his shoes and wondered if he should invest in the Clorox company.

Louis left New Orleans and headed back to Alabama. He had driven only a block or two before stopping to change a tire. Everyone carried two or three spares. With so much debris and rubbish in the streets, flat tires were expected. Louis continued and pulled off the interstate at the first Mississippi exit near Bay Saint Louis. He had full cell service.

"Hello Kathy, it's Louis."

# 29

THE PLAN TO REBUILD NEW Orleans from the ground up was one of the largest construction endeavors ever undertaken, except for war reconstruction. Federal funds, insurance proceeds, grants and private donations flowed into the city at unprecedented levels. The money attracted honest contractors from across the country; it also lured grifters, swindlers and con artists. Skilled workers, including roofers, plumbers, carpenters and electricians, arrived from nearly all fifty states attracted by high wages and plentiful jobs. Many unskilled workers came illegally from developing nations enticed by the advertised fifteen dollars per hour for manual labor. Most arrived from South and Central America, but some laborers came from as far away as Indonesia and Thailand. These workers planned to stay for a year or two, making as much money as possible and sending most of it back home to support their families.

Unscrupulous contractors took advantage of these undocumented workers. Kathy's ex-husband, Stewart, organized work crews to shovel out houses, remove mold-infested furniture and refrigerators full of rotting food, and rip out flooring and sheetrock. He used pick-up trucks and generous promises of cash to round up these work crews. Undocumented workers usually gathered in certain areas waiting for contractors to come along with job offers. The Winn-Dixie parking lot on Carrollton Avenue near Iberville Street was a favorite location.

Stewart could hire thirty undocumented workers a day just from the Winn-Dixie parking lot. He promised fifteen dollars an hour for twelve-hour days, payable in cash at the end of each month. The only equipment he provided were shovels and cheap paper breathing masks, the sheetrock type; there were no gloves, eye protection or bleach. He operated eight teams of seven workers each. They worked hard in very unhealthy situations, ripping out mildewed carpets, shoveling raw sewage and pulling out walls covered with black mold.

Near the end of each month, before payday, Stewart anonymously reported his own work crews to the Feds. Immigration and Customs Enforcement (ICE) used blue and white cars that resembled NOPD cruisers, except these had a thick blue stripe across the back doors. One undocumented worker was always assigned to be a lookout. He yelled when an ICE vehicle approached, "Federales!" When officers arrived, the undocumented workers fled. Fear of deportation and arrest kept them away.

Stewart liked to park nearby and watch the workers run from the ICE officers. "They look like roaches in the night," he said. Stewart never paid any of the wages he promised. At the start of the next month, he simply went back to the Winn-Dixie parking lot and hired new eager crews attracted to his same worthless guarantees and empty promises. The process began again.

"This is the easiest money I have ever made. With zero expenses and nearly a 100% profit margin, it's impossible not to get rich! I made thirty grand last month!" Stewart liked to brag.

The New Orleans mayor also got in on the game, and although he spent most of his days in Texas, he still found time to shake down New Orleans' city contractors. He usually met his marks at Larry's Grill for an early breakfast. "We can talk freely here. Don't worry," he said to nervous businessmen.

The mayor made hundreds of thousands of dollars in bribes from companies hired to rebuild the city. He accepted payment in cash, checks and wire transfers. Contractors gave the mayor fully paid trips to Hawaii, Chicago and Vegas, and a private limousine in New York City. Some provided jets for the vacations and expensive shopping sprees for the mayor's wife. He claimed these trips were "fact-finding endeavors" intended to research a blueprint for the reconstruction of New Orleans. "I have never accepted a bribe or kickback of any kind," he said in response to a reporter's questions about the junkets. The mayor was foolish to accept these trips for other reasons as well. He finalized many of his corrupt deals at these expensive resorts and hotels. Las Vegas was his favorite location. However, once he crossed state lines the political extortion became a federal matter.

Mayor Glapion started a family business offering home flooring, granite, carpeting and tile. Truckloads of free granite were delivered to the business from city contactors. He insisted there was nothing inappropriate about any of these deals. However, the FBI disagreed and began secretly watching everything. The arrogant mayor had no way of knowing that the busboy refilling his water glass at Larry's was an FBI agent.

Level Lock executives met with the mayor explaining the importance of raising the elevation of homes restored with Road Home funds. They wanted every house raised above median flood stage. "That means the first floor of every house should be ten feet high! That is ridiculous!" The mayor said the Road Home program would never require something like that. The executives disagreed and argued that it could be done for thirty thousand dollars per house. The mayor did some quick math; hundreds of houses at thirty thousand dollars each. He smiled. The clever mayor had a better suggestion.

"What if we establish the thirty-thousand dollar grants as proposed, but require a more reasonable elevation adjustment? Let's say three feet. It should cost significantly less to raise a house three feet as opposed to ten, and I can set specific contractor requirements within the grant language that only Level Lock can meet. That will eliminate your competition and generate even more cream to skim off the top of a massive pile of cash, right?" The Level Lock executives kicked that idea around and welcomed the mayor as a new silent partner.

"If the Feds spend billions to rebuild levees and protect the city, then the three feet additional elevation should be acceptable flood protection for private homes."

They complimented the mayor on his brilliant suggestion. "Your honor, we look forward to a long and prosperous relationship."

# 30

TULANE PLANNED TO REOPEN IN time for the sum-
mer semester. They used the Claiborne Avenue baseball field on the
north side of the campus as the location to construct temporary housing for returning employees. The portable modules were made from
shipping containers, and were quite comfortable and strong. Con-
structing living quarters from containers was common in remote oil
fields and offshore on deep water drilling and production platforms.
Tulane made these living arrangements to encourage employees to
return home. "They are comfortable, strong and safe. Tulane security
will patrol the area constantly, and university food service staff will get
a school cafeteria up and running," Wilson said.

The university constructed temporary housing because the FEMA
trailers and Road Home program offered no guarantees regarding
police protection, utilities, and delivery and setup timelines. Tulane
needed to get faculty and staff back quickly, as much work needed to
be done in a very limited time.

"I have everything for the FEMA trailer and reconstruction funds. My
Road Home check should arrive any day now. Contractors are lined
up and ready to rip out the floors and walls at the house. I will do
most everything else myself. I plan to live in the FEMA trailer and
work on Montegut Street in the evening and on weekends when I'm
not needed at Tulane." Louis thanked Wilson for the university's

housing opportunity. "If things change I will certainly take you up on the offer."

Wilson and Louis also discussed Mon Luis. "I love that old Creole house. It is perfect and Willow loves Spring Hill College. She was elected to the freshman class student government and works on the school's newspaper twice a week. Her grades are good and she volunteers for Spring Hill's chapter of Habitat for Humanity. Willow is doing great and has many new friends, but I know she does miss Tulane." Wilson was glad to hear Louis's encouraging news.

"Although I must admit, Jan seems really homesick for New Orleans."

"I can understand that. Feel free to stay at Mon Luis if necessary, but try and get back to New Orleans pronto. We need you here at Tulane!" Wilson said.

"I will have the Road Home check and a FEMA trailer soon. Things are finally working out. See you in a few weeks. By the way, I'm just wondering. Is Puncher welcome at Tulane housing?"

"Of course, Puncher is always welcome."

As if on que, Louis received a FEMA notice regarding his trailer setup. He was given a two-week time window and asked to verify his social security number for the Road Home funds. The check arrived Saturday morning in a plain envelope with the regular mail.

"What the hell! Why are two names on the check?"

Jan asked Louis what he thought would happen after he added Leon to the property deed. "Are you really that dumb? Sure looks like he screwed you," she said.

Louis ignored Jan's sarcasm and called the FEMA adjuster.

"The check payee line reads exactly like the property deed recorded in the conveyance office at the Civil District Court building. That's the law. If a mortgage, lean or equity line of credit exists against the property, then that third party has a claim on the FEMA funds as well.

This is how the banks protect their interest. In most cases, financial institutions will endorse the checks without any trouble. It is in their interest to see collateral value restored, since they hold the mortgages. You shouldn't have anything to worry about." The FEMA adjuster went on to explain that some banks have established escrow accounts to assure that FEMA funds are spent correctly and to prevent contractor fraud.

"For Christ's sake! I own my house free and clear! There are no mortgages or leans, or anything like that!"

The adjuster pulled up Louis's information on his screen. "It is right here, clear as day. There are two names on your property deed, you and someone named Leon. The check appears to be correct."

"Leon doesn't own my house! I was told I could remove his name from my deed at any time. The conveyance clerk said so. If I get Leon's name removed, can I get a corrected Road Home check in my name only?"

"Yes, but that will be between you, Leon and the conveyance office. Good luck."

Louis left Mon Luis early enough to be one of the first in line at the conveyance office when they opened at eight-thirty. He parked in the Hyatt parking lot across Poydras Street from the Civil District Court building. It was seven-fifteen in the morning, but already at least fifty people were waiting. Louis pulled multiple numbers and sat down. When his first number was called, he said nothing and continued to wait. "51, 51… going once. Ok-52. Next!" Louis waited longer because he wanted to see the same clerk that had promised him it would be easy to remove Leon's name when the time came.

"You said lawyers do it all the time. You said it was a simple process to remove Leon's name from my deed. Well, I need to do that now."

"I do remember you. Yes, it is that simple." Louis relaxed a little. "I just need to see your affidavits. Do you have three notarized affidavits and certified copies signed by both you and Leon?"

"No! I do not have any affidavits."

"We can't do anything without the proper legal documents. You are welcome to come back once the paperwork is signed and notarized in triplicate form." The clerk was about to call the next person in line when Louis spoke up.

"You said lawyers do this all the time?"

"Yes they do, and it is a simple process when the paperwork is in order. It only takes a few minutes to file everything. You asked if it was easy, you did not ask anything about the necessary legal documents. Get your paperwork together and come back. NEXT!"

Leon was expecting Louis's call.

"I figured you would be calling soon," he said.

Louis explained the situation and asked Leon if he would sign the necessary affidavits so he could deposit the FEMA check and start work on the planned repairs. "I can't afford to get to square one with the restoration work without this check. Everything is ridiculously expensive since the storm, especially building materials."

"It's expensive because everyone is trying to bamboozle everyone else. There is a lot of gouging going on around here. At first, everyone was desperate. Now with all this federal money flowing in everyone is greedy. Desperation and greed don't mix." Leon asked how much the Road Home check was. "That is a lot of money!" He was quiet for a minute. "I won't sign your affidavits. However, I will endorse the check if we open a joint bank account with equal ownership. I want 50%. Remember, both our names are on the Montegut Street deed. Don't even think about forging my signature. If you try to cut me out, the Feds will consider that fraud," Leon said.

"How can I rebuild if you are taking half my Road Home money? I think that *is* fraud! Besides, this is my house. My father bought it in the early 1960s. The note was $114 a month. He made every payment on time for thirty years. After I inherited it, I did all the remodeling work with my own hands! I was raised in that house and my daughter was born there!"

Leon explained that this wasn't a swindle at all, only good business. He said he didn't get rich by being a softhearted pushover. "Business is business and I am a successful businessman. I expect to get 50%, one way or another. If you renovated the house with your own hands once, you can do it again and save money."

Louis had no choice. He agreed to Leon's demands. "I will open the joint bank account."

"Okay, that sounds like a square deal. Since we are renegotiating, I want more money. Now I expect 60%!" Leon took advantage of Louis's emotional attachment to the property and used it against him.

Banks protected people with mortgages by setting up escrow accounts and dispersing funds to contractors as renovation work was completed. Some homeowners complained, but the escrow accounts prevented exactly this type of fraud.

At least the Montegut FEMA trailer delivery went as expected. It was set up between the street and the front porch on strong cinderblock foundations with wooden steps leading to the front door. Sewer lines and electrical hookups were done in a professional manner. It was very small, but comfortable. Louis planned to work at Tulane and get the house back to a livable condition by working long hours at both. He expected Jan to stay in Mon Luis while Willow finished the year at Spring Hill.

"I'm not staying in this Creole rat hole a day longer than necessary. Willow is old enough to take care of herself." Jan insisted on getting back to Montegut Street.

"You are going to find that old house much more comfortable than living in a FEMA trailer," Louis warned.

# 31

THERE WAS NO RENT EXPENSE involved with the
FEMA trailer, but utilities had to be paid monthly just like any other
housing. Wilson did not charge rent at Mon Luis, but utilities had to
be paid there as well, and grass had to be cut and general maintenance
kept up to date. The estimated material costs for the Montegut
restoration was rising as price gougers flooded the city. Most of Louis's
rebuilding funds had been stolen by Leon. Louis spent over fifteen
hundred dollars on fuel in one month driving back and forth to New
Orleans. Jan was demanding new clothes and a new car. "I can't help
it if all my stuff flooded. Katrina ain't my fault," she said. The city
wanted twenty-five hundred dollars for fees and rebuilding permits.
Louis also learned that a new city ordinance would require him to
raise the elevation of the first floor three additional feet. That could
cost thirty thousand dollars of his Road Home funds. All of this was
putting a horrible strain on Louis's health and marriage. Jan seemed
distant and distracted.

Louis had not worked at Tulane long enough to qualify for unemployment benefits. The only income he'd received since Katrina was
two small monthly Bayou Contracting payments from William-Mark
and three hundred dollars from the Red Cross. Louis's savings was
gone and he was nearly broke. Even though he'd started working back
at Tulane again, there was no way to make all these ends meet. He
could not take a higher paying construction job, because he needed
the Tulane tuition waivers for Willow's education and he needed the

afternoons available to work on his house. Willow offered to find a full-time job, but Louis wanted her to focus on school. She would need to stay at Spring Hill at least until the summer semester.

Louis was having a difficult time sleeping. He had not slept an entire eight hours since before Katrina. Usually he felt exhausted and tried to fall asleep early. Louis's mind always started racing, thinking about finances, his failing marriage, all the things he needed to get done, the money he'd lost to Leon, and the stupid business deal he'd signed with William-Mark giving away the Level Lock franchise, not to mention his flood insurance nightmare.

After a half hour, his stomach always began to turn. Louis tried to ignore the discomfort, and then turned onto his back and rubbed his stomach in a circular motion. This seemed to help temporally. No one likes to throw up, and Louis always did everything he could to avoid it if possible, at least until he realized delay was hopeless.

He tried to be as quiet as possible in the bathroom, but Jan usually woke anyway. She said the same thing every time. "It will be better in the morning." Then she covered her head with a pillow and went back to sleep. For Louis, it was never better in the morning; same stress, just a different day.

He came across an employment ad for tour guides that offered flexible hours, generous pay and commissions. Louis always thought he would enjoy being a guide in the city he knew so well and loved so much. Perhaps he could conduct tours on weekends, working around his busy schedule. The employment advertisement said tourists were coming back to the city in large numbers and good paying jobs in the industry were plentiful again. They especially wanted to hire people familiar with the areas around the Superdome, Convention Center, Lakeview, Gentilly and the 9th Ward. It occurred to Louis that these were the areas hardest hit by Katrina.

Louis accepted the 'Katrina Tour' job because he needed money, but he would not enjoy it. Driving tourists around in a large bus so they could gawk at destruction, desperation and despair was not his idea of rewarding employment. Also, he was expected to wear a silly blue uniform jacket and cap. It looked like something from the Greyhound bus company, and Louis hated it. Jan told him to, "get over the uniform thing and support your family."

The tour company said Louis's personal story of Katrina survival would be of great interest to the tourists. "They love to interact with Creole people." Louis was amazed at the large numbers of people coming to tour a destroyed city. They responded to ads on travel websites: 'drive past levees that failed and see the resulting devastation that displaced hundreds of thousands.'

Louis accepted the job because he hoped some of the tourists would end up donating to the city's rebirth, or contributing time and energy in other ways. He did his best pretending that someone on his bus could be a CEO planning to move a business here, or a hedge fund manager or a Middle Eastern sheik eager to help the city. But most visitors were middle-class families from the Midwest looking for a different type of exciting vacation filled with unusual adventure, entertainment and amusement.

Part of the on-the-job training involved riding along with experienced tour guides, learning the ropes and memorizing scripts. The bus drivers had a microphone to deliver the approved tour monologue as the bus rolled past devastated neighborhoods. "The tourist love hearing gory details. The gruesome specifics sell best," Louis's trainer said. The bus stopped at an intersection on Claiborne Avenue. It occurred to Louis that this was the very same spot where he first realized cars were submerged at the intersection beneath him. Many unfortunate souls were entombed inside those flooded cars.

"Dude, tell them your story about the Sea Horse motor and that old boat. Tell them about the submerged cars you saw and the all those dead bodies. They will love that." Louis's trainer handed him the microphone. "Go head! Tell them!" All the tourists stared at Louis, anticipating an exciting story.

"People lost their lives right here at this intersection. No one deserved to die like that. It is all very sad. Those images never leave me." Louis turned off the microphone and sat down. It was the first time he had been back to this exact location since the flood. The tourists were quiet.

"Way to go, dude. Buzz kill." Louis's trainer took back the microphone and continued with his upbeat monologue.

At the next stop Louis took off his cap and handed it to the trainer. "Thanks for the opportunity, but I quit." He got off the bus and started walking home.

In January, the city council finally passed an ordinance banning the entry of Katrina Tour busses into neighborhoods. The law read in part, "It is important that these residents not be victimized again by having their ongoing suffering exploited and paraded for commercial gain." However, the rule was ignored by the tour bus companies, and not enforced by corrupt NOPD officers taking kickbacks from the tour operators.

Even under his difficult financial circumstances, Louis did not need money bad enough to do the Katrina bus tour job. Besides, he was picking up more and more hours at Tulane. The campus devastation was overwhelming, but the rebuilding process was moving along ahead of schedule. There remained much work to do, but very few maintenance and facilities workers returned to their Tulane employment. Many former employees decided to start over in new cities with good schools, honest politicians and higher flood-free elevation. Who could argue with that?

At lunch Louis liked to spend his time studying Tulane's historic pre-Civil War slavery documents at the Amistad Center, the collection he personally helped save and protect from Katrina. Louis was proud to have done something important. Saving the collection for future generations was a significant contribution to the rebirth of New Orleans and to the preservation of the city's unique culture. He found inspiration in these stories of hardship and perseverance. His problems were peanuts compared to what his ancestors faced. That part of New Orleans history could never be explained to silly tourists on a two-hour Katrina bus tour.

Louis moved up quick at Tulane, and was now a supervisor in charge of a heavy equipment crew doing land and subsurface utility work. The pay increases he received reflected his added responsibilities. Louis's new plan was to focus on his Tulane responsibilities and restoring Montegut Street, having both ready by early summer.

Wilson always gave Louis outstanding reviews and said, "The rebirth of Tulane would not be possible without him!"

Louis was only a mile or two from Montegut Street when he got off the tour bus and began walking home. He expected a work crew to start stripping the house down to the studs today. They also had to drag everything outside to the curb for pickup later in the week. His sofa, refrigerator and dining furniture was already hauled out and piled on the sidewalk. Most likely, some of the horrible smells came from the rancid food inside the frig.

Health officials advised everyone to dig five-foot-deep holes in their backyards, remove the rancid food and bury it in plastic bags before placing the refrigerators on the curb for pickup. The putrid, disgusting smells were too much to handle. Many people dug big holes and pushed everything in, entombing refrigerators with their contents forever like graveyard coffins. Trying to follow the rules, but unable to stomach the decomposing petri dish inside his fridge, Louis wrapped it with duct tape, wrote 'bio hazard—do not open' with red spray-paint and waited for the city to pick it up. "Oh, my God! That is disgusting!" Louis lost his stomach.

He hated to see the bright orange Katrina X-Code spray painted on the front of the house, but now at least Louis understood what the codes meant. The left side of the X was used to identify the rescue team that searched the property. Code 3-505 indicated that the house was searched by Alpha Co. Parachute Infantry Regiment, 82 Airborne Division. The top of the X indicated the date it was searched: 8-29. The right side warned of hazards present. The F/W indicated flood water. The bottom of the X indicated the number of live and dead victims found in the structure. DB was for dead bodies found, LB was live bodies found, 0 was used if no bodies were found inside.

The mildew cleaning crew consisted of six men and one woman, all from El Salvador. The women appeared to be pregnant. They did not have gloves, much less quality breathing masks. Louis was especially worried about the pregnant lady. Last weekend or so, he stored the box of masks from Heather's hardware store under the carport with some other cleaning materials. Louis called the foreman over, opened the box and handed him six masks. "No money," the foreman said in broken English. He opened his wallet to show Louis that he had only two dollars.

"No money necessary." Louis demonstrated how the mask's adjustments worked. "The air inside is very dangerous. Everyone must wear one of these, all the time!"

Jan was inside the FEMA trailer trying to get settled in. It was set up on a cinder block foundation a few feet from the house, utilities were hooked up and the air conditioner was running. Louis filled Puncher's water and food bowls, then went inside. "These people have been working all morning in deadly mold and mildew conditions, and you could not offer them the breathing masks? That lady is pregnant for Christ's sake!" It was difficult for Louis to conceal his anger. "And what about Puncher? Did it ever occur to you to check his food and water? What have you been doing?"

"In case you haven't noticed, I have been busy setting this trailer up. I am sorry I can't do everything to your satisfaction."

Jan tried to change the subject. "I have some really good news," she said. "William-Mark offered to raise the foundation three feet at no charge. Isn't that nice of him?!"

"Why was William-Mark here?" Louis asked.

# 32

LESLEY WAS NOT A PROFESSIONAL lobbyist, but she understood government and was passionate about public education. She met with BESE members and the Governor's Director of Education Policy where she introduced the charter school concept as a potential solution to the city's public education crisis. "Charter schools will have considerable autonomy in many areas, including instruction and mission. Each school will serve the unique interests of a diverse student body. Hopefully, it will be somewhat like repeating the Harris County success multiple times across the city," she said.

Money is the mother's milk of politics. Lesley addressed the cost concerns expressed by a legislative committee. "There is a federal grant earmarked for charter school development. Based on our situation, Louisiana should qualify for over $20 million. We have over one-hundred schools moving from a failed system toward the most promising reform opportunity in the nation's history!"

Lesley's plan to reform the New Orleans Parish Public Schools evolved into the most revolutionary and controversial attempt at education reform in American history. It was the first time independent, non-profit charter schools operated with substantial autonomy in a competitive educational marketplace. Independent charter schools had the freedom to design their own unique curriculum and hire nonunion teachers, set disciplinary guidelines and write overall mission statements. Some worked closely with Tulane. Because of these reforms, 7,500 employees of the failed Orleans Parish public school system were terminated, making way for the new, market-driven, charter school system. Moreover, many of the chronically failing public schools were closed for good, and then reorganized as part of the new charter school model.

"At the stroke of a pen the entire New Orleans public school system has been transformed. Public school children in New Orleans will, without question, get a better education," Lesley said. She expected over 60% of all public school students to attend a successful charter school within a few years.

Lesley promised significant overall improvement in most academic statistical measures. She especially wanted to see gains in the city's graduation rates and in overall performance on standardized tests. "School leaders used to think of the old system with a powerful, unchecked, corrupt school board was the ideal way to go, but now those ideas seem unpalatable," Lesley reminded everyone that before Katrina nearly 70% of public school students were attending failing schools. "We are changing that!" although she did acknowledge that there is a long way between 'not failing' and excellent. "Excellent results at all schools are the ultimate objective," she said.

Reforming an entrenched system is difficult. People who gain from the old political structure will do everything to stop change as they fight to protect self-interest. However, those benefiting from reform have only promises. They are not inclined to fight in the trenches, as promises are cheap.

Unemployed members of the old public schools made some good points, and said any post-Katrina improvements were only temporary. "Conditions after Katrina are distinctive. Well-meaning do gooders from around the country are coming here. Anyone who wants to be a part of education experimentation will head to New Orleans. If you want to be an investment banker you go to New York. If you want a job in technology you move to Silicon Valley. If you want to dismantle a minority run school district you come to New Orleans. These opportunists will destroy our schools, then go back to Chicago or

California, or wherever else they came from. What happens to New Orleans once they all leave?"

Fired teachers sued, school board members sued and politicians complained. They said special needs children were left out of charter schools completely. They said charter schools simply expelled difficult students. "Charter schools are skimming the cream off the top and leaving the most difficult challenges for others to deal with. Of course, the performance record looks good for charter schools."

As the population of New Orleans began to increase back to more normal levels, some of the schools under the Orleans Parish School Board began to reopen. New board members were elected, a new superintendent appointed and experienced teachers rehired. FEMA funds were used to rebuild the school buildings. Some of the city's best schools remained under the old structure, including Lusher Elementary, Edward Hynes Elementary, Benjamin Franklin High School on the campus of UNO, McDonogh 35 and Warren Eastern High School. All schools in New Orleans were improving at a remarkable rate. The beneficiaries were the New Orleans school children.

Lesley gave speeches around the country and said the achievements obtained in New Orleans schools across-the-board, both charter and traditional, were real and long-lasting. "Our accomplishments are a function of permanent structural changes put in place after Katrina. They are not a one-time event caused by a non-replicable temporary infusion of teaching and leadership talent," she said.

# 33

THINGS WERE BEGINNING TO LOOK up everywhere. Schools were reopening, restaurants were back, tourists were returning, and almost one-hundred and fifty thousand residents were home, a good number, but still a small fraction of the pre-Katrina population. The Eiffel Restaurant was the first on Saint Charles Avenue to reopen. The wait, even with reservations, was long but worth it. Everyone was eager to get back to normal, and Mardi Gras was just around the corner.

The mayor was opposed to having Mardi Gras this year. He said it was too soon to celebrate. Mayor Glapion was also concerned about jeopardizing federal money. "If we are in good enough shape to have Mardi Gras, then Congress might think we are in good enough shape to cut our FEMA funds," he said. He was also worried about police protection and crowd control. "The national guard and the state police should take over these activities. What about damaged areas of the city? Thousands of homes and businesses still sit unoccupied. The parades should be consolidated to one Saint Charles Avenue route. What about medical incidents? On average, the typical Mardi Gras weekend generates over three thousand medical emergencies. We are not equipped to handle that. It is hard to celebrate anything when so many people have not been able to return home. There is still too much that needs to be done," he said.

The lieutenant governor thought bringing back Mardi Gras was generally a good idea. He lived in New Orleans and was always interested in running for mayor. He could be counted on to oppose anything Glapion suggested. "People need it. It is like city-wide therapy. The city has been hard hit, but we must move forward and enjoy life again. It will help get us back on our feet. Not having Mardi Gras is like not having jazz music." He supported the idea, but had mixed feeling about the parades passing near the convention center. "Just too much suffering went on there," the lieutenant governor said.

Louis supported the lieutenant governor's position. He agreed with holding Mardi Gras in New Orleans again because he did not want to spend it away from home. Mobile locals think their Mardi Gras is bigger and better than New Orleans. That could be believed only by someone who had never seen Bacchus, Endymion, Rex, Orpheus, or any large New Orleans parade for that matter. Mobile float riders do throw Moon Pies! That does make them unique. "Even a shorter and less elaborate New Orleans Mardi Gras celebration is still better than being away from home," Louis reasoned.

Trying to avoid additional political conflict, the mayor offered a workable compromise. "We can support 28 parades instead of the usual 34, and instead of parading for eleven days it should be reduced to eight this year. That is assuming the lieutenant governor can deliver on his commitment to provide one-hundred and fifty state troopers for additional crowd control duties. Our current reduced medical capabilities should not be a problem, since crowds will be greatly reduced as well."

The city council approved the Mardi Gras deal as presented. "It won't top the $150 billion dollars tourists spent here pre-Katrina, but at least we are moving forward," said the councilman from District A just before the vote was called. "All in favor? Any opposed? Motion carries." The city council approved the Mardi Gras resolution unanimously by a voice vote. The *Times-Picayune* celebrated the council's decision with a dramatic one-word headline: "Rebirth"

People from New Orleans tend to be creatures of habit. Once they find something they like they stick with it, sometimes for generations. Neighborhood friends often buy Saints season tickets in the same Dome seating sections year after year. Many have sat in the same seats since the stadium opened in 1975. They attend Sunday mass at the same neighborhood Catholic church where they grew up, regardless of what part of the city they now call home. They passionately pull for their high school football teams, even if they graduated fifty years ago. Children and grandchildren attend the same Catholic schools, and they stay loyal to the hospitals where they were born. When a local asks, "where you from?" they want to know your hospital and high school.

Louis and his family spent every Mardi Gras day on the corner of Saint Charles and Napoleon Avenue. It had been their spot for generations. Fat Harry's bar is on one side of Saint Charles and the old First Baptist Church is on the other. The bar provided .25 cent beer and the church provided bathrooms. Everyone from Louis's neighborhood had favorite spots in the same area. These were the people he grew up with, the friends he made his First Communion with, the people he went to high school with. They were old girlfriends and old best friends. They were aunts, uncles, cousins and neighbors. They were his community.

Electric utility poles ran parallel to the Saint Charles Avenue streetcar tracks. They were in the perfect location to tie up ladders with chains and ropes. Secured to poles, eight-foot ladders worked best, high enough so float riders could see the children sitting on top, and stable enough not to fall over when crowds pushed and jumped for beads. Homemade seats lovingly constructed of plywood and painted eye-catching colors were bolted to the tops of the ladders. A broomstick fastened across the front from side to side kept children from falling forward. They sat perched high above the crowds waving their hands, "Throw me something, mister!" Willow saw her first seven Mardi Gras day parades sitting in the same seat and ladder Louis used when he was a child. It had been repainted and repaired many times since Louis's dad built it in the 1950's, but to Louis's eye it was perfect.

Before sunup on Mardi Gras day, blankets were spread on the neutral ground near the ladders before the large crowds arrived, marking off the territory of various families and groups. They brought lawn chairs and ice chests. Louis always liked to bring two, twenty-five-piece boxes of spicy Popeye's Fried Chicken, one dark meat and one white. Others liked to bring potato salad, chips or homemade sandwiches. Everyone contributed. Louis's uncle always dragged along a large ice chest he used to keep a single Tupperware bowl of potato salad cool.

"That's a big ice chest for such a small bowl of potato salad!" Louis liked to needle his offbeat uncle.

"Yea, but it's really good potato salad! It's not Mardi Gras without it! You know dat! Besides, why does da president fly around in a giant 747? A smaller airplane would work fine, but the president is special. So is my potato salad!"

It was important to get things set up beforehand, because the walking groups passed early; sometimes they arrived at Napoleon and Saint Charles before 8:00 a.m., and the drinking started long before that. No one wanted to miss the 'feet on the street.' The Jefferson City Buzzards and Pete Fountain's Half-Fast Walking Club each had hundreds of members. Sometimes the Half-Fast Walkers were all dressed in red tuxedoes; it was quite a sight. They walked, danced and drank their way down Saint Charles carrying canes decorated with paper flowers. Women greeted them with kisses in exchange for flowers. Some were asked to do much more. If they wanted a paper flower bad enough, they readily submitted. Women proudly displayed their flowers the way Scarlett showed off her fist full of buttons.

Each walking group had their own 'freestyle' jazz bands following close behind. It seemed they all played, "Do You Know What it Means to Miss New Orleans." Louis could listen to Louis Armstrong's version of that song over and over. He never grew tired of hearing it. He also loved to sing along with Professor Long Hair, "If you go to New Orleans, you ought to go to the Mardi Gras."

It wasn't long after the walking groups passed when two NOPD tow trucks and a New Orleans Public Service, Inc. utility truck leading the

Rex parade turned onto Saint Charles. A cane pole attached to the truck's roof measured height clearance along the route. The NOPD mobile communications unit followed with the chief of police sitting in the glass observation bubble waving to the crowds. The United States Marine Corps band was first in Rex. Rex always had military bands marching first.

Two truck parades followed Rex. These were the parades that came to mind when Louis saw the delivery trucks lined up for Tulane's move-in day. It took hours for the homemade truck floats to pass. The first few trucks were decorated elaborately and competed for best float awards. The winners won the honor of lining up first next year, but the quality of the homemade truck floats deteriorated as the day wore on.

Watching the truck floats roll by soon became monotonous and tiresome for the adults. The children never grew tired of catching thousands of beads all day long. The adults retreated to the relative quiet of their lawn chairs, ate chicken and potato salad, and drank lots more beer. Louis had an old aunt that loved Miller Beer Ponies. She drank them through a straw and was usually sloshed by noon. Throws rained down even in the back of the neutral ground. After a while it became too many to pick up. The ground was covered under a blanket of plastic beads and trash. Louis counted thirty-two empty Miller bottles around his aunt's feet. "Bring me another beer for Christ's sake! What's the matter with you people?" Some people get quiet when they drink; others get mean. Louis's aunt was as mean as a snake.

Costumes were always popular. There were people dressed as crawfish, Saints football players, priests and nuns. New Orleans loved making fun of politicians, and satirical costumes always had a popular edge. Most of the sexually explicit erotic action took place in the French Quarter, especially on Bourbon Street near Esplanade Avenue. Saint Charles and Napoleon were poles apart from the Quarter. It was a family area, and much of the Mardi Gras activity reflected that. Louis saw a group walk past; one person was dressed as strips of bacon, another as a banana, another as a carton of milk and the last was dressed as a box of cereal. They carried a sign calling themselves 'The Breakfast Club.'

The Katrina Mardi Gras was a far cry from every one that came before. Louis's aunt and uncle were living somewhere north of Memphis. There was no famous homemade potato salad this year. Most everyone from the old neighborhood was gone as well. The walking groups had only a few dozen members, and the paper flowers were gone. The two sweet old ladies that made them by hand were living with family in Tampa. There were no blankets or ladders this year, as the crowds were small. The truck floats combined into one very small parade. No one had the time, energy or money to build floats.

"This is lame," Jan said as a few poorly constructed trucks with only a few riders passed by. She was ready to leave and threatened to go sit in the car. "I should be watching the Pacific Ocean from a Malibu beach house, not at this depressing parade."

Louis stood on the Saint Charles Avenue neutral-ground side for the entire parade and made a point of encouraging the riders. "Nice float, my brother! I love it! Thank you."

There were still people dressed in costume, but this year they were made of available materials and reflected the city's difficult situation. Louis saw many revelers dressed as mildew eradication teams. They wore the same masks and plastic suits now common everywhere in New Orleans. One group carried a sign that read: 'The Mildew Mardi Gras.' Another couple covered themselves with green and black body paint and said they were 'Mold and Mildew.' Others dressed as Willy Wonka. The mayor said New Orleans had always been a chocolate city, and would always be a chocolate city in the future. Other than mildew, Willy Wonka was the most popular getup.

Louis parked at Tulane so that he could avoid the gridlocked traffic after the parades ended. It was somewhat of a long walk from Napoleon Avenue to the university, but it saved a lot of time in the long run. It also gave them a chance to see the progress Tulane had made getting everything up and running. Willow had not seen the campus since she saved Sloan from the thugs. She did not relive Katrina nightmares, but Willow was surprised by the lingering memories she found difficult to shake. Seeing the restored campus helped. Willow wanted to get back home to the life she missed. The campus was looking great.

"Tulane's president just announced privately to university employees that classes are expected to start again next semester!" Louis surprised Willow with good news. "The emails will go out to students next week," he said.

# 34

SHEETROCK WAS NOW WORTH ITS weight in gold, but it became nearly impossible to find available in New Orleans at any price. Louis could manage to haul a few sheets at a time from Alabama, but that would take forever and his cost in time, effort and fuel would be prohibitively expensive. Still, he wanted to get the house finished as quickly as possible, as life in the small FEMA trailer was getting old fast.

Louis was thrilled when he learned Chinese manufactures were preparing to meet the sheetrock demand at reasonable prices. The Taishan Tianjin Plasterboard Company had already shipped fifty million pounds of Chinese drywall to New Orleans. Tianjin is the city in China where the company is headquartered. These first shipments of inexpensive drywall were scheduled to arrive soon. Louis ordered enough to finish the entire house, and expected it to be delivered to his doorstep by week's end. Just in time, since the foundation work was done and Louis was finishing the electrical and plumbing.

William-Mark had Level Lock workers raise the Montegut Street foundation as he promised. All the work was done on time and professionally. "How you like dat elevation job?" William-Mark asked Louis as he pointed out the additional pillars and footings they added for increased strength. "It's all no charge as promised, not a penny. Dat's what friends do." Louis was skeptical and suspicious about anyone doing something for nothing, especially someone like William-Mark.

"For Christ's sake! Would it kill you to show a little more gratitude? William-Mark is a busy man. He didn't have to help us." Jan angrily called Louis a thankless ingrate.

Louis did the plumbing work and electrical on his own, and had everything ready for the required city inspections. He was a licensed roofer from his days owning Bayou Contracting, but Louis was not a certified plumber or electrician. He could not proceed with installing sheetrock until the city inspector signed off on his plumbing and electrical work first. Louis saved thousands of dollars by doing everything himself, but  city building rules required licensed contractors to verify that everything was done 'to code'.

"It all looks great. Just have your licensed builder sign these forms and provide his state and city contractor's number, and we are set to go. You did hire licensed professionals, right?" The inspector promised to be back in two days. "If you have problems, try calling one of the names on this list." The inspector handed Louis a list of "friendly" contractors. "They understand how things get done around here," he said. "By the way, I could order you to rip everything out and start over. But we don't want that, do we? Call one of these names."

Louis asked legit contractors for advice, but they did not do the work and were unlikely to sign off on the permits. However, there were plenty of unscrupulous names on the list of 'friendly' contractors. All the money Louis saved doing his own work went to paying off the fly-by-night contractors willing to falsify the city's permits.

"Bring your paperwork by and I will sign everything. Cash only, no checks, cards or rain checks. Just cash on the barrelhead. I don't give credit," the crooked contractor said.

"Don't you need to at least look at my house first?"

"Why would I need to see your work? I'm sure it's great. This is not extortion; consider it an incentive," the contractor said.

It occurred to Louis that he could have paid bribes to the crooked city inspector directly instead of jumping through all those hoops.

Certainly the graft payments made its way back to him anyway. Corruption was rampant.

"Why does it smell like eggs?" Jan was first to notice the odd odor of the Chinese drywall stacked in the center of the unfinished living room.

"It will be fine once it is installed and painted. I'm sure the smell is no big deal," Louis said. "It is odd that nothing is printed on it, no company name, country of origin, nothing. Very strange."

Working every evening and on weekends, Louis finally had all the sheetrock nailed up, but floating it was a difficult job. He did all the sanding by hand, and was amazed at the amount of dust the job created. Louis used the mold breathing masks instead of the paper drywall masks, but still his eyes burned and his throat itched. The dust penetrated every crease and caves on his body not covered by clothing. His hair was a matted mess and his sweat turned the dust into cement that was nearly impossible to scrub off. He needed to hire sheetrock professionals, but could not afford them.

Louis installed wood laminate flooring downstairs and carpet in the upstairs bedrooms. Trying to please Jan, he paid extra attention to the master bedroom and bath. Louis put in the jetted tub she'd always wanted and a nice, double, his-and-her washbasin arrangement with manmade marble and nice tile work. Jan was always angry about the water droplets Louis left on the sink and mirror each morning after brushing his teeth. "Separate washbasins should solve that problem," he said.

Jan offered to help. "I think I can do some of the painting once you have the drywall ready," she said.

Tulane was in a last-minute rush to get things finished, so Louis was working more and more hours on the campus. Lately, he'd worked weekends as well. Painting the bedrooms would take a lot of time and energy he did not have. Jan said she could figure it out. "How difficult could painting be? Just roll it onto the wall. I got this." Louis suggested she buy the paint from Sherwin-Williams.

"Quality paint will be somewhat more expensive, but it should cover in one coat. Makes things much easier, and actually less expensive in the long run," he said.

Louis had just done a sixty-five-hour work week at Tulane and he was dog-tired. Jan finished painting the master bedroom and bath, and was eager for him to see it. Somehow Louis found the strength to act enthusiastic.

"It all looks perfect, and you did a great job painting the crown molding and trim. Very nice work. The walls look like professional painters did it. I also like this color. It's different, but I like it, kind of green and kind of blue. It's nice."

"I'm glad you like it. It is a custom color! No one else has this exact hue. It is amazing how many different tints come from just three primary colors. It took us a long time to come up with it. You wouldn't believe all the paint they have," Jan said.

"It took 'us' a long time?" Louis was puzzled. "Who is 'us'?"

"Well, William-Mark offered to help. Was I supposed to turn him down?"

"Are you telling me William-Mark picked out the paint color for my damn bedroom? Are you kidding?"

"You said you liked the color, didn't you?"

"Forget about the damn paint. That is not the issue. I want to know what is going on between you two! Why is William-Mark always around, and what is he doing in my bedroom?"

"You are being a little too theatrical, don't you think? Get some sleep. You have been under a lot of stress since Katrina and you're worn out. William-Mark worked hard to find a color he thought you would like. He wants to be helpful. That's all. For heaven's sake, we are just friends. He is your friend, too! I think tomorrow morning we should talk about marriage counseling."

Louis worried about another big expense, but was willing to consider the counseling idea. He was too exhausted to put up a fight. "Okay, I guess it is worth a try." Louis sat down on the bed and fell asleep quickly.

The therapist said bumps in the road are common, especially for couples that have been together for a long time. "There are certain relationship problems that seem to be most common, and they always involve communication, sex, money, conflict or trust problems. I am trained to be helpful in these situations." The marriage counselor said he preferred to meet privately on an individual basis first. Then he would bring everyone together to work out their differences and, "get everything on the right track." He said in this case he would like to see Louis first.

"I will start by explaining the common reasons many marriages end, analyzing the most important justification for failure last. Strong communication is essential to a strong marriage. Never raise your voice, and always use body language in a positive way. Don't lie or overreact, and never say things you can't take back." Louis was not at all surprised by the therapist's shabby office or casual dress. Since Katrina, nothing was as it should be. He had a degree from Delgado Community College hanging behind his desk, but it was too far away for Louis to see the fine print. The counselor noticed Louis trying to read it. "I am certified by the National Institute of Marriage Fulfillment. It is a very prestigious institution, but my certificate was in the flood and I just haven't replaced it yet."

"How much is all this going to cost?" Louis asked, but the therapist changed the subject without answering.

"You should always find time for sex. Make it a priority to be together and do it during the day, not at night when everyone is tired. When couples plan a sexual rendezvous, it increases the anticipation. It can make the encounter more intense." All of this was nice information, but Louis did not hear anything so far that was worth his time and money. A sexual rendezvous in the middle of the day certainly sounded great, but nobody had time for that. "Except perhaps Jan and William-Mark," Louis whispered under his breath.

"I'm sorry, did you say something?"

"I am just trying to survive from week to week, working too many hours, and I feel exhausted all the time. Sex has not been a high priority," Louis admitted.

"Let's talk about conflict. Don't keep responding the same way to problems. If what you did in the past caused more trouble and marriage unhappiness, then you should do things differently if you want a different result. Don't ever be jealous."

Louis thought about that for a long time. He usually responded to Jan's tug-of-war with indifference, not anger. Louis was always afraid of her overreaction or her immature silent treatment, which could last days and make everyone uncomfortable. If he did anything different, he wondered how Jan would react. The status quo, while unpleasant, was at least predictable.

"What about money? Financial stress can kill an otherwise strong marriage. The key here is to be completely open, even when things are financially tight; honesty is most important. Don't expect your spouse to live by a budget if you are stashing away cash in secret bank accounts. I have seen people hide money for a future vacation, new home or antique automobile. The purpose of the deceit may be noble, but dishonesty never is. It is these small lies that slowly destroy a marriage. Have you ever hidden money from Jan?" the therapist asked Louis. "If you are hiding money from her, most likely you are ignoring Jan's hopes and dreams as well. She gave up Hollywood to live in the 9th Ward. She sacrificed everything for you. Have you been selfish?"

"I never thought about it like that, but it was for Willow's education. For years I hid cash in our bedroom ceiling. Each time I had a little extra, I socked it away. I knew Jan would want to spend it or lose every penny of it at the Biloxi casinos! I was not saving it for some selfish reason, for crying out loud!"

The therapist was quiet for a few minutes, giving Louis time to consider what he had just said. "Do you see my point? You expected Jan to live a very Spartan lifestyle, yet for years wads of cash were hidden in her bedroom ceiling. Do you see my point? Dishonesty and indifference is the issue here, not your motivation."

"We have discussed sex, conflict, finances and communications. These are very important components to a happy and fulfilling marriage experience. I intentionally left the most important factor for last. It is by far the most meaningful because none of the other healthy marriage aspects can endure for long without it. Do you care to guess what it is?" The therapist answered his own question before Louis had a chance to respond.

"It is trust! That's right, trust!" He placed his hands down flat on the desk for effect and looked Louis directly in the eye.

"When one partner distrusts the other it is usually because the accuser has done something wrong, and it usually involves an affair. We call this 'Guilt Transfer.' It is a theory first developed by a Stockholm doctor in the 1960s. It has been further refined and developed since then. If the accuser was willing to cross the line, then they assume their spouse would as well. It makes a guilty spouse constantly suspicious and paranoid. Louis, could your distrust of Jan and William-Mark derive from something haunting you? You are the accuser in this scenario. I can't help if you are not forthcoming. Have you had an affair?"

Louis explained how he never intended for things to go as far as they did with Kathy. He enjoyed her company, but never wanted to jeopardize his marriage. Certainly, he was never planning to fall in love with her. "I have not seen her since before Katrina. I have tried to give up my desire for Kathy because I did not want to give up my marriage, but it is hard."

"Do you see parallels here? It's possible that Jan and William-Mark are just friends. Didn't William-Mark rebuild your foundation for free? Didn't he help paint? Because you crossed-the-line with Kathy, you assumed Jan would do the same thing. If you want your marriage to survive and grow, you will need to give up contact with Kathy completely, meaning no calls, meetings or sexual encounters. This is the only way to handle your 'Guilt Transfer.' What does Jan know about Kathy?"

"Jan came across some messages Kathy left on my phone after the storm. That's about it," Louis said.

"To reestablish trust in this marriage, first you will need to admit to your failings as a husband and explain everything to Jan in an open and honest way. You must accept total responsibility for everything. It will also be helpful if you apologize and reestablish your friendship with William-Mark; truthfully he is a good friend. That will convey a clear sign to Jan that you trust her again. Go, my friend. Rebuilding trust is a difficult undertaking, but you must make the first move and start now. You have a lot of difficult work to do."

Louis looked at his cell phone for a long time. He just could not find the courage to call Kathy. Finally, he pushed her number and his stomach turned as his heart broke. Kathy picked up on the first ring. "It is so wonderful to hear from you. How are you and when can I see you again?" Kathy asked.

"We need to talk," Louis said. He explained 'Guilt Transfer' and the difficulty his troubled marriage faced. Louis carefully related all he learned from the therapist. Kathy asked if this meant everything was over. She realized Louis was hurting, so she tried to make things easy for him. "I have never heard of 'Guilt Transfer,' nevertheless your marriage is very important. I have been through a difficult divorce and I would not wish that on anyone. You are making the right decision," she said, trying unsuccessful to appear strong.

"I am so sorry. I am so sorry. I never intended to hurt you," Louis said over and over. Kathy tried to understand, but still she cried. "Louis, please don't forget. Can you promise? I need to know you will always remember. Please remember me?"

Louis's heart was ripped from his chest. The anguish was unlike anything he'd ever felt before. None of this was easy, nevertheless the therapist said saving his relationship with Jan had to be a priority. Realistically, Louis knew the love left his marriage long ago, but he trusted the therapist's advice. After all, he had helped save many marriages.

Clancy's finally reopen after the storm. Jan had been asking to go there for months. "Let's go to Clancy's tomorrow night. I want this dinner to be a new start for us." Louis said the therapist was very helpful. "I'm glad we decided to do the counseling sessions. It was worth the time." Jan was surprised that Louis was willing to invite William-Mark. "Any friend of yours is a friend of mine," he said.

Louis reserved a quiet table near the back wall. He ordered a bottle of red wine, Jan's favorite, and an oyster appetizer. Louis poured three glasses of wine and proposed a toast. "To my wife Jan and my good friend William-Mark, I hope this evening is the start of a new beginning." Louis said the therapist visit was a good idea. "I was reluctant at first, but he taught me to see things differently. I think I have been selfish." The waiter came by and presented the dinner specials. The Redfish sounded most wonderful.

"I'll take me da Redfish and more of dem ersters," William-Mark said.

Louis knew he had to be truthful and forthright to save his marriage. "I have not been completely honest and have made mistakes, most of that is because of 'Guilt Transfer.' Do you recall the cell phone messages you asked about from Kathy? I said she was a coworker from Tulane. Well, that was not exactly honest." Louis also apologized to William-Mark. "I acted stupidly because I was insecure. Thanks for helping Jan pick out the paint color, and the foundation work was great. I don't know where we would be without your help. I am glad Bayou Contracting is working out. That benefits all of us."

"What part about Kathy was dishonest? The friend from Tulane part or the phone messages part," Jan asked.

"It's over now." Louis avoided giving a detailed answer.

The waiter brought the salads and refilled the wine glasses. William-

Mark took the opportunity to order another bottle of $75-dollar wine for Jan and Louis. He ordered beer for himself. "I am happy to see restaurants coming back. Things are slowly improving everywhere. Dis is a wonderful dinner, but I feel like a fifth wheel. Dis should be just between you two, and don't worry about da bill. I got dis," he said.

Louis explained his unfounded suspicions to William-Mark. "The therapist really helped me. I am content with things now. I want you here because I want to mend fences with you as well. There is nothing wrong with Jan having close friends. Please stay."

Louis realized there was a difference between contentment and passionate love. He was trying to find a way to be content in a loveless marriage. It was the best he could hope for.

William-Mark cupped his hands over Louis's and looked directly into his eyes. "I want to speak from da heart, if I may. You are a good man, Louis. I am happy we are podnas. Dat therapist did a remarkable job, especially da 'Guilt Transfer' concepts. He may have saved a good marriage and a rewarding friendship." William-Mark proposed a toast to the therapist and said he was the "man of da hour." He clicked his beer bottle against Jan and Louis's wine glasses.

"To da therapist!" Jan and Louis repeated William-Mark's toast, "To the therapist."

# 35

**WILLOW'S TIME AT SPRING HILL** Collage was ending. She'd made good friends and loved the school, nonetheless she was eager to get back to New Orleans and Tulane. Still, she would miss many aspects of life in Mobile and Mon Luis Island. "Can we come back to visit? I want to catch crabs off the pier and fish for flounder in the Bay again. I love this old house so much," she said.

"I'm sure we can arrange that. As a matter of fact, I have already asked Wilson that very same question. He gave me the keys! He said we can come back anytime. He is happy the old house is loved again." Louis said he also wanted to keep in touch with the friends he'd made on the island. "I'm looking forward to spending Saturday mornings at the hardware store."

Willow wondered if they could plan summer crawfish boils at the Mon Luis house. "What a great way for my Tulane friends to meet my Spring Hill friends. That would be so much fun. Tulane students all love the Creole-Cajun culture. A crawfish boil on Mon Luis Island would be perfect."

One of the happiest days in the life of a Katrina survivor was when their FEMA trailer was delivered outside their home and set up. The next happiest day was when the trailer was removed. It meant things were getting back to normal. Louis watched the truck hook up to the towing attachment at the front of his trailer. A work crew disconnected the electrical and plumbing fittings, removed the cinder blocks and checked the tires. Louis watched until the trailer was pulled down the street and out of sight. "Good riddance," he said.

FEMA delivered 145,000 trailers to the New Orleans area. Most had unhealthy levels of formaldehyde from the particleboard used in their construction. The trailers caused nasal cancer, nosebleeds and aggravated asthma. Congressional testimony said they were built, "fast and not intended to last." Everyone was given the option to buy their trailers for seven cents on the dollar. It came as no surprise when almost no one took the government up on that 'generous' offer.

"People love that new car smell. That's formaldehyde, It's no big deal," per the mayor. People don't live and sleep in cars. They did spend months living in the poorly ventilated unhealthy trailers and consequently many became ill. Louis was happy to move back into his newly renovated spacious and healthy home. It was better than new.

The home was not a palace by any measure, but it was comfortable in a lower, middle-class sort of way. The bathroom fixtures came from a special sale at the Habitat for Humanity warehouse. Most everything else came from Home Depot and Lowe's. About the only thing Louis splurged on was his new coffeemaker. It was made in Germany and did nearly everything. Louis loved the hot foam on top of his café au lait. The laminate flooring resembled real wood, and the artificial granite on the kitchen countertops looked almost real as well. The base and crown molding in the bedrooms were made of white vinyl. It was inexpensive when compared to real wood and did not need to be painted. Louis was proud to give Jan the grand tour. He only wished his dad had lived to see the old house looking so good.

Jan complained about Puncher's hair on the new rugs. That was one of the first things she noticed. "He can't be allowed inside. I'm sorry!" she said. "Who would want to allow a mangy mutt like Puncher inside to ruin a new home anyway?"

Louis had anticipated Jan's reaction to Puncher, and used some extra wood to build a comfortable doghouse for him. It was in the shade near the back fence. Puncher stayed in the yard whenever Jan was home. "I guess we are both in the doghouse these days," Louis said as he introduced Puncher to his new home in the backyard. When Jan left, Louis always let him back inside. Puncher's favorite activity was chewing Milk Bones on the new rug in front of the flat screen, especially when Willow sat next to him and rubbed his ears.

Willow loved the renovation of her bedroom and bath. Of course, she would finish college in a few years and move out on her own. In the meantime, Louis wanted her to have a safe and comfortable place to call home. "Dad, if you have time, please stop at Walgreens and pick up some eye drops." Willow was the first to say her eyes felt irritated and itchy. Louis assumed it was from springtime pollen common in the New Orleans air. Willow also complained of headaches.

"You know, I have had a sore throat for some time now," Jan added.

Louis's expensive German coffeemaker was the first appliance to fail. "They just don't make things the way they used to." He went to Walmart and replaced it with a twenty-five dollar Mr. Coffee. It seemed to work just fine. Louis thought the problems he was having with the air conditioners and televisions were because everything was made with cheap foreign labor. "Nothing is made in America anymore," he said. "It's a real shame."

Lawsuits were flying everywhere in New Orleans trying to assign blame for the floods on anyone with deep pockets. A lawyer sent three letters within two weeks, but Louis ignored them all. He assumed it was just another class-action solicitation from a starving ambulance chaser. When the forth letter arrived, Louis decided he should open it. He was sitting at the kitchen table enjoying his first cup of morning coffee.

"Have you noticed an unusual rotten egg smell in your renovated home? Have appliances failed? Is anyone complaining of headaches, sore throats or irritated eyes? If you installed Chinese drywall, we want to represent you." The letter said the Chinese companies may be libel for negligence, product liability, breach of warranty, fraudulent misrepresentation and fraudulent concealment.

"Chinese drywall used in New Orleans contains dangerous levels of sulfur and strontium," per the lawyer. "Assigning liability will be difficult, because it is nearly impossible to positively identify the manufacturers. We plan to sue everybody, including importers, builders and installers."

The last paragraph addressed important steps homeowners should take immediately. "DO NOT STAY IN THE HOUSE. Have the home's electrical system inspected and remove all Chinese sheetrock promptly. Expect market value depreciation in any home containing Chinese drywall. Call our law firm. We will recover the losses you are sure to incur."

Louis slid the letter across the table without saying a word. Jan picked it up and began reading.

"The letter says they will sue the installers. Don't you realize you are the installer here? Are we going to sue ourselves? Ugh! I can't take this anymore." She placed the letter back in its envelope, pushed her chair under the table and walked away.

Louis finished his coffee, picked up his lunchbox and headed to Tulane. It was a long day at work, yet he did come up with a plan for dealing with the contaminated sheetrock. It wasn't great, but it was a start. He could buy one of the FEMA trailers from the government for almost nothing, have it hauled back to his property and set it up just like the first one. Louis figured Jan would not mind staying in a trailer for a few additional months while he redid the sheetrock again. With so many trailers available, Louis was sure he could find one in very good condition. He would charge the expense on a credit card, planning to pay it all back after the lawyers sued the Chinese. Louis assumed Jan would go along with the plan, because after all it was the best he could do. Louis did not know that all FEMA trailer sales were going to be stopped and canceled because of health concerns associated with them.

Jan was in the front room working on her computer when Louis arrived home late that evening. He was eager to discuss his plan. She turned the screen around so that he could read the article she just finished.

"Don't you watch the news? The government is not selling the trailers anymore. They are unfit for human habitation and you want me to move back into one? I can't take this anymore! I can't keep living like this. I should have been in Hollywood, but instead I spent thirty years in the 9th Ward! I'm sorry, Louis, but William-Mark bought a condo at the Pontchartrain Place Condominiums. It is a three-thousand square foot penthouse on the top floor with a large balcony, and views of the marina and lake. It even has a grand piano and floor-to-ceiling glass walls! A boat slip is included. William-Mark is looking at a forty-five foot Bertram yacht. He invited me to stay there if I like," Jan said.

Louis was puzzled. "What about Willow and me? Are you planning to live in William-Mark's condo alone? I did everything the therapist suggested. What about the 'Guilt Transfer' concepts? I thought we were making progress."

"You can keep this dump. William-Mark had a lawyer handle this. The house is yours. You get Montegut Street, William-Mark gets Level Lock and I get the lifestyle I want! We all get what we want. Therapist? You are a fool, Louis! Therapist? For Christ's sake! There is no therapist! That man is a recovering alcoholic with three failed marriages. He runs a used car lot on Lime Street in Metairie. That guy has been friends with William-Mark since the fourth grade. William-Mark paid him one thousand dollars and a bottle of cheap whisky to act like a therapist. All that 'Guilt Transfer' foolishness was just made-up crap!" Jan handed Louis an envelope with the legal documents giving the Montegut Street house to him. "It's over, Louis! My ship has come in! Take the house as a gift and move on!"

Louis was taken completely by surprise. "Why would you two do that? Why did you have to make me look so foolish? You tricked me into hurting Kathy. That did not have to happen. She cared about me. I could have been happy!" Louis said.

"I did all of it because it was the only way I could be sure you would not run and tell William-Mark's wife and screw everything up again!

This is my last chance for the life I want. I am already packed. Whatever I left here you can keep! Bye-bye, Louis." Jan was gone.

"Don't be angry with your mother. She just wants more out of life than I can provide. No one can blame her," Louis explained to Willow.

# 36

**THE MAYOR'S EXTRAVAGANT LIFESTYLE BEGAN** to draw attention. The small cottage he claimed to rent in Houston was really a three-thousand square foot home overlooking a golf course that he secretly owned. His wife frequented the most expensive shops, drove a new Cadillac Escalade, and spent three hundred dollars each week to have her hair done at the M Salon, Houston's most exclusive. For the past two weeks, the mayor was vacationing at a Jamaican resort "researching," hurricane impacts on low-lying areas. It was his frequent trips in Level Lock's corporate jet that caused the FBI and the US Justice Department to take notice.

It was early afternoon. William-Mark left his penthouse condo and walked across West End Blvd. The Bertram yacht he planned to purchase was docked just across the street at the West End Marina. He wanted to do one more walk-around inspection before the sale, as he just loved looking at it. William-Mark spent the morning with Jan. They passed the time screwing in each room, on the outdoor balcony, on top of the grand piano and on the granite kitchen countertops. "We need to christen every room. It's good luck!" Jan insisted on trying different positions each time.

"I'm up for dat!" William-Mark was agreeable.

The penthouse condo was expensive, but if it made Jan happy then it was worth the expense. "I love it! I think Malibu would be just like this!" she said. William-Mark planned to buy a nice two-bedroom unit on the fifth floor until Jan said it looked like something a local bank vice-president of modest ambition would aspire to. "I'll take da penthouse. It's an all-cash offer," William-Mark said to the real estate agent. Jan was resting and decided to stay inside and take a shower. Afterwards, she planned to watch the sunset over the lake from the penthouse balcony. Sex with Jan was so good it was almost spiritual. William-Mark said it was transformative, like being 'born again' without having to be saved to Jesus or speak in tongues.

The boat looked perfect and he liked its name, 'Lucky Duck.' William-Mark could not believe it would belong to him in a few days. He was so distracted by the Lucky Duck's beauty that he did not notice the man standing nearby on the dock. He was casually dressed in gray pants, a polo shirt and dark sunglasses. He approached William-Mark. "You mind if I smoke?" He lit a cigarette before William-Mark could answer.

"I don't give a fuck what you do, podna. Do I know you?"

"I'm Allen Peterson, Special Agent US Justice Department. Can I ask you a question?" He flashed his badge.

"Do I need an attorney or no?"

"Actually, the Justice Department just wants your help. You are not a target of any investigation, just a person of interest now. We do want to see every transaction related to Bayou Contracting and Level Lock Foundation Repair since Katrina. We are not after you. We are after the mayor. If you take the wrong path and make the wrong decisions, then your status will change and you will be considered a target of multiple federal probes. You have a very limited time window. I trust you will make the right decision."

"You and da Justice Department can kiss my ass. Get da fuck out of here."

"That is not the reaction I was hoping for. Perhaps you are as dumb as we thought." Allen used the boat's polished wooden railing to put out his cigarette and he tossed the butt into the lake. "You remember National Lampoon's "Vacation"? Griswold was thinking about buying that crappy station wagon and the salesman said, 'You think you hate it now, just wait until you drive it.' Well, I'm like that, too. You think you hate me now, just wait until you see me in court."

"Can I ax you a question? Why you need to burn a hole in da fucking boat. I don't even own it yet. What da hell is wrong with you?" William-Mark asked.

"Don't go far; we will be in touch."

"Don't worry 'bout me, you fucking nickel dick!"

A few days passed and William-Mark thought he was out of the woods. He was at home enjoying a quiet Sunday evening. He planned to sneak away and visit Jan at the condo for a quickie. Things were working out great. With the condo close by he could visit Jan and return before his wife even noticed he was gone. William-Mark called these encounters 'booty calls.' Jan called them 'play dates.' He parked the Lincoln in the usual spot at the back of the third-floor parking garage adjacent to the condo. Unconcerned about getting caught running around with Jan, William-Mark said his wife was like, "a cigarette butt dat you found discarded on da sidewalk. If you are really lucky it may have a few good drags left."

A black Ford sedan pulled up behind William-Mark's Lincoln, blocking the way. The passenger jumped out. Allen Peterson waived a brown envelope in the air. "William-Mark stop right there. Time is up. I told you I would see you again." He tried to hand the grand jury subpoena to William-Mark. "This is an ad Testificandum order, which means your appearance before the grand jury is demanded. Do you understand?"

William-Mark refused the envelope, but it made no difference. Agent Peterson threw it on the ground at William-Mark's feet. "You have been served! See you in three weeks."

The lawyer was an ambulance chaser who ran commercials on late-night TV. His name was the only one William-Mark could think of. He said he could handle any legal matter, even Special agents, the US Justice Department or the US Attorney. "I have a degree from LSU School of Law and passed the bar exam on the third try. That's not bad, because nobody fully understands the Napoleonic Code. It's a Louisiana thing." The lawyer said he would not be allowed inside the grand jury room, but he would wait in the hall. "I'm paid by the hour, even if I am just sitting on a bench in the federal building reading magazines. My time is valuable." He wanted five thousand dollars up front.

Special Agent Allen Peterson presented William-Mark with a non-prosecution immunity agreement. "Sign this and you will not be prosecuted for anything discussed with the grand jury, so long as you are completely truthful. It is a good deal." He advised William-Mark to discuss the agreement with his attorney.

"If you plan to answer every question correctly and honestly with no bullshit, then you should sign this. It will keep you out of jail. It looks to me like they just want you to confirm information what they already have. Evidently they are close to filing charges against powerful people. If you lie they will also charge you with perjury! It is a dangerous double-edged sword," William-Mark's lawyer said. "What da hell. Give me dat pen." William-Mark signed the immunity agreement without reading or understanding it.

It was impossible not to notice the large camera mounted above the door at the far end of the hall. William-Mark and his lawyer arrived at the Federal Courthouse early and sat on one of the uncomfortable wooden benches lining the walls. Other witnesses were also there sitting with their lawyers. William-Mark recognized some of them as officers of the Level Lock Company, but no one said a word to each other. He stared at the camera. "Is dat thing on?" he asked before flipping it the bird. From time to time federal agents and prosecutors walked out of the grand jury rooms and down the hall toward adjacent private offices. They never made eye contact with any of the people waiting in the hall. William-Mark and his attorney sat all day, but were never called into the jury room. "Dat was a waste of time. Are we going to wait all day tomorrow, too? I guess you want to be paid for babysitting me?" William-Mark said.

"This is all part of their act. The feds are trying to intimidate you, and they are watching you every minute of the day. They are studying your reactions each time someone is called in and each time someone comes out. They want to soften you up before they call you in to testify. This dog and pony show could go on for days."

By the third day, William-Mark was tired and frustrated. The door opened and he was called into the grand jury room just before lunch. "Good luck," his lawyer said without putting down his magazine. "I am sure you will do fine."

The feds were operating three grand juries at the same time. Allen Peterson instructed William-Mark to sit in an old-style oak office chair placed at the front of the room facing the jury members. "Remember when I said you would hate me? Just wait!" Allen smiled in a fuck-you sort of way. William-Mark expected twelve grand jury members, not the thirty-six he now faced. Most of the questions were asked by the US Attorney and Justice Department lawyers, but the jury members could also ask questions. Allen swore William-Mark in and read the immunity agreement aloud. "Is this your signature?" he asked.

"Yes."

"It is now time for lunch," the US Attorney announced as uniformed agents escorted the jury members out. "This grand jury reconvenes at one-thirty."

William-Mark walked past his lawyer and went into the bathroom where he threw up. He had never been so nervous. Still reading a magazine, his attorney did not notice him walk past. William-Mark was sweaty and pale. He splashed cold water on his face and felt somewhat better. "That was quick. Are you done? You look like shit," his lawyer said as finally looked up from the magazine.

"No, I ain't done! How da hell would you know? All you do is read dat stupid magazine."

William-Mark's lawyer said he would feel better if he ate something, and he suggested oyster po'boys. "I just threw up. I don't want no po'boy." William-Mark sat on the uncomfortable bench and waited. "Remember, you are still sworn in." William-Mark was led to the same chair he used before lunch. He was instructed to stand while the jury members reentered the room. Then the questions started. "Have you ever seen a hundred-dollar bill? Have you even seen five one-hundred dollar bills at one time? Do you know anyone who carries that much cash around? Have you ever seen boxes filled with hundred-dollar bills? Have you ever cheated on your taxes?"

William-Mark wondered what all this had to do with Level Lock. "We ask the questions, not you. Please answer."

"Of course I have seen hundred-dollar bills and no, I have not cheated on taxes."

The government lawyers asked about his failed fish-raising business and his 'dish industry' work. "Did you report tips?"

"I don't remember all dat stuff."

They asked about the lakefront penthouse condo he paid cash for and the boat he planned to buy. Peterson showed pictures of Lucky Duck to the grand jury.

"I'm a good businessman. What can I say?"

The US Attorney reminded William-Mark that he'd signed the immunity agreement that required truthfulness, but that he was free to leave the room and speak with his attorney at any time.

"My lawyer don't know nothing. Why you ax all these stupid questions? What does dat have to do with Level Lock? Do you want to know everything I did wrong since da third grade? I stole a candy bar once, and I screwed da girl next-door when I was thirteen. I started smoking at nine. I cheated in high school and I stole a carburetor off a 1966 Impala. I was arrested for drag racing on Banks Street in 1979. Dat should 'bout cover it."

The real questions started after William-Mark finished his rant. "Have you ever seen the mayor at the Level Lock warehouse?" The questioning went on for five more hours.

"How did Level Lock win hundreds of millions of dollars in city contracts?"

"I don't know."

"How did Level Lock skirt public bid laws?"

"I don't know."

"Have you ever seen or delivered checks, cash or wire transfers form Level Lock accounts to any elected official."

"I don't recall."

"Why did Level Lock get such favorable treatment from the city?"

"I don't know." William-Mark tried to explain that he knew absolutely nothing about running the business or the financial details of any transactions. "I got paid a lot. I don't know why. They just kept giving me da money. So, I kept taking da money. Ain't nothing wrong with dat! I was paid to be da consultant. Ain't my fault they never axed me to consult on nothing!"

# 37

"WE SET UP HUNDREDS OF These FEMA trailers after the storm and we removed dozens over the last few months. This is the first time we are bringing one back." The crew had Louis's trailer hooked up and ready to use in a few hours. Louis bought a FEMA trailer just before the government stopped selling them. He figured he would need it for only a month max, and he had no other options anyway. With Jan gone and Willow moving back into her Tulane dorm, he figured him and Puncher could tough it out. "What's the worst thing that could happen?" he wondered.

Louis supervised the restoration of Willow's dorm building himself. Tulane's recovery was a remarkable achievement and a tribute to the university's leadership. More than thirty thousand students applied for the twelve hundred freshmen class open enrollment spots. The campus looked great and students from around the country wanted to be a part of the rebirth of a great university.

Heather ordered sheetrock from the American Gypsum and Drywall Company. "They do most all their manufacturing in the Dallas area. They are a fifty-year-old American company. We can trust them." She arranged to have the new sheetrock delivered directly to Montegut Street. Using her Mon Luis Hardware's commercial ID number, she could buy it at contractor cost and she picked up the delivery charge, billing the hardware store's delivery account. "Pay me back sometime later. No worries," she told Louis.

Ripping out the Chinese sheetrock was going to be slow and messy, but at least there was no mildew and mold, or rotten wood or damp insulation, for Louis to deal with this time around. With Tulane nearly back to normal, his work schedule was less stressful with reasonable hours. He expected to work two to three hours on the house each afternoon. Louis still used the breathing masks just to be safe. He was so careful to do a perfect job restoring the house because he wanted Jan to be happy. It was hard to rebuild, yet so easy to rip it all apart. Montegut Street seemed to be a metaphor for his life. All Louis ever got from hard work was more work.

"I hope you don't mind, I figured you could use some help." Clarence already had much of the Chinese sheetrock ripped off the walls on the first floor when Louis returned home Monday evening. He piled it up in the center of each room, making it easier to haul outside. "Lesley is spending a lot of time on the charter school movement, so rather than just sitting around doing nothing I figured we could get this sheetrock thing knocked out quickly," Clarence said.

"The success Lesley is generating with school reform is remarkable. Families are moving back to New Orleans for the good schools! That is amazing! Lesley has done more to rebuild New Orleans and any politician ever has," Louis said.

"The city now has more charter schools than traditional public schools! They are all doing great, traditional and charter!"

Louis had been using a regular claw hammer to pry the drywall apart. It was a slow and time-consuming process. "How did you get so much of it ripped out so quickly?" he asked Clarence.

"Watch this." Clarence used a large, three-foot-long crowbar that was flattened out on the short end. "It is designed for this type of work. They call it a cat's paw." He first located the wall stud, then dragged the cat's paw down, popping the long end up each time he hit a nail. Within a minute the entire eight-foot-long sheet fell to the floor. "I have another cat's paw for you. We should have this finished in no time at all," Clarence said.

Louis had a radio playing in the background as they ripped the sheetrock out. He was so involved with the task at hand that he paid little attention to the special news reports concerning the mayor. "It looks like the mayor is going to be indicted!" Clarence said. "I'm sure he deserves it." Louis said every encounter he'd ever had with politicians ended badly. He mentioned the tax assessor, Tulane's Willow Street Stadium, the BESE Board, the city's building inspector and the knuckleheads he saw at Russel's Grill. "Every politician I ever met would run into interstate traffic to pick up a nickel."

The reports indicated that certain businessmen and other associates of the mayor had already accepted plea deals in exchange for lighter jail sentences. "The plea deals would involve asset forfeiture, limited jail time and testimony in court against the mayor." Legal experts expressed their views on the radio news programs.

William-Mark was facing 35 counts on various corruption and bribery charges. Each count could carry a maximum ten years' jail time. If he went to trial, he faced a life sentence without the possibility of parole if convicted on all counts. Considering his choices, the Justice Department's offer seemed attractive. "They want your testimony against the mayor, that's all. They could care less if you rot in a federal shithole prison in New Mexico for the next fifty years. The Justice Department is going to squeeze your nuts until your eyeballs pop out. That's what they do. If I was you, and I'm glad I'm not, I would take the deal. You have no choice. The sword of Damocles is hanging over your head." William-Mark's lawyer advised him to testify against the mayor. "Per Allen Peterson, you have twenty-four hours to accept the deal or it is off the table."

"Who da hell is Damocles? I guess I won't be buying da boat."

"Buying a boat is the least of your worries." William-Mark's lawyer explained that the Feds wanted everything forfeited, including the penthouse condo, his primary home, the Lincoln, all bank accounts and other financial assets, and all assets owned by Bayou Contracting, including Level Lock. They even wanted his clothes and watches.

"You will lose everything, but in exchange for your testimony you will be a free man in six months. It's actually a very generous offer."

"How you doing, baaaby? I'm sorry, but you are going to have to leave da condo."

"Okay, that's not a problem at all. I haven't started lunch yet. Are the painters coming early?" Jan asked.

"No, it's not da painters. Da Feds are on their way. Dem no-good bastards seized everything. You have about twenty minutes to take your stuff and get out."

"What am I supposed to do? I don't have any money. I have no place to go!" Jan cried.

"I'm sorry, baaaby. I guess I fucked dis all up."

The next call William-Mark placed was to his wife. "How you doing, baaaby?"

"Hello Louis. It's me, Jan. It would be a mistake to throw-away a thirty-year marriage. Think of everything we have been through. I always thought we would grow old together. We need to talk." Jan left many messages like this on Louis's phone. He listened to all of them. She even had the nerve to ask if she could borrow a few dollars.

# 38

MOST PEOPLE NEVER REALIZE HOW important simple everyday things are until those things are lost. Louis was thrilled just to have regular mail delivery again. He even looked forward to reading junk mail. Louis received an important-looking certified letter from an uptown law firm with a fancy name. The postman had him sign a receipt. Louis brought the letter into the kitchen where he eagerly opened the envelope with a kitchen knife. This was about the time he expected to get news on the Chinese drywall lawsuits and his settlement check.

The letter was not related to the Chinese issue, it was from a law firm hired by Leon, the owner of the warehouse leased to Bayou Contracting. The letter claimed the warehouse lease agreement, secured by the Montegut Street property, was now three months in arrears and declared in default. Yes, Louis paid Leon to remove his name for the Montegut Street property deed, but the Bayou Contracting third-party lease with William-Mark was a separate legal matter.

"William-Mark has stopped making the required payments and is avoiding calls." Louis was given thirty days to correct the situation. "This urgent matter demands immediate attention! The Montegut Street collateral will be sold in accordance with the lease agreements. A forfeiture sale will be conducted on the courthouse steps unless the lease is fully reinstated and current. Nevertheless, the lessor may elect to accelerate the warehouse lease, in which case the only way to stop the property sale would be to pay off the terms of the lease in full." The lawyers included a copy of the lease for good measure. "Thank you for your time and attention to this important matter." The letter was signed by a lawyer with the letters 'Esq' after his name.

Louis realized that he should be prepared to bid at the courthouse sale to protect his interests. He was broke! If Leon's lawyers were the only bidders that showed up they could essentially steal his home for a minimum $5,000 bid. Leon would then resell it at full market value and a clear title. Louis would end up with only a $2,500 check in exchange for the home he loved.

Louis eventually called Jan back. She answered the phone on the first ring. After a thirty-year marriage, Louis felt he should hear her out. He thought it was best to be completely honest about the money. "You should know that in thirty days I will be homeless," he said as he explained the lease problem. He read the letter to her.

Jan said he never should have signed that lease agreement. "I told you! Perhaps you are just not cut out for business. Every time you get a few dollars, things go terribly wrong. If you won the lottery you would be broke again in a few months. You let everybody take advantage of you. It's sad. I guess borrowing a few thousand from you is out of the question considering your circumstances." She promised to call back soon.

It was very early. The sunrise was still two or three hours away. Louis was too stressed to sleep. He checked the balance in his bank accounts: $2,238.15. Leon got half of Louis's Road Home money after Katrina and now he wanted more. Louis wondered why he ever agreed to add Leon's name to his property deed or sign the third-party lease agreements. Perhaps Jan was right; maybe he was just a stupid businessman. Louis climbed out of bed and made a pot of coffee, got dressed and sat alone in the dark at the small table in the corner of the kitchen. He rested his head in his hands.

Puncher wondered what was going on, then went to his favorite spot in the living room and went back to sleep. Louis lost track of time. His coffee got cold before he finished it. He refilled the hot coffee, sat back down and wrapped his hands around the cup. The warmth felt reassuring. He watched the hands of the wall clock sweep around its face and he half-remembered some good times with Jan in the Montegut home, but the images were like fragments of a dream forgotten in the morning. Louis sat and watched the kitchen clock that was still determined to remind him of more lost time. Why not sit around and waste a few minutes this morning? After all, Louis felt he already squandered thirty years with very little, if anything, to show for it. He was lonely, broke, and about to lose the home he loved.

Louis finished his coffee, got up from the table and took the wall clock down. He wrapped the cord around it and dropped it in the trash can. He rinsed out his coffee cup, put it in the dishwasher, gave Puncher a milk bone, and then walked outside. Louis was not in a hurry; he had plenty of time. It was still an hour before sunup. His stress caused physical pain. Louis leaned against his car's fender and held his stomach. It felt like he had been punched hard in the gut.

The drive to Tulane was easy this early in the morning. Very few cars were on the road, and all the traffic lights on Saint Claude Avenue blinked yellow. He drove with the windows down and the radio off. Louis took the same route his father used for the Tulane football games held at the old Willow Street stadium. He hoped his father knew that he'd done his best. Losing the house was bad enough, but disappointing his father's memory was heartbreaking. Louis was completely spent, physically and emotionally. Some people always said he was a loser. Now he believed they were right.

He parked in a spot reserved for employees in front of Tulane's Gibson Hall. All the spots were open, yet Louis still followed the rules and parked in the appropriate place. The eastern sky was just beginning to reflect the first faint signs of daybreak. Louis walked the short distance to Saint Charles Avenue and turned left toward Loyola University. An empty streetcar rumbled past; the conductor waved and smiled. The first hint of morning was beginning to peak over the horizon. It was going to be a beautiful day.

Louis knew the massive front doors of Holy Name of Jesus Church would be locked at this early hour. He walked around to the side entrance, opened the door and entered the peaceful sanctuary. He always sat in the same pew. The stain-glass windows on the east side were first to welcome the new day. Louis leaned his head back and stared at the ceiling. He loved watching dust particles moving in the sunbeams. He imagined they were dancing to celebrate the start of a new day. *How did these problems become so overwhelming? What would this new day bring, gift or curse?* The solitude Louis sought was disturbed by the sound of someone opening the side door. It opened and closed, but Louis did not hear any footsteps. Somewhat curious, he turned around. Louis expected to see a priest or some early morning parishioner.

Louis stood up. He felt unable to move much more than that; his heartrate accelerated and his knees felt weak. He managed only a few awkward steps. Kathy was nervous, unsure what Louis's reaction to seeing her again would be. She was still standing near the door with her left hand covering her mouth. Anxiously, she ran her fingernails across her lower lip while fighting back the tears running down her cheeks. Kathy took a few timid steps, and then ran to Louis. He cradled her face between his open hands for a moment, and then wrapped his arms around her. They embraced and kissed while swaying back and forth. This time he was never going to let her go. Kathy tilted her head sideways against Louis's shoulder. "I knew you would be here," she whispered.

# 39

WILLOW'S MON LUIS PARTY WAS an immense suc-
cess. All her Tulane friends loved the Cajun Creole culture. It was one
of the things that helped lure them to New Orleans for college in the
first place. Her Spring Hill friends were thrilled to meet college students from Tulane. Over twenty-five showed up from Tulane and at
least that many from Mobile. Tulane provided two fifteen-passenger
vans; Wilson handled the transportation. Louis and Kathy did most
of the cooking. They boiled one hundred pounds of crayfish and fried
almost that much catfish. Louis put his financial troubles aside and
decided to enjoy himself. At this point he figured it was all out of his
hands anyway.

A Tulane student from Westchester, New York wanted to help Louis
with cooking the seafood, so he shared a secret family ingredient.
"This is something my grandmother always did when preparing
seafood. She was the best cook around. You are going to be amazed at
how good this makes everything taste." He took a tablespoon of
cayenne pepper and proudly sprinkled it into the boiling pot. "Just
wait! You will love it!" he insisted.

"Is that your family's secret?" Louis rubbed his chin and looked puzzled. "A tablespoon of cayenne pepper?"

"Watch this," Kathy said as she added three full cups of cayenne pepper, potatoes, corn, Andouille sausage and more Zatarian's crab boil

into the pot. The Tulane kid used a small spoon to sneak a taste of the creole concoction. "My God, that's going to be soooo good!" He used a paper towel to wipe away the sweat accumulating on his forehead. Louis cut open a burlap sack and added fifty pounds of crawfish to the boiling pot.

Willow enjoyed teaching her New York friends how to catch softshell crabs. It was the perfect time of year for that. They put inner tubes around ice chests and pulled them with ropes around the shallow areas of the bay. They filled some chests with beer, and others just ice. Willow gave out nets that resembled those used to catch butterflies. "The crabs tend to hide in shallow water under logs, sticks or anything else they can find. They especially like old tires. Don't be afraid to move things around. The crabs don't bite!" she said.

Kathy and Louis sat under a grand old Live Oak tree, Spanish moss dripping from the massive branches. "I always feel protected under these old trees. They have seen a lot of history." Louis used some of the moss to make pillows. They passed the evening in the cool shade. When the group finally made it back they had an entire chest-full of large softshells.

Louis, Kathy and Wilson cleaned the crabs first, and then coated them with the same spicy creole fish-fry mixture used for the catfish. "Those are the ugliest things I have ever seen. No way would I ever eat one of those!" Louis advised the skeptical Tulane students to just wait and see. The fried softshell crab poboys were a huge hit. "That is one of the best things I have ever had!" They all had plates piled high with catfish, crawfish and the poboys. Louis took pictures of the sandwiches. Other people have pictures of significant others, family or lovers on their phones. People from New Orleans have photos of softshell crab poboys.

Willow and Kathy decided it was time to start the real party. Willow used Pandora to keep her favorite Cajun and Creole Zydeco music. She especially loved the music of Zachary Richard with his contemporary interpretations, Michael Doucet, and of course Wayne Toups. "It's Zydeco time!" Willow said, using the creole word for dancing.

Kathy saw the puzzled look on the Tulane faces. "That's a fais do-do for all of you who don't speak creole," she joked, knowing that if they didn't understand creole words they most likely wouldn't understand Cajun French either. Kathy and Willow held hands together and began teaching the Cajun two-step. They got along like close sisters. Louis loved watching the affectionate interaction between them. He got up from the table and joined his two favorite girls on the dance-floor. Soon everyone was doing the Cajun two-step.

Louis and Kathy had that lover's look. They constantly were sneaking short kisses. When Louis looked at Kathy, she blushed. They held hands throughout the day. After the eating and dancing was done, they disappeared for almost an hour. Willow noticed this and winked at her dad. She had never seen him so joyful. "All these years, I never knew life could be so sweet," he said. Willow enjoyed seeing her dad like this, and she loved Kathy for making him happy.

Larry's Grill had been open for a few weeks. Reopening it took longer because it was located so close to the failed 17th Street canal levee. Damage was extensive. Louis craved the onion mum, but had too much going on to worry about that. He was happy Kathy took the initiative and made reservations for them. She also invited Willow. Kathy always wanted to include Willow.

They were seated in a corner booth. Louis sat with his back to the dining room. He had been craving the mum all week, and thought about skipping the entrée all together and just enjoying the mum, but he thought Kathy and Willow would be concerned about his health. "What if I order a salad with the mum? Would that be healthy enough?" They all laughed.

"Dad, order whatever you want. This is your night. Order two mums if you want."

Service was very slow, so Kathy opened her purse and placed a thick brown envelope on the table. "I have something for you," she said. Willow had tears in her eyes. "Open it, Dad!"

Louis read the documents in disbelief. "How can this be possible? How did you do this?" He stood up and wrapped both Kathy and Willow tight in his powerful arms. Louis reviewed the paperwork again. Willow had never seen her dad cry.

It was a clear title and unencumbered deed to the Montegut Street house along with the canceled lease agreement. The envelope also contained a ten-thousand-dollar certified check signed by Leon's lawyers. Louis thought that money was lost forever after William-Mark missed lease payments. "It turns out Leon's agreement was not a properly executed contract. It pays to have good attorneys in the family. My family lawyers are better than Leon's," Kathy said with a playful wink. "My uncle said Leon's lawyer backed off quickly after he was served with a countersuit and civil claims."

The waitress approached their table. "Can I take your drink orders?" Louis recognized that voice and turned around. "Hello Louis."

"Jan? What are you doing here?"

# 40

KATHY WANTED NOTHING MORE THAN to be
married in Holy Name of Jesus Church at sunrise. She thought both
failed marriages had a fair chance of annulment under the circumstances. "Every parish priest has the power to annul marriages in specific situations using a process called 'ecclesiastical tribunal.' The
annulment is called a declaration of nullity. It is as if the marriage
never existed in the first place! Surely we qualify on both counts! You
and Jan were incapable, and my husband was deceitful from day one!
We can have a beautiful Catholic wedding at Holy Name. A sunrise
service would be most wonderful! I know Grandmother would have
loved that," Kathy explained.

"Ecclesiastical tribunal? Declaration of nullity? Are you sure about
this?"

Louis wore a new suit and Kathy looked remarkable in a snug-fitting
black dress and pearls. The black dress and white pearls looked great
with her fair complexion and blond hair. They sat in uncomfortable
wooden chairs outside the priest's office. Kathy nervously held her
grandmother's rosary tight in her hands; her head was down. She
prayed quietly.

The priest began the meeting by explaining how marriage was viewed
by the church. "Canon Law presumes that all marriages are valid until
proven otherwise. Marriage is the sacrament by which two people

become one flesh before the eyes of God. Annulments are issued in the rare occasions where deceit or incompatibility has been proven." He looked at Louis first.

Louis felt uncomfortable and squirmed around in his seat.

"Louis, you claim incompatibility, but you have been married over three decades. Why did you not come before the church thirty years ago? You also claim Jan has been deceitful, and you mention William-Mark and a fake therapist. Have you been honest with her always? Have your loved Kathy while still married to Jan? Who has been deceitful here?"

The priest asked Kathy if her husband was any different before the marriage. "No. He has always been like this," she said.

"Stewart has not changed, but you have." The priest suggested that Kathy had become restless. He asked if they remembered the original wedding vows they both took. "I promise to be true to you in good times and in bad, in sickness and in health. I will love and honor you all the days of my life." He said the church does not give annulments simply because new lovers want to commit adultery. "The commandments are not a compact between equals; they are the word of God! They are not negotiable. You should both be here asking for forgiveness, not annulments! Adultery is a mortal sin! Behavior like this leads to purgatory. Your souls will be lost forever. In the eyes of the Church, you are unwelcomed sinners!"

Louis took Kathy's hand and they stood up. "Sorry to have wasted your time," he said.

Kathy said nothing, but left her grandmother's rosary on the priest's desk as they walked out.

# Epilogue

**SLOAN MARRIED A JUNIOR HEDGE-FUND** manager. The marriage lasted thirty-two days. She kept all the wedding gifts.

The 'Life is like a po-boy! Fill it with good stuff!' banner remained hanging at the Convention Center for years. It was recently replaced with a new one.

Warren Eastern High School is now a charter school operated by the reorganized Orleans Parish School Board. It is separate from the charter schools managed by BESE. Warren Eastern has made a remarkable turnaround. It has received multiple national awards and was visited by the First Lady.

Kathy's ex-husband, Stewart, learned he was under investigation by the United States Department of Labor. He fell off the grid and ran to southern Guatemala. Most of his wealth disappeared with the collapse of Lehman Brothers. Stewart now raises chickens for a living, and does odd jobs here and there to make ends meet. It is poetic justice that he now lives like the undocumented workers he cheated.

The Mayor of New Orleans was convicted on bribery and money-laundering charges. He received a ten-year sentence and will not be released until 2024.

After the economic collapse of 2008, Krueger was investigated by the Securities and Exchange Commission. He was accused of using insider information to manipulate stock prices. It was also alleged that his TV show was nothing more than an elaborate 'pump and dump' scheme. He bought shares of worthless corporations, and then recommended them on his TV show. After the price went up, he sold. His show was canceled and his securities licenses revoked. He never did send the signed picture he'd promised Louis.

William-Mark testified against the mayor. The government dropped most charges against him, but he did spend six months in a minimal security federal prison in Texas. His wife used her law firm connections to destroy him in divorce court. Upon his release, there was no one at the prison gate to meet him. He plans to get back into the 'dish' industry.

The New Orleans Parish School System became a national model for educational reform. The charter school program is now studied by school districts around the country. Lesley is in demand as a consultant and advisor.

Lesley and Clarence restored the riverfront New Orleans home they loved. They also purchased 1121 Duck Pond Branch at the beautiful Callaway Gardens. They try to spend at least one weekend each month there. Lesley continues to study the remarkable success of the Harris County schools in Georgia. She believes they may possibly be some of the best public schools in the nation; most impressive are the AP Economics and AP US History programs.

Willow finished her Tulane undergrad degree and wears the Newcomb acorn ring with pride. She graduated in 2010, forever remembered as The Katrina Class. She earned a Tulane law degree three years later. Willow accepted an associate position with an important New Orleans firm. She tries to spend her weekends at Mon Luis, and she talks with Kathy and Louis daily. In 2011, Tulane began talking about building a new campus football stadium near the original location of the historic Sugar Bowl on Willow Street. Willow organized supportive student and neighborhood groups. The stadium opened in time for the 2014 football season. The September 6th first game against Georgia Tech sold out in fourteen minutes. It was thirty-nine years after the original Sugar Bowl was demolished.

Leon parlayed his real estate expertise into a mortgage finance business. Attracted by the higher returns, he invested everything in Collateralized Debt Obligations, which nearly destroyed the global economy when they collapsed in 2008. He lost everything.

The thugs that chased Willow and Sloan have not been seen again.

Jan is kicking around working at various New Orleans restaurants, still saving for a ticket to Los Angeles. She often leaves messages for Louis asking for money. They go unanswered.

Tulane University is stronger than ever. The university's survival and rebirth is a tribute to the remarkable courage displayed by the school's leadership. Tulane's history and its future are interwoven into the fabric of New Orleans.

To date, Puncher has consumed 18,437 milk bones and counting. He is always at Louis's side.

Kathy convinced Louis to take a few Tulane night classes. As an employee, he could take them through the School of Continuing Studies at no charge. He registered for Louisiana History and Political Science. Louis continued to do very well and eventually was accepted in Tulane's Historic Preservation program within the School of Architecture. His timing was perfect, as he finished the program just as the rebirth of New Orleans was gaining momentum. His preservation expertise has been in great demand as hundreds of historic New Orleans homes are restored.

Clarence and Louis both helped Steve rebuild his flood-damaged home. His mother received medical treatment and is doing fine. It turns out she makes some of the best pralines in New Orleans. She sends some every week to Montegut Street. Steve and his mother are both happy to be home.

Kathy and Louis spend their time between her Robert E. Lee Blvd. house and Montegut Street. Wilson gave them a lease on the Mon Luis property for $1 per year as a wedding gift. "I know the old place is in good hands. I'm happy it is a loved family home again," he said. Kathy and Louis had a small sunrise wedding ceremony at Mon Luis. In the eyes of the Catholic Church, they remain unwelcomed sinners headed for Purgatory.